Welcon

After stints working in entertainment and advertising, Amy True turned to chasing her one dream: writing romance. She can often be found in her local writing spot sipping her favorite iced tea (with a touch of lemonade) and putting together playlists for her next books. When she's not daydreaming about her next cinnamon roll hero, Amy is traveling with her family, reading good books, and plotting her next small-town romance. While she grew up only ten minutes from Disneyland, which inspired her love for storytelling, she now calls Arizona home.

Also by Amy True

Ivy Falls

Meet Me in Ivy Falls
Finding Love in Ivy Falls
Welcome Home to Ivy Falls

AMY TRUE

Welcome Home to Ivy Falls

hera

DK | Penguin
Random
House

First published in the United Kingdom in 2025 by

Hera Books, an imprint of
Canelo Digital Publishing Limited,
20 Vauxhall Bridge Road,
London SW1V 2SA
United Kingdom

A Penguin Random House Company
The authorised representative in the EEA is Dorling Kindersley Verlag GmbH.
Arnulfstr. 124, 80636 Munich, Germany

Copyright © Amy True 2025

A CIP catalogue record for this book is available from the British Library.

Print ISBN 978 1 80436 803 9
Ebook ISBN 978 1 80436 805 3

This book is a work of fiction. Names, characters, businesses, organizations, places and
events are either the product of the author's imagination or are used fictitiously. Any
resemblance to actual persons, living or dead, events or locales is entirely coincidental.

Printed and bound in Great Britain by Clays Ltd, Elcograf S.p.A.

Look for more great books at
www.herabooks.com | www.dk.com

For librarians, who fight every single day for the power of the written word. Your bravery and dedication to literacy will always be a shining light, even in the darkest parts of the world.

Chapter One

PIPER

A Latte Bath

We were in that odd summer lull in Ivy Falls. Two weeks past Fourth of July and sweltering in a tight, wet hug that would grip my small Tennessee town until the leaves turned a rich autumn orange in late September.

I hustled around the coffee bar in the Pen & Prose, collecting discarded napkins and mugs filled with the last dregs of the morning's coffee. Customers milled around the bookstore, most of whom I guessed were here for the air conditioning more than the stacks of bestselling hardcovers and vegan cookbooks.

After I dumped the mugs into the sink with hot soapy water, I went back to cleaning up, cursing the college bro we'd hired for calling in sick again.

More than once my long braid slid over my shoulder and I gave it a good sniff.

Nothing except the slight hint of my vanilla-scented shampoo.

My soon-to-be sister-in-law, Torran, swore I had olfactory fatigue. I didn't know I'd lost my sensitivity to the scent of coffee until I came home from work one day and she confessed that I smelled like I'd bathed in a vat of espresso. There were worse things to smell like, but I couldn't shake the feeling that most days I wandered around the town square reeking of eau de Sumatra blend.

I sniffed my T-shirt, tugged at the collar, shaking it out when Penny, the P&P's manager, said, 'Piper, can you take the iced vanilla latte over to Silvio in the corner?'

She tilted her chin to the drink sitting in a pristine clear mug on the counter. Penny usually worked the register in the main part of the bookstore, but with us down a person at the coffee bar, it was all hands on deck.

I grabbed the mug and walked in the direction of the small marble table, dodging kids running back and forth between the children's area and around the overstuffed armchairs where the community book club was having their monthly meeting.

As I passed Old Mrs Vanderpool, she gave me a small wave and my footsteps stuttered. I was still getting used to that – the kindness in her eyes. How she made a point of always offering a gentle smile when she saw me. As Ivy Falls' self-appointed matriarch, she made it her business to know about everyone's lives in town – whether you wanted her to or not. My past was at best rocky and the fact that she went out of her way to be sweet always shook me a bit.

I slid the coffee toward Silvio and his deep brown eyes twinkled. When I was a kid, I raced past his hardware store as fast as I could because he always found a reason to yell and shake his fist. Over the last year he'd grown softer, more charming. His hair used to be a cloud of wiry white tufts, but was now trimmed nicely around his ears. He looked content petting Old Mrs Vanderpool's teacup Yorkie, Baby, who snoozed on his lap.

My guess was that the change in him, and his hair, had to do with all the time he was spending with Old Mrs V. She'd tried to be sly, keep her own life private, but every few minutes her gaze slid in his direction as the ladies discussed the latest Abby Jimenez novel they loved.

After I delivered the drink, I went back to wiping down the tables and counter. Customers browsed the aisles, pulling books from the shelves and making themselves at home in the cozy spots the owner, Tessa, had created throughout the store.

The P&P was its own sweet little box of dark paneled walls and muted lighting. It reminded me of an old English study where a good cup of tea and the right book were the only ingredients needed to create a perfect day.

I was busy loading more cups into the sink when my childhood friend, Maisey Bedford, hurried toward the bar, her short molasses-colored curls bouncing out in every direction. Before she could say a word, I opened the small fridge below the bar and yanked out a pitcher of sweet tea, thinking she might need a shot of caffeine. Last week she'd told me she was running on fumes because her two small kids, Ada and Jordan, had gone full mutiny on their afternoon naps.

She landed on a leather stool, plopped her hands onto the bar, and I pushed the glass of tea in her direction. She mumbled something like 'Thank the heavens' and took an eager sip.

'The kids with Joe?' I asked.

'Yes, he's working remotely at the house today.'

'Good. I'm always glad when I get to spend extra time with you.'

She drained her glass quickly, tapped it against the mahogany counter and said in the worst cowboy impression ever, 'I'll take another, barkeep.'

I laughed, filled her glass and went back to cleaning mugs when a tall, dark-haired guy with black-frame glasses walked into the seating area and sank into an oversized gray armchair.

Maisey glanced over her shoulder. 'Oooh, he's a cutie.'

'Probably another tourist who wants to check out the town thanks to Torran and Manny's TV show.'

'There are certainly more of them these days, especially since *Meet Me in Ivy Falls* has become so popular. People still showing up at your house and being all weird?'

For over two years now, Torran and her business partner, Manny, had been shooting a home renovation show for the Hearth and Home network. It started out as a one-season deal, but after the first couple of episodes aired, the show took off and so did tourism in what was once a crumbling Ivy Falls. These days it wasn't unusual to see people taking photos of themselves in front of some of the more recognizable spots around town. One of those spots included the show's most popular renovation: my childhood home on Huckleberry Lane, where I currently lived with my brother, Beck, and Torran, his fiancée.

'It's tapered off since we put up the fence.'

'I know the show does a lot to highlight the town, but I would've never guessed it'd bring around so many looky-loos.'

When my brother came back to Ivy Falls and outbid Torran on the house we'd grown up in, he kept it from me until I arrived for an unexpected visit. I was ninety days into my sobriety then and thought I could handle it, but watching Torran and Manny help Beck restore

4

the run-down place, knowing my deceased parents would never see it, catapulted me right off the wagon. It'd taken another trip to rehab, and lots of therapy before I returned home hoping for a second chance. I was two years sober now and never looking back.

I focused on cleaning glasses, trying to ignore the shy glances the guy kept flicking my way.

'Does he think this place has table service?'

Maisey's voice must have carried because he stood and approached the bar.

'Can I grab a menu?' he asked with a deep Southern lilt to his voice.

'We only serve coffee and tea. Some specialty pastries in the morning but those are gone,' I said.

'Oh.' His pale blue eyes narrowed with an odd kind of curiosity. 'Have we met before?'

Maisey snorted into her tea.

'Nope,' I said roughly.

He was cute with broad shoulders and a thick curl to his hair, but I could tell a tourist by a mile and he was definitely an out-of-towner.

'Did you want to order?' I said.

'How about a sweet tea? Lots of ice, please.' He swiped at his sweaty brow. Pulled off his glasses and wiped them clean with a napkin. It was a little too deep into summer to be wearing a blue blazer and khakis.

Yep. Definitely a tourist.

I went to work on his order as Maisey questioned him like she was a covert agent for the CIA.

Where was he from?

Why was he visiting Ivy Falls?

Was he going to buy any books?

I bit into my lip, trying not to laugh. Maisey was *a lot* sometimes and I loved her for it.

A group of preteens sauntered into the store. Some had skateboards tucked under their arms. Others carried kick scooters. As they approached the bar, I started filling up water glasses because their flaming-red cheeks said they needed it.

Once I passed the plastic cups to the kids, the man managed to take his drink and extricate himself from Maisey's interrogation, all without answering any of her questions, which was impressive.

'What's the latest on the wedding?' Maisey said, re-adjusting her small body on the leather stool.

A few months ago in a corner of the store, Beck had asked Torran to marry him. They'd met in that same spot as kids and it was a full-circle moment. Since that day, they'd had a lot of wedding issues to navigate thanks to Torran's show – none of which they could agree on.

I ignored Maisey's question and went back to scrubbing a mug with a little too much force.

'Pipe,' she pressed. 'Are Torran and Beck going to let Hearth and Home film it?'

I let out a heavy breath and set the mug back in the sink, ignoring that anxious itch in my spine.

Maisey stopped mid-sip. 'Are they still arguing about it?'

My attention went to the delicate hummingbird tattoo on my wrist, and I used my fingers to trace the outline of its periwinkle wings. 'Arguing is a strong word.'

She reached out and placed her hand over my frantic-ally moving fingers. 'Why is it stressing you out?'

It was impossible to hide anything from her.

'They keep rehashing the same concerns. Wanting to keep it small and intimate, while also feeling pressure from the show's producer, Lauren. She keeps pushing them, insisting that if the network films it, it'll send ratings through the roof. That it'll translate to a bigger contract for next season and more money.'

'Well, shit,' she hissed through her teeth. 'That's like putting dog poo frosting on a pretty cake.'

I laughed, which I needed, because things at the house were thirty steps past tense. It was another reason I needed to find a place of my own. I was twenty-seven and should not be living in my brother's house.

'Are you still thinking about moving out?'

Since we were little girls playing dress-up and having imaginary tea parties, Maisey has had the keen ability to read my mind, understand my inner turmoil. It was unnerving at times.

'Yes. I've been saving up for a while, and I'm still getting money from the trust my parents left for me.'

She swirled the straw around in her drink while I went back to washing glasses. 'Joe's boss renovated those two apartments above the law practice to bring in extra income. I could ask what the rent's like.'

'That would be great.'

She tapped her fingers against the counter. Took another gulp of tea. 'I know I say this a lot, but I'm so glad you're home,' she sniffled.

'Don't get all weepy, Maise. I swear I'm not going anywhere.'

'I know.' She wiped at her cheeks. 'Sorry. I'm exhausted because my body hasn't quite figured out how to deal with the kids not sleeping in the afternoon.'

7

She took another long pull on her drink, draining it down to the bottom again.

'Want another?'

'Sure. I'm going to take my time before I have to go home.'

Silvio called to me across the room and pointed to his empty glass. As I started another drink for him, Old Mrs Vanderpool rushed to the counter.

'Piper, can you please make that a decaf? Dr Sheridan says Silvio needs to cut down on caffeine because of his high blood pressure.'

'Don't you think he'll notice?' I said.

She gave a lazy wave. 'He likes the foam and sugar more than the caffeine.'

Maisey chuckled as I agreed to the request.

Old Mrs V hovered near the bar, her lips twitching like she had more to say. 'You going to see Miss Cheri this week?'

'Yes, but I'd bet ten bucks you already knew that.'

That made Maisey chuckle again.

'Well, good,' Old Mrs V said gruffly. 'You be sure to tell her your thoughts. How you can bring a fresh set of ideas to the show.'

Ever since I'd expressed interest in the volunteer director position for the theater's upcoming production of *Mary Poppins Jr.*, Miss Cheri, who managed the theater, and Old Mrs Vanderpool had been hounding me about it. When I first came back to Ivy Falls after rehab, people gave me those lingering, worried stares. Nothing was a secret here. Pretty much everyone knew I'd been the cause of the destruction of the Huckleberry Lane house, which almost cost Torran, Beck and Manny everything.

Old Mrs Vanderpool never gave me those judgy looks though. Instead she quizzed me about my jobs, and later about my interest in the theater, even commenting on how she'd loved the shows I'd been in as a child.

She leaned in as if her authoritarian voice could somehow be contained. 'You've got this, hon. I see something special in you. The town will soon see it too.'

Maisey nodded along even as Old Mrs Vanderpool huffed at her eavesdropping.

'Thank you,' I said quietly. 'Let's just see how the meeting goes.'

She gave another quick glance in Silvio's direction before scurrying back to her meeting.

'Isn't she laying it on a bit thick?' Maisey said.

'She was close to my parents when they lived here. Since I've been home, she's been kind, like she thinks I need another person in my corner. Which is nice, because I'm pretty sure most of the ugly stares I got when I first came back have all but disappeared thanks to her.'

'Yeah, I'd much rather have Old Mrs V in my corner than against me.'

'That's the truth. Remember how she practically ran that guy out of town when he said he wanted to start a nightclub inside the old knitting shop?'

'That was one hell of a town council meeting. Never seen so many red faces and irritated stares in my life. Thought for sure Amos was going to launch himself over the council's table and grab that guy by the lapels.'

I shook my head. Town meetings were notorious for being equal parts serious business and sideshow antics.

'Oh, Amos would have if Deputy Ben hadn't been giving the guy his own stare down,' I said.

'Old Mrs V was in rare form that night. I think it took two sentences about picketing and chaining herself to the door and that guy couldn't get out of here quick enough.'

I smiled at the memory of her going toe to toe with the guy, her small, resolute chin tipped up as she traded barbs with him.

Silvio waved his mug at me again and I went back to working the espresso machine. As I grabbed the milk from the fridge, my gaze snagged on the cute guy with the sweet tea. He spent a lot of time scrolling on his phone and rubbing at the dark stubble on his chin.

Maisey followed my stare. 'Guesses on what he does for a living?'

'In that outfit, he's either a car salesman or a realtor.'

'Not with those shoes. They're Berluti Oxfords. They cost twenty-five hundred bucks.'

I'd argue with anyone else about the price, but Maisey studied fashion design at UT Knoxville, and avidly followed the latest trends at New York and Paris fashion weeks. 'Um, wow. Okay, then he's a spy.'

'Nope,' she said with a pop. 'James Bond couldn't afford those babies on an MI6 salary.'

Just as I was about to suggest billionaire tech tycoon, the preteens came back toward the counter. Their leader, Dex Swanson, was a head taller than most of them and had a talent for finding trouble. More than once, Barb and Susan had to walk him out of Sugar Rush for shoving four donuts into his mouth at once and challenging other kids to do the same.

He raced around holding a young-adult book over his head and taunting a smaller blond-haired boy. 'Mason likes to read about kissing!'

I grabbed Silvio's drink and moved out from behind the bar. Dex kept cackling and jumped on his skateboard, careening in my direction. I spun away but not before he clipped the edge of my sneaker and I stumbled forward. The glass mug flew out of my hand in a sharp arc, landing with a crack on the arm of the gray chair where the dark-haired guy sat. Coffee showered the front of his blazer, soaking the crisp white shirt underneath.

'Oh, shit. I'm so sorry!'

Old Mrs Vanderpool moved from her table, shaking a finger at Dex.

Penny came flying across the room. 'Out, all of you! And don't think I'm above ratting you out to your mother, Dexter Swanson!' Like a bodyguard, she corralled all of the kids out the front door.

Maisey rushed me a handful of napkins. I patted at the man's shirt and then lower to where his pants were soaked.

Olfactory fatigue reversed, because this guy reeked of vanilla latte.

He shuddered under my touch, and when I looked up he gave me a puzzled smile.

Yeah, maybe touching the zipper on a stranger's wet pants is a bridge too far.

'I got it,' he said, taking the napkins from my hand. His fingers dragged over the top of my skin and my heart took off like a shot.

'Let me grab you a wet rag,' I sputtered.

'It's okay.' He gave me an amused smile. Dabbed at his shirt, which was pointless, because he was drenched. 'What do I owe you for the tea?'

'Oh no. After this…' I flung my hand out to the milky brown mess dripping off the chair. 'It's on the house.'

'All right. Thank you.' He shoved his wallet into his back pocket, a conflicted look crossing his face. 'Maybe I'll come back here again. It's a nice place.'

'Next time, I promise you won't get a latte bath.'

The grin he gave me made my insides flare. 'I'm counting on it, Piper.'

He left through the front door, and I scrambled around the chair to clean up the sticky mess. Maisey knelt beside me and sopped up the brown puddle with a rag.

'Well, that was interesting,' she said.

'Yeah, those kids come in when they're bored, but it's the first time they've acted so out of control.'

'I wasn't talking about the kids.'

'What do you mean?'

She inched back with wide eyes. 'You didn't notice?'

'Notice what?'

'If that guy's a stranger, how did he know your name?'

I arched a brow. Pointed to the stitching on my apron.

'Oh.' She huffed out a laugh and went back to cleaning up.

Her question stayed with me though. There had been a soft, yet eager, look in his eyes. Like he had wanted to ask a question but was too afraid to speak another word.

Chapter Two

FORD

A Shock To The System

My socks squished inside the designer dress shoes my mother had bought me. She swore they weren't that expensive when she handed over the cardboard box with the gold-leaf design on the side. I made the mistake of looking them up online and became nauseous: $2,500. That kind of money could buy important medicine. Food or water for people who needed it. What a fucking waste.

I pushed away the knot in my gut and headed in the direction of the apartment I'd rented off the square. It was a newly renovated space with a small bedroom and even tinier kitchen, which was great because I didn't own much. That was the exact reason my mother had bought me the ridiculous shoes. Insisted I wear them today for our family brunch.

The thick summer heat beat down on my head, making the scent of the vanilla latte soaked into my pants chokingly pungent. A vision of the woman from the bookstore filled my head. That itch at the back of my brain returned, insisting I knew her, but I still couldn't figure it out.

I crossed the street, passed the town's only stoplight, and kept walking. The doughy smell of fresh bread floated out of the nearby bakery. At a place called the Dairy Dip, kids sat at metal tables licking at the ice cream streaking down their cones.

After traveling much of the world, Ivy Falls was a shock to the system. I was used to the frenzy of people, honking horns and food vendors shouting about whatever they were cooking that day. This place had a calm rhythm that was nice. Peaceful.

My phone went off again. How many times was my mother going to call?

When the ringing stopped it turned to buzzing. She'd moved on to texts.

I let out an annoyed breath and started scrolling. None of it surprised me.

> Where are you?

> Why aren't you answering your phone?

> Leaving brunch without saying goodbye was rude. I taught you better than that, Crawford!

Her ranting continued on text after text, and I shoved the phone into my soggy pocket without answering.

This was the reason I'd stayed away from Tennessee for so long. My mother meant well, but she didn't understand a damn thing about me.

Unlike my older brother, Grayden, I was not made for the old-money society life that came with growing up in the small community of Harpeth Manor. It was ten miles from Nashville, but it might as well have been Jupiter with the way people behaved like their existence was the only thing that mattered. My family adored the country-club lifestyle, but I had zero interest in spending my days comparing stock tips, playing golf and dating the latest debutante back from law school.

Beads of perspiration trickled down my neck, and it reminded me of my time spent in Africa. How the heat and humidity clung to me like a second skin. The way the hazy tangerine sun melted into the horizon at dusk. Each night the subtle lap of waves from the Atlantic lulling me to sleep. My friend, Kip, called it nature's own version of white noise.

Senegal. Damn, I missed it. The staff on the floating hospital ship, *Humanity of the Seas*, was my second family. The clinic shifts were long and chaotic, but I'd never felt more invigorated or useful as a physician.

On my first day, the medical staff threw me into the deep end. By the time I got into a groove weeks later, I was seeing dozens of patients, charting and quickly clicking with the nurses and surgical staff. It wasn't long before I was making connections with the ship's crew and the entire community on board.

Over my four years on the ship, I'd only left twice. Once was to do a stint with Doctors in Service working in a field hospital. The other was to return home for a brief visit. That time away had taught me quickly that my place was on the *Humanity of the Seas*. My last stint was for eighteen months and, when it was close to ending, I made my mother a deal: I'd return to Tennessee for six months.

While I was gone, I'd hoped my parents would finally accept the path I'd chosen. Sadly, I'd been back less than three weeks now and nothing had changed. My dad continued to lecture me about my obligations to my legacy in Harpeth Manor and goading me every chance he got about the small salary I made. My mother wasn't much better, taking every opportunity to set me up, against my will, with any girl she deemed appropriate to be my future wife.

Four years and I was still fighting the same fucking battles with them. The hope that they'd understand why the work I was doing was so important faded more with every passing day.

My strides grew longer as I walked by pastel-colored buildings housing a candle shop and a music store. Red and purple flowers spilled out of moss-covered baskets anchored to light poles along the small, narrow streets. This place was idyllic compared to the cold and colorless world of Harpeth Manor.

At the end of the block, I pushed through an ivy-shrouded gate that led to a small wooden staircase. Once I reached the top, I walked through a door into a hidden hallway. The day Diego from Gold Star Properties showed me the place, I rented it on the spot. It was quiet and secluded. Everything I wanted after living in my parents' house for two weeks too long.

What struck me first about the apartment was the exposed brick and piping overhead. The warm yellow light that spilled into the space thanks to a massive sliding glass door. It was both rustic and homey, which was a big change from the eight-thousand-square-foot monstrosity I'd grown up in.

I headed for the bathroom and turned on the shower. As I peeled off my coffee-stained shirt and blazer, I laughed. Getting a latte bath had not been on the agenda for today, especially when that bath came from the most beautiful woman I'd ever seen.

Piper, the bright yellow stitching on her apron said. Maybe we'd met in Nashville? Or in Harpeth Manor? My mind kept spinning but I still couldn't place her.

I stepped into the shower, scrubbing the sugar and coffee off my body. The knots in my neck were back. My stress levels always skyrocketed the minute I came back to Tennessee. The pressure from my parents to fit into their perfect mold was like a bad headache always lurking in the back of my mind. When I told them my plans for the summer, that I'd be living forty-five minutes away from Harpeth Manor, their faces morphed into their regular masks of disappointment. When were they going to learn I wasn't the golden boy they could brag about to all their friends?

After toweling off and throwing on some shorts, I slid on my glasses and moved to the caramel-brown couch that came with the apartment. Once my laptop was open, I scrolled for a few minutes until a new email appeared. The subject line made my heart race. The contract for my next stint on the *Humanity of the Seas* was pretty much all boilerplate. It listed out the typical items: my role as a staff physician, date of arrival and how I'd board the ship in Senegal's capital city of Dakar. I'd promised my parents I'd come back to Tennessee, I just didn't tell them I wouldn't be staying for the full six months.

My phone buzzed once more, this time a different number than my mother's.

'Hello, Gray,' I answered.

'Ford, you have to call Mom back. She's absolutely blowing up my phone over today.'

'Sorry. I needed some time to calm down after she totally blindsided me.'

'Come on, Missy Flynn-Boyd is a cutie. Could it have hurt to trade some small talk at brunch? Have a mimosa or two with her?'

'Gray,' I sighed, tugging my hand through my wet hair. 'It was wrong to take off, and I'm sorry, but Mom got me to the country club under false pretenses. She swore it was going to be family only, and then Missy shows up. She's nice and all, but that wasn't why I agreed to brunch.'

'Believing Mom was your first mistake. Claudia Cannon Beloit Foster always has a plan.'

I groaned. 'Why do she and Dad refuse to listen to me?'

'Because they think they know better than you.'

'In this case, they don't. I mean, hell, I did what they asked for a while. I went to Vanderbilt for undergrad and medical school. I even did my residency a few miles away at Meharry. What else do they want from me?'

'They want you to buy into a practice here. Get married and have babies so you'll be chained to Harpeth Manor for life.'

'What about you? Why isn't she harassing your ass? You're thirty-five.'

'Mom's given up on me. I've already told her I don't want to get married. That I'm going to work at the bank, play golf on the weekends, and then retire to Lake Como and never come back to Tennessee. You're her last hope, Obi-Ford Kenobi,' he chuckled.

'Not funny, Gray.'

An uneasy breath filtered through the phone. 'Listen, I get it. Mom can be overbearing sometimes, but she means well. The accident last year shook her up, and she is unflinchingly focused on being a grandmother one day soon.'

'That's not happening. She needs to set her sights back on you.'

'Nope. I enjoy being a bachelor way too much.' The phone went muffled and then he said, 'Gotta go. My tee time is up.' He paused. 'Let her cool off a bit and then call her, okay?'

I grumbled an agreement and let him go.

A knot tightened in the center of my chest. We'd been in port along the coast of Senegal when I was notified that my mother was in a car accident. I stayed in contact with my dad, who raged about some idiot texting and running a red light, and the surgeries needed to fix her shattered femur, tibia and fibula. Once it was over, Mom spent a couple of months recuperating. Before the incident, she'd been determined to get me back to Tennessee. After, she was like a dog focused on a steak sitting at the edge of a kitchen table. Her sights never veered from her one goal: getting me home for good. It was the only reason why I'd agreed to come home for six months.

I glanced at the sticky shoes sitting next to the couch. Since I was a child, I'd never fit the Harpeth Manor mold. I hated prep school. The starched uniforms and even stiffer personalities. It was like everyone knew what was expected of them. Get good grades. Go to an Ivy. Move back to the suffocating little burg, marry, procreate and add to the long line of old-money families. Maybe that made some people happy but it was never for me.

When I showed my parents my first contract for *Humanity of the Seas* it was like a bomb detonated in my father's head. Without my permission, he'd already spoken to his country club friends about me joining one of their family practice clinics. On the day I had to leave, only our housekeeper said goodbye when I left for the airport.

Looking back at the contract on my laptop, I scrolled to the bottom of the document and added my signature. I'd made a promise to stay in Ivy Falls for a short time, but then I was going back to Senegal where I belonged.

Determined to ignore my phone, which was buzzing again, my thoughts veered back to the beautiful woman in the bookstore. I couldn't help but wonder if she lived close by. She had to in this one-stoplight town.

I picked up my coffee-soaked clothes and dumped them into the washing machine. That scent of vanilla latte hit me again and I saw Piper's panicked eyes. How my body flamed when she tried to dry me off.

No way. I wasn't going there. But even as I turned the knob, the washer filling with a gurgle, my mind went back to the bookstore. I wasn't sure I could stay away from it, especially now that I knew she worked there.

Chapter Three

PIPER

Second Home

What I loved most about Ivy Falls was the way the tight-knit community looked out for each other. Yes, they could be all kinds of nosey, but there was never a doubt people cared. The town and its residents were familiar, reliable, and it made my heart content.

It felt good to know that when I walked into the square, each of the small, independently owned businesses like Minnie's Market and the Ivy Falls Inn would still be there, waiting for customers both old and new. I'd had so much chaos in my life, but now I found comfort in the dependable and reliable. Something I never thought I'd want or need.

I walked past Sugar Rush and the hardware store. Silvio was in his regular spot on the sidewalk, using his old broom to sweep away dirt. He'd started moving slower over the past year. It was why Old Mrs V had been such a nag. He'd had more than one fall in the store but refused to cut his hours or hire anyone to help him manage the business. In my time away, I'd forgotten that being stubborn was practically a way of life in Ivy Falls.

At the end of the street, I turned the corner and years of memories descended like a warm summer rainstorm. The

Ivy Falls Children's Theater had been my second home as a kid and nothing had changed about it since I left. It had the same droopy shale roof, weathered black sign and industrial steel doors that had seen better days.

The last time I'd walked inside this building was a month before my family left for our year-long RV trip across the country. I was twelve and played a mouse in a production of *Cinderella*. I loved the singing and dancing. How every single person in the cast felt like a friend. It was one of the last happy memories of my childhood. Six months later my parents died, and Beck was badly burned in an RV explosion and my life was never the same.

I stopped in front of the theater's doors, my hands trembling at my sides. Acting was the one thing I hadn't completely screwed up, but I still hesitated. What did I know about being a director? My performing experience amounted to a few local commercials, small parts in community productions and several failed auditions while I tried to pursue a career as a professional actress in New York. I glanced over my shoulder to the street that led toward my house on Huckleberry Lane. For a second I thought about running.

No. I'd agreed to meet with Miss Cheri and I was done breaking promises.

Two steps inside the building and I heaved in a full breath. I wanted this, I just had to be strong enough to go after it. That's what I'd told Dr Catherine, my therapist, last week, and I wasn't backing down, no matter how hard my heart thumped against my breastbone.

I marched across the red-carpeted lobby to a set of double doors that led to the administration wing of the building. Miss Cheri told me her office was the third one on the left and I walked down the quiet hallway, coming to a stiff halt in front of a closed oak-colored door. With a shaky hand, I gave a quick knock and her sweet voice called out, 'Come in.'

Miss Cheri had not changed much in the years since I'd been gone from Ivy Falls. Her black hair was in that same fringy pixie cut that made her wide blue eyes pop. The edges of her deep purple skirt flowed out in a swirl as she jumped up from behind the desk and encircled me in a warm hug. Just like when I was a kid, she smelled of patchouli and rose.

'Thank you for taking time to see me.'

'Of course!' She released me and pointed to the plain wooden chair in front of her desk.

Before I sat, I took in the small, square office. Every inch of the walls was covered in old theater posters. I couldn't help but smile at some of the shows I'd performed in. *The King and I. Newsies. A Christmas Carol.* Coming into this theater was a lot like coming home, and I regretted the fact that it had taken me so long to return.

When I finally eased myself into the chair, Miss Cheri shuffled a mound of papers into a tidy stack on her desk. 'I was so pleased you expressed interest in the director's job the day of the P&P's grand reopening. But...' She tapped her fingers against the desk's aging wood. 'Since then you've acted reluctant. Thought maybe you'd changed your mind.'

I let her comment sink in. The idea of directing the show sounded great at the time, but over the last few months I'd gotten inside my head. Worried that I wasn't in the right mental state yet to take on such a big responsibility. It wasn't until Old Mrs V cornered me at the Sugar Rush last week, pressed me on it, that I gave it more thought. Decided I was ready to go back to what I loved. What brought me so much joy. The theater.

'I am a little hesitant. Do you think I can handle it? I remember a few of the directors from my shows, and they were all kinds of stressed out until opening night.'

She took a long pause. Maybe someone else had stepped in, or she'd decided that my past was too much of an issue to allow me to do the job. Or maybe she'd heard through the Ivy Falls grapevine that I couldn't even deliver a damn latte without showering a customer in it. A flash of that poor drenched guy flew through my mind, and I quickly shook the image of him, and his sweet smile, away.

'Piper, there is no other person in this town who is better suited for this job, but I only want you to take it if you feel like you're ready.' Her gaze went to the poster for the production of *Cinderella*. 'You were a fixture here as a child. I remember that show in particular like it was yesterday. We couldn't keep your tail on even though we sewed it to your costume multiple times.' She started to laugh. 'If I recall correctly, Prince Charming took a spill straight across the stage because he tripped over it.'

'You can thank Beck for that. He loved to yank on the tail to be annoying.'

She gave me an amused grin. 'I bet he loves having you home.'

'He likes the fact that I insist on doing most of the cooking and cleaning, which makes life easier for him and Torran.'

She gave my hand a firm pat before her eyes went serious. 'I know this theater holds a lot of memories for you. Your family was always here, with your dad and Beck helping with sets, and your mom insisting on bringing food to feed the entire cast and crew. I can understand how being here might be difficult.'

She was right. Every inch of this building was a reminder of a happier time with my family. Of when I was a carefree kid. My only worries being which part I'd get in the next show and if I'd remember my lines.

'It is difficult. I've immersed myself in every part of this town, except for this place because of what it meant to me. Who I was in this space before everything in my life exploded. Literally.'

She bit into her wobbly lip. Miss Cheri was one of my mother's closest friends. They'd traded recipes and sat next to each other at book club meetings. The day we left Ivy Falls to travel the country in the RV my parents bought, she was the last one to hug my mother goodbye.

'I do have one question and I need you to be honest.'

'Go ahead,' she said.

'Will my taking the position cause problems? Pretty much everyone knows about my past. My struggles. Parents might object to me being around their kids. If it's going to be an issue, I won't take the job.'

She straightened her shoulders and clenched her jaw. 'How many people do you know who have gotten a second chance in Ivy Falls?'

'There've been a few.'

'This town may be into everyone's business, but they also have big enough hearts to see when someone is putting their best foot forward. Learning from their mistakes and making a new life for themselves. Anyone who has been around you for the last year sees how you've been working your tail off. That all you want is the best for this town. I can't think of anyone who deserves this job more.'

25

She pushed up the sleeves on her cream blouse and gave me a determined stare.

'The question is can you do this while having two jobs and going to school? I won't let you work yourself into the ground. Your mother, bless her soul, would never forgive me.'

This was another reason why I'd hesitated about the position. While I'd stopped taking classes at the community college, because I still had no idea what I wanted to do, working at the café and managing the coffee bar at the bookstore was still a lot. I also had to consider my commitment to my therapy sessions once a week. But every morning when I woke up, a hollowness in my chest warned I was missing something. It hadn't taken long to figure out that something was creativity. A pull to immerse myself in the arts again.

'I'm holding off on classes for a while, which means I can shuffle my schedule around to make it work.' My gaze wandered back to the show posters.

'You miss it,' she offered quietly.

'I do. While New York wasn't the right place for me, I did enjoy the energy that came from going to auditions. Losing myself in a character if only for a few minutes.'

'That's the way I felt with the opera. Even if I had the smallest role, I didn't care because I ached to be onstage. Needed to feel the hum of the creative process filling the air. That feeling, like your soul is snapping to life once the music begins, is something a true performer never forgets.'

As a young woman, Miss Cheri had performed with a few opera companies. She'd graduated from the Bienen School of Music at Northwestern and had sung all over the world, including the Sydney Opera House and the Opéra Garnier in Paris. She'd met her late husband in New York and they eventually moved to Ivy Falls to start a family. Every once in a while, we could cajole her into singing an aria for us, and the beauty of her voice made more than a few Ivy Falls locals blink away tears.

'Rehearsals start at one o'clock tomorrow. Auditions have already taken place, and the kids are ready to go.' She pulled a yellow file out of one of the drawers in the desk and handed it to me. 'This is the script. Feel free to read it over. Make notes.'

She must have noticed the tremble in my hand as I took the file.

'The kids can be a handful, but I'll be here if you need anything, honey. I believe in you.' Her voice went thready. 'So does Mrs Vanderpool. All we need is for you to have confidence in yourself. Can you do that?'

I opened the file and read the block letters inked across the script: *MARY POPPINS JR*. The summary of the show spilled out across the page and adrenaline flooded my veins.

The scary voice that usually knocked around inside my head, the one that screamed I'd never be able to build a new life, that my darkest demons weren't gone, clawed at my chest. I closed my eyes and tried to picture my favorite place like my therapist instructed, but there were only flashes of all the wrong roads I'd chosen. Instead of letting the fear take hold, I reminded myself of how far I'd come. How many of those demons I'd slayed in the past two years.

I opened my eyes to find Miss Cheri staring at me cautiously.

'Yes,' I said, gripping the pages of the script. 'I can definitely direct this show.'

Chapter Four

FORD

Poisoned Pessimist

The buzzing noise on my bedside table woke me from a deep sleep. I let out a groan. *Please tell me my mother is not calling at two a.m. to lecture me.*

I grabbed the phone, and when I saw the number I quickly answered.

'Kip? You okay? It's the middle of the night.'

'Oh shit. Totally forgot about the time difference, man.'

Kip was the director of maintenance and one of my closest friends on *Humanity of the Seas*. My first day on board, I'd been sitting at a table all alone nursing a cup of strong black coffee and hoping my terrible case of jet lag would pass. All six-foot-five of him folded into the chair next to me and he started up a conversation about American football, saying he'd heard I was from the States. He'd grown up in Ohio and went on a long ramble about how he missed going to noisy bars on Sundays and watching all the games. It didn't take long for us to become fast friends after that.

'I wanted to check in because rumors around here say you're coming back.'

'Yeah, in October. Contract is for six months this time.'

'October, huh? What are you doing in the meantime?'

I reached over and turned on the light, shifting back against a mound of pillows. It was another nice thing about renting a furnished place, there were little extras like four fluffy pillows filling the bed. A big difference from the lumpy, old mattress and threadbare sheets on the ship. 'Took a job at a small clinic. Filling in for a doctor who went on a three-month sabbatical.'

'A small clinic? Why?'

'It's forty-five minutes from my parents.'

'Ahhh. I get it. You're hiding from them.'

'No,' I grumbled. 'It's a good job. Tomorrow is my first day.'

'It's gonna be a lot slower than things around here, that's for sure. I hear the guy they brought in to replace you is having a hard time adjusting to the pace. You know how things pick up on screening days. The long lines of people waiting to be seen.'

'He'll be fine once he gets into a routine.'

'Maybe.' He sighed. 'But not everyone catches on as quickly as you.'

'How would you know? You're busy fixing leaky toilets and faucets all day,' I teased. Kip had a much bigger role on the ship, making sure that all the facilities were in running order, but I loved to rib him about the tasks he hated most in the world.

'You forget how quickly word spreads around here, especially when people are getting their asses kicked.'

I let out a small huff of laughter. That was a truth I knew too well. Many of the clinic nurses teased me in the early days of my first contract because I insisted on micromanaging every aspect of the job like I'd done in residency. It got on the nurses' nerves and one night during dinner they cornered me. Told me if I didn't stop hovering they were going to order the kitchen staff to cut off my caffeine supply, and on the ship strong coffee was life.

'So you're living away from your parents? I take it things aren't great?' His voice went hesitant like he knew he was wading into a minefield.

'Too complicated to talk about in the middle of the night.'

'That bad?'

'Same shit. Different day. They keep asking me what I'm going to do next. My dad is the worst. Three times now he's tried to set up meetings for me to join private practices. And my mom—'

'Wait, let me guess, she's already picked out *her* bride of choice.'

'Close. She's inviting me to brunches under the guise that it'll be only family, except when I get there a girl I know from my past shows up like some old-fashioned setup.'

'Damn. Your parents make my folks look like saints.'

Kip was from Cincinnati. His dad was born there but his mom lived in Senegal until she was ten before her family moved to the United States. For most of his childhood, she spoke about missing her home. Even tried to teach him French, which he admitted didn't take. After Kip graduated from high school, he backpacked around most of the world, eventually ending up in Senegal. Like his mom, he loved the place and never wanted to leave.

'Speaking of women, there's a new girl working in the dining hall and she's gorgeous. Her name is Vivienne, and her red hair is the same color of the sky at sunset.'

'And how many times have you asked her out?'

30

He went quiet before saying, 'Twice now. I even invited her to that rooftop bar at Les Mamelles Lighthouse to have a drink. Listen to music.'

'Turned down both times?' I ribbed him.

'No, asshole. She said she just needed time to acclimate to the ship.'

Kip was a nice guy but not so slick with women. When we had weekends off, he'd shown me his favorite parts of the country. Saint Louis for its annual jazz festival. Toubab Dialaw, a bohemian village with one of the most beautiful beaches I'd ever seen. In every place he'd confidently approach a woman, but then his brain short-circuited and he stumbled over his own words. It didn't help that most people spoke French and his fluency skills weren't so great. In one instance, he told a woman at a restaurant she was *très Jeudi*. She rolled her eyes, walked away, and Kip shook his head in confusion.

'Was it wrong to tell her she was very pretty?'

'No,' I cackled. 'But you just told her she was *very Thursday*.'

He dropped his head in his hands. Grumbled that he should have paid more attention to his mom's attempts to teach him her native language. After I'd witnessed several of his crash and burns, I started calling him a hopeless romantic. He, in turn, called me a poisoned pessimist when it came to dating – which wasn't far off.

'What about you? Any beautiful women where you're at? What's it called?'

'Ivy Falls, and I have absolutely no time for that. I'm going to do my job. Relax a little. Count the days until I can get back to the ship.'

Even though Piper flickered through my head, there was no way I was telling him about our coffee mishap.

Plus, I meant what I said. I didn't have time for dating. I was only here to kill time until I could return to Senegal.

'I'm going back to bed because they need me at the clinic by seven.'

'All right. Miss you, bud. This place is boring without you.'

I pictured him standing in the framed doorway of his cabin, his tennis shoes squeaking against the yellow linoleum floors. How the early morning crew moved outside on the decks, their boots clomping with powerful thuds. The way the ship swayed along with the tides, the powerful scent of brine and salt floating in from the North Atlantic.

The time couldn't go by fast enough here.

'I'll be back before you know it.'

'Don't fall in love with some gorgeous girl and keep me hanging. I need my wingman back.'

I let out another laugh. There was no chance of that happening.

Chapter Five

PIPER

Emotional Sensors

Today was all about good luck charms. I was wearing my favorite T-shirt, my softest jeans and a pair of worn-in purple Converse that felt like slippers. The topaz and jade rings I'd collected from all my travels sat perfectly on my fingers. Even though I'd shampooed it twice, the scent of coffee still lingered in my hair so I tied it back in a braid with my best scrunchie. It felt silly to wear every special talisman I owned, but I needed this first rehearsal to go smoothly because it would set the tone for the whole production.

I pulled in a full breath before I opened the doors to the lobby of the theater. Fake potted plants and red velvet benches sat in the corners of the room. More framed posters of shows like *Avenue Q* and *The Heights* lined the walls. To the right of the entrance sat the glass-encased box office with its arched window and single high-back chair.

I could do this. They were kids. I was a kid once. How hard could it be?

With confident strides, I marched toward the theater doors and yanked them open. What I saw inside had me quickly slamming them shut.

That urge to run again overtook me until I considered the way Miss Cheri had looked at me with such confidence yesterday. How she swore I could handle this.

I stiffened my shoulders, tipped up my chin and flung the doors back open.

The scene inside the theater was what I imagined the circus would look like if all the animals and clowns were let loose at once.

More than a dozen kids raced around the hundred-year-old space. Some were screaming. Others were singing along to a rap song blaring out of a portable speaker.

The pungent scent of old paint and decaying wood swept over me as I stalked down the center aisle. Small puffs of dust floated up around my feet as I moved. I'd spent a lot of time here when I was a kid, but I didn't remember the place being so ancient and musty.

When I reached a set of side stairs, I climbed them and marched onto the stage. The entire time my mind was spinning.

Why had I thought this was a good idea?

I didn't know anything about kids.

And, sadly, did I even deserve to be here after everything I'd done?

I pressed a hand to my lips. Grounded my feet on the stage. My pulse raced. A thousand dire scenarios swirled in my head. I closed my eyes. Counted out what I could hear, smell, feel. My pulse slowed and rational thought took over.

If I understood anything, it was acting. It'd been my passion since I was a kid. Hell, I had my first small role here when I was seven playing a cub in a production of *The Lion King*.

I steadied my feet before placing two fingers against my lower lip and blowing out the loudest whistle I'd ever conjured.

The chatter stopped immediately.

'How'd you do that?' a boy standing below the stage asked. He quickly followed it with, 'Can you teach me?'

'That's not on the schedule today,' I said in the most adult voice I could muster. Kids started to talk again, chase each other up and down rows, until I called out, 'If you want to be part of this show, you will find a seat by the time I count to five.'

This had always worked for my mother when she was pissed at Beck and me, and I hoped it'd work now.

The kids kept laughing, running, until I said, 'Five, four...' I paused. 'I can call parents.'

It didn't take long for them to put their butts in the red upholstered seats in front of the stage. Like magic, the music disappeared too.

'Good,' I said firmly. 'Looks like you all understand instructions.'

The weight of a dozen stares landed on me. My hands began to shake again and I shoved them into the pockets of my jeans. Again that doubt about whether I was capable of doing this job raced through my brain.

It'd been over two years since I'd gotten my shit together. I wanted to be a bigger part of the Ivy Falls community; that was why I'd volunteered for this job. But kids were emotional sensors, and they'd smell fear on me in an instant.

I rolled back my shoulders and pulled the folded paper out of my back pocket.

'Welcome to the first day of rehearsals for *Mary Poppins Jr*. I'm Piper Townsend, the volunteer director for the

35

show. Today, we're going to do a read-through of the musical.'

A boy in the front row who looked to be around twelve shot up his hand. 'Is this going to be like the movie my mom made me watch? It was ancient and the animation was kind of sketch.' The kids around him snickered.

'No. This is going to be a shorter version made for younger actors. And I'll have you know that both Julie Andrews, who played the nanny Mary Poppins, and Dick Van Dyke, who played Bert, won numerous awards for their roles in the movie, so it'd be good to show a little respect.'

The room went quiet and I went on.

'I'll call out your names and the roles you're playing based on the recent auditions. I want you to come to the stage and fill the seats.' I pointed to a circle of plastic chairs set up behind me.

Some kids stared with wide eyes. Others played on their phones.

I started with the character of Mary Poppins. A teen girl named Autumn popped up and moved to the stage. Next, I called out who would be playing the chimney sweep, Bert. A familiar kid with shaggy brown hair approached. Dex. A few days ago, he'd taken me out with his rogue skateboard at the P&P.

My mind flashed to that cute guy I'd dumped an entire iced latte all over. How I'd stupidly tried to dry him off in not-so-appropriate places. My heart sped up and heat filled my cheeks.

This was what I did. Let myself spiral over things I couldn't change. I focused on my breathing and the kids who were waiting on my next directions.

Dex sauntered up the stairs and gave me a mischievous grin like he remembered the coffee disaster too.

The rest of the cast found their own chairs. I walked to a small table set stage right and grabbed a round wicker basket. 'First rule. No phones during rehearsals. You'll get them back when practice is over.'

The kids grumbled but willingly dumped their phones. I set the basket under the table and grabbed a stack of papers. A wayward, frizzy curl drooped over my cheek and I tucked it back behind my ear.

'Let's begin with an easy question. How many of you have done a musical before?'

Autumn raised her hand. 'This is my fourth year. I played Dorothy in *Oz!* – last year's production.'

'Great. You can help me show the new kids the ropes.'

Her gaze danced over the rings on my fingers and then moved to my faded gray T-shirt.

'What's CEE BEE GEE BEE?' she asked.

'It was a legendary spot in New York where some amazing bands and musical artists used to play. They closed it down a long time ago.'

'I heard you were an actress,' she said eagerly. 'Did you live there?'

That got everyone's attention.

'Yes. I had an apartment in Greenwich Village.'

'Why did you come back here? This place is boooooring,' Dex said snidely.

A few kids giggled. The others stared at me like wide-eyed barn owls.

'Ivy Falls is where I grew up. In fact, I did a few shows in this theater myself when I was younger.'

None of them were impressed except Autumn, whose stare was now fixed on the two small gold hoops pierced through the cartilage on the top of my left ear.

'Why don't we get started,' I said, moving around the circle. 'These are your scripts. You can make notes in the margins if you want, but do not lose them. We don't have the funding to order a ton of replacements.'

The kids started flipping through the pages.

'We'll start at the beginning with me voicing the intro. When you see your character's name, you'll read that line.'

Two boys to my left shifted anxiously in their chairs.

'Your lines can be read simply for now. When we get more practice, you can add your own voice to it.'

Autumn raised her hand. 'Miss Piper.' She blushed. 'Is it okay if we call you that?'

'Sure. That works.'

She smiled and said, 'Will we hear the music too?'

'No. Right now we'll focus on your lines.'

'When will we get to the music?' Dex asked.

'If we can get through the script in the next day or two, music will come after.'

Dex looked around the room. 'How will we hear it? I don't see a sound board.'

I arched an eyebrow. 'Why didn't you raise your hand when I asked about who'd done a show before?'

Dex shrugged. 'I haven't acted. A friend's older brother is part of the theater tech team at Ivy Falls High.'

'I'll accompany you all on the piano first. When we get farther into rehearsals, we'll work with an instrumental recording that will be used during the actual performance.'

'You play the piano? Cool,' Dex said.

Maybe this kid was not going to be a problem after all.

Before we started with the script, we played an introduction game. By the time we were done, the kids were smiling and laughing.

Okay. This isn't so bad.

We started from the top and the kids read their lines. Autumn, who was a bit older than most of the other actors, took to Mary Poppins' motherly role quickly. Dex wobbled a bit with some of Bert's lines. More than once, I caught him staring at Autumn.

Oh no, preteen hormones. I was going to have to keep an eye on that.

By the time we got through the first act, the kids were begging for a break. I agreed and let them know where the bathrooms were. Miss Cheri appeared from the wings and set out a few snacks for the kids. It didn't take long for them to swarm the table, stuffing their mouths with pretzels, granola bars and gummy bears.

She rushed up to me wearing a wide grin. 'I was watching from the wings. You're a natural with them.'

'I'm not sure about that.'

'Well, you're certainly better than Ferris Johnson. He may be a great handyman, but he was a disaster at being the co-director of last year's production.' She rolled her big blue eyes. 'That man could not carry a tune, even if you put it in his wheelbarrow and encouraged him to push it across stage.'

As the kids continued to chatter and eat, her stare narrowed on Dex. I didn't like the quick look of concern.

'Problem?' I said.

'Uh, remember what I said yesterday about the kids being a handful?'

'Yes.' I waited for her to go on.

'Dex can be a bit of a wild one. His mom, Rachel, recently took a full-time job working for Maisey's husband over at his law office on Silverlake Street. She signed him up for this, hoping it would keep him, well, occupied.'

I couldn't help but think about him and his skateboard at the P&P.

'Should I expect trouble?'

Her eyes pinched at the corners. 'His parents' divorce was final earlier this year. He's been struggling with it.'

Dex stood a few feet away telling a story to all the kids. Judging by their rapt attention, it was clear he was a natural performer. I noticed more than Miss Cheri would understand. The posturing. The commanding voice. The way he held himself up like he was confident. It was all an act. A crippling need to belong. Fear that if people could see inside his head all they'd notice was his worry and fierce desperation to fit in.

'That's good information to know. I'll keep an eye on him.'

She gave a hesitant nod. 'I'm gonna head back to the office. Let me know if you need anything.'

When she was gone, I gave the kids a five-minute warning.

They continued to chatter, and I went down the side stairs and took a seat in the front row. My attention went back to the script, writing notes in the margins about costume ideas and blocking.

My phone beeped in my back pocket. I pulled it out and let out a heavy sigh. Of course it was Beck checking on me. At least he kept it short.

I loved my brother but sometimes he was beyond smothering. Not that I could blame him. I'd given him a hell of a lot to worry about since our parents died twelve years ago.

That swell of panic filled my chest. This show was a big deal to the town. It was always part of the Ivy Falls end-of-summer celebration. Once the opening show was over, people filled the streets for a festival complete with cotton candy, hot dogs, fresh-squeezed lemonade and about a half-dozen bounce houses for the kids.

I could not screw this up.

The mantra I'd learned in treatment filled my head. *Face. Forgive. Forward.*

Face your issues.

Forgive the past.

Move forward into the present.

I'd chuckled when the therapist in rehab first spoke about it in a group session, but over time it'd become a touchstone for me. A reminder that I owed myself some grace. That the past did not define me as a person.

I repeated the mantra several times until my heart slowed. I opened my eyes and stared at the stage. In the corner, all of the kids were standing in a circle. Some were laughing. Others kept darting looks in my direction.

'What's going on?' I said, climbing the steps to the stage.

The kids surged back in a wave and Dex was left in the center. A defiant look covered his face.

'Care to tell me what you're up to?'

He shrugged.

41

I scanned the group but no one was talking.

'We can't get back to rehearsal until someone tells me what you're hiding.'

'*We* are not hiding a thing.' Autumn jabbed her finger at Dex. 'It's that idiot.'

A few kids laughed.

'First, we are not calling names. Second, Dex tell me what you did.'

His mouth went firm as he crossed his arms over his chest.

'Please do not make me call your mother.'

His lips pinched thin but he stayed silent.

Autum groaned. 'The moron thought he'd be funny for his friends so he shoved a gummy bear into his ear. Now,' she gave him an irritated glare, 'he can't get it out.'

Blood pounded in my ears. My palms started to sweat. I'd only been with the kids forty minutes and there was already a crisis. What would their parents think? I had to handle this calmly, rationally, because this incident would tell the kids exactly what kind of director I'd be.

'Dex, did you really do that?' I asked with a gentle voice, taking a few steps toward him. Sure enough, I saw a hint of red poking out from his ear canal.

He gave another annoying shrug.

'Have you tried getting it out? Shaking your head or something?'

'I tried,' he huffed. 'But it only pushed it in farther.'

I rubbed a hand over my forehead. Shit. This was bad.

'Please don't call my mom.' His voice had a panicked edge I didn't like. 'This is only her second month at the law office. She needs that job.'

A tight ball of anxiety crowded my chest as the kids watched me. If I lost my temper, they'd never trust or respect me. I had to show them I could be cool in a situation like this one. That they were in good hands.

I turned to Autumn. 'Go to the office and ask Miss Cheri to come out here and go over the rest of your lines.'

'Okay, but where are you going?' she asked.

'Dex and I are headed to the Ivy Falls Community Health Center.'

be provided, *just to show them* I would be *good* in a situation like this. That did seem to get a nod. I agreed to Amsterdam, too. To the villa and all the diversions we had on here until you were satisfied with that
...oise, but where are you going, she said.
...De... and I are headed to the Ivy Falls Community Health Center.

Chapter Six

FORD

No Lasting Damage

To be honest, I wasn't a train guy. I'd taken them in every part of the world. India. Canada. All over Europe. But I never understood the appeal. The shifting and rocking of the car and incessant intercom garble grated on my last nerve. Even the Eurostar, while an engineering marvel, was a little too much, with my ears popping every ten minutes as the train raced underneath the English Channel toward Paris.

But as I stood in the hall facing the waiting room of the Ivy Falls Community Health Center, all I saw was train wallpaper, and a track built overhead for a tiny engine. The nurses periodically blew the tiny whistle for the children (and the adults too), who all grinned ear to ear whenever the jarring noise bounced off the walls.

I waited near the door because, according to Shirley, the head nurse, every patient arriving today wanted to meet the person filling in for Dr Sheridan, who was taking a three-month sabbatical to travel with his wife, Sylvie, all over the United Kingdom and Europe.

Once I was done meeting and greeting the waiting patients, which was a strange, yet amusing, experience,

I raced back to the office to catch my breath and grab a handful of trail mix before my next appointments arrived.

The office was so small that if I stretched out both arms I could touch the walls. When I'd interviewed with Dr Sheridan two weeks ago, he'd apologized that they didn't have a separate office for me. That they'd had to expand as Ivy Falls grew, and that I'd have to make do with his space while he was gone on what he called his 'second honeymoon'.

He'd kindly cleared most of the clutter from the old wood desk that was covered in nicks and water stains. I wasn't about to complain. It was an office. With a door. When I worked on *Humanity of the Seas*, my single-berth cabin was less than 700 square feet and had to act as both my living and personal workspace outside the clinic. It was cramped and claustrophobic too much of the time.

I dipped back out into the hall and found the tiny kitchen reserved for employees. A small coffee maker sat on the counter. I poured myself a cup, and the nutty scent made me think of the bookstore. Of Piper.

The minute I saw her standing behind the mahogany bar, that long dark braid lying so perfectly over her shoulder, I was stunned into silence. She reminded me of a woman in a Degas painting I saw at the Musée d'Orsay. The confident figure gazing at something in the distance, not noticing that every eye in the room was focused on her and her unforgettable beauty.

In Harpeth Manor every girl had perfectly cut and colored hair. They were beautiful for sure, but there was always a sense of longing in their eyes. Like they wanted something more – which I understood. The time I spent in Senegal allowed me to carve my own path. Make my own choices. Now that I'd returned from what my parents called my 'Misspent Years of Charity', they thought they could talk me into staying.

It wasn't the life I wanted, and deep down they knew it, but my mother still took every opportunity to throw an eligible woman my way. The scene at the country club a few days ago was by far the worst.

My parents had insisted we were having brunch as a family. They lured me in with the promise of seeing Gray. Even though it meant I had to wear a stiff blue blazer and khaki pants in the wet summer heat, it was worth it to spend time with my brother. I should have known it was a trap when Missy appeared and my parents invited her to join us. Claudia Cannon Beloit Foster was like a hound scenting a fox. Laser-focused on one thing: getting a wedding ring on my left hand.

For most of the brunch we traded small talk. We'd gone to school together, and Missy brought me up to date on what most of our friends were doing. She went on to talk about all the new restaurants in Nashville she wanted to try. Places where they were playing live music. My mother watched us with eager anticipation, more than once interjecting her own comments, including how she was happy that I was home for good. My father bitterly added how he was glad I was done with my 'ridiculous gallivanting'. I gripped my napkin under the table, biting back all my angry comments.

After we finished our drinks, I told Missy it was nice to see her, excused myself to go to the bathroom and promptly walked out the door. I drove the forty-five minutes back to Ivy Falls, ignoring the constant calls and texts pouring in from my parents.

Too frustrated by their refusal to listen to what I wanted, I paced the brick-paved streets of Ivy Falls, the heat almost unbearable until I slipped into the little bookstore. The last thing I expected was to encounter a beautiful woman. Or be doused with an iced latte.

Days later and Piper still floated through my mind on a regular basis. The memory of her touch, that embarrassed smile as she brushed her hand over my pants, played on a constant loop in my head.

My phone buzzed on the desk. Another text from my mother. This one apologized for ambushing me. I pushed the phone into my pocket and shoved another handful of nuts into my mouth.

There was a slight tap on the door and Janice, the office manager, popped her head inside. 'Doing all right in here?'

'Yes, just taking a quick breather.'

She inched into the room, tucking her white hair neatly behind her ears. 'Shirley says you've already seen eleven patients this morning. That's quite the record. Even on his best days, Doc Sheridan couldn't get to more than seven by lunchtime.'

'They've all been easy cases. Allergies. Small colds.'

She glanced over her shoulder and took another step into the room, closing the door behind her. Why did I get the feeling I was about to be scolded?

'The doc usually takes his time with folks. Asks not only about their health, but about their family and job too. He...' She hesitated, her mouth pinching at the corners. 'Well, feel free to slow down with the patients.'

'Have I done something wrong?'

'No. It's only that you're new to Ivy Falls and—'

'People are used to Dr Sheridan,' I finished.

'Yes, and they want to get to know you too.' She gave me a weighted look. 'But that can't happen if you're slapdashing them out the door.'

'They do know I'm only filling in, right? That he'll be back in a few months.'

She waved a hand at me. 'That doesn't matter. If you're treating them, you're family.'

I took a thick gulp. Family? These people didn't know me. Hell, my own parents cared more about their social status than whether I was happy.

Like she could sense my mood change, she took another step toward the small desk. 'Before he left, Doc told me you spent time on a ship off the coast of Africa caring for those who needed your skills. It's no different here. When people walk in that door, they trust you. Believe you care about Ivy Falls. All I'm saying is give them a chance to get to know you.'

On the ship, we were on a tight schedule. Every day we had clinic, a long line of patients waited in the corridor sometimes for hours. There wasn't time for small talk. To get to know them. All they needed was a physician's attention, and I was laser-focused on making sure they got the care they deserved without getting into too much detail about their lives. Janice's narrowed eyes and tight jaw made it clear that a different approach was needed here.

'I hear you, and thanks for the heads-up. Been practicing medicine for several years and I guess I still have things to learn.'

'Every job is different and the people here need a gentler touch.'

'I'm beginning to understand that.'

'Good,' she said with a satisfied tone. 'Take a minute. Get a sip of that coffee and another handful of trail mix.

When you're finished, head to Room Three. There's a walk-in that needs your immediate attention.' She hesitated near the threshold. 'This place is special. You'll see that soon enough.'

Piper's warm brown eyes flashed through my mind again.

She glanced to the busy hallway and said, 'I'll let you have a little peace now.'

Once she was gone, I sat back in the leather chair. Dr Sheridan had cleaned off his desk, but his personal touches filled the room. Pictures of his family sat on one part of a bookshelf. Other items like his framed college degrees and congratulatory plaques covered the rest of the space.

I wasn't like my brother in the sense that I was against getting married and having a family. I just didn't see where it would fit into my life. I wanted to keep working in Senegal, using my skills to help those who couldn't get medical care anywhere else. It was impossible to think how a relationship, or a family, fit into any of that plan.

When I first met Dr Sheridan, I was taken aback by his casual demeanor. The twists of his white hair, and the psychedelic splash of color that covered his casual button-down. He may have looked like a hippie, but the way he spoke about medicine and the people in this community said he had an intelligence to be admired.

I was used to the frenetic pace of the ship's clinic. The need to get through as many patients as possible, but this place required a different approach. I could do what Janice asked. Take my time with the people if that's what they needed. It was only three months anyway.

My phone buzzed in my pocket again. Another text from my mother. She was overbearing, and irritating, but she was also my mom.

49

I left the office and walked down the hall to Room Three. After I knocked once, I poked my head in the door. A kid, maybe twelve or so, sat on the exam table. He was chatting, laughing with a woman who had rich dark hair swept back from her face in a braid. My heart stuttered when she turned to look at me.

'What…what are you doing here?' she gasped.

'I'm the physician filling in for Dr Sheridan while he's away.'

'I heard something about that. But nobody said…'

'That you'd welcome that person to town with a latte bath?' I turned to the kid sitting on the table. 'Thanks to our friend here.'

He gave me that preteen stare down. 'Ooops. Sorry about that,' he said like he wasn't sorry at all.

I tried not to laugh as Piper's face went three shades of red.

'Dex, be nice. This man is your shot at getting that candy out of your ear.'

'Candy?'

'Yep. Dex thought it'd be cute to show off for his friends and shove a gummy bear deep into his ear.'

'Why'd you do that?' I asked.

''Cause Jake Anderson dared me I wouldn't,' he huffed.

Piper gave him a concerned look.

'So are you two related? Is he your son?'

'No! Of course not. You think I'm old enough to have a kid this big?' she said like she thought I was an idiot.

'No. But you're here, and… you were chatting… and…'

Shit. I need to stop talking.

'For your information, Dex is part of the summer musical I'm directing over at the community theater.'

'Oh, that makes sense.'

Yeah, I was sounding even dumber now. What was it about this woman that made me so damn flustered?

I turned my attention back to Dex. 'Where are your folks?'

His shoulders sagged. 'My dad lives in Knoxville, and my mom is working over on Silverlake Street.'

'I called her as we walked over here,' Piper said. 'She said you have permission to examine him.'

At that moment, Shirley slid in the door. Her red hair tucked into a tight bun. 'Dex's mom, Rachel, called. Said she can't get away for a few more minutes, but that she signed a medical release for the theater program in case of emergency.'

'Fine. Let's get started.'

I grabbed the otoscope off the wall and walked toward the exam table. My gaze clashed with Piper's. There was something about her that was magnetic. I couldn't put my finger on it. Of course she was beautiful, but there was a quiet resilience hidden beneath her steely attitude. A steady thrum to her personality that drew me in. Made me want to know more about her.

'I need you to move so I can look in his ears.'

'Oh, yeah. Right.' She scooted away to sit on a nearby chair.

Being gentle, I looked in one ear. The kid had jammed the candy pretty deep into the ear canal.

'Shirley, can you grab me a pair of forceps?'

For the first time since I'd entered the room, the kid's tough demeanor crumbled.

'What's that?' he gulped.

She opened the sterile package and handed them to me. I held them up for Dex. 'These are like tweezers and will help grab the candy.'

'Will it hurt?' he squeaked.

'No, it may feel uncomfortable for a minute though.'

The kid's worried gaze flicked to Piper. Without hesitation, she pulled her chair close and reached for his hand. The silver rings on her fingers glittered in the pale light of the room.

'How old are you, Dex?' I asked.

He puffed out his chest. 'I'll be thirteen in August.'

I tried to grab the candy but could only grasp small bits. Shirley stepped closer and I whispered to her about another idea I had and she left the room.

'Yep. That was the year of "The Great Brother Battle" for me.'

'What's that?' Dex asked.

'The summer I turned thirteen my older brother, Grayden, who was sixteen at the time, was a real pain in the a...'

Piper arched a brow at me.

'He was a menace, always harassing me and my friends. Constantly challenging us to do stupid things like jump off our roof into the pool.'

'Cool,' he gushed.

Piper's arched brow morphed into a scowl.

Yeah, probably should not be giving the kid ideas.

'One night when I was hanging out at my favorite pizza place, my brother came in with his high-school friends. He bet me I couldn't eat an entire large pepperoni pizza and drink a full liter of soda in under ten minutes.'

Dex's eyes gleamed. 'You totally took that bet, right?'

'Yeah, and I paid the price.'

52

His look turned puzzled. 'How?'

'I took that pizza down, not a crumb left. Drinking the liter of soda was easy too. Thought for sure I'd beaten my brother, but five minutes later the cutest girl in middle school showed up. She smiled at me and I proceeded to throw up all over her flip-flops.'

'Ooooh, gross,' Dex laughed. 'Were there chunks and stuff between her toes?'

Piper pressed a hand to her mouth but not before I saw her smile.

'Tons of chunks. She and her friends hated me for the rest of middle school.'

Dex gave a hesitant smile. 'Wish I had a brother. I'm an only child.'

'Do you have a best friend?'

'Yeah. Jensen Banfield. We've been buddies since second grade.'

'And do you play video games? Skateboard? Hang out regularly?'

'Yep,' he sighed, finally showing a flicker of vulnerability. 'He invites me over a lot because my mom's always working.'

'See, you do have a brother then. Blood might not unite you but friendship does.'

Dex cocked his head like he was giving it serious thought. I caught Piper's eye and her steady gaze said she approved of the way I'd handled his worries.

Shirley returned a minute later with another sterile package. She pulled out a curette and handed it to me.

'Continue to hold still, buddy. I'm going to use this to scoop out the rest of the candy.'

Piper's stare never left Dex. For his part, he managed to stay frozen as I worked the candy out of his ear. Piper was good with him. Knew to smile when he tensed up. Squeeze his hand when he winced.

There was something gentle, kind in her demeanor that made me want to move closer. Look into those deep, thoughtful eyes and ask about her life. If she was originally from Ivy Falls. How long she'd lived here.

A small knock on the door forced me to look away. In a flurry, a woman with curly white-blonde hair flew into the room.

'Oh, Dexy! What did you do?'

Piper instantly moved out of the chair. 'Sit down, Mrs Swanson.'

The woman gave Piper a scathing look before she said, 'Is my baby all right, doc?'

'He's fine. I'm almost done.'

She held her son's hand and he wilted. 'Sorry, Mom. It was a dare and I had to do it.'

'We've talked about this, Dexy. You don't have to perform to get people to like you.'

Piper inched back against the wall like all she wanted to do was disappear.

'I know, but I thought it'd be funny. People did laugh.' His chin dipped. 'Until they didn't anymore.'

She patted his hand, but the tense set of her mouth said this wasn't the first time he'd pulled a stunt like this.

It took ten more seconds before I pulled out the remaining red chunks from his ear. I checked the canal once more with the otoscope. 'Looks clear. You may be sore for a little bit, but no lasting damage.'

Mrs Swanson stood and reached for my hands. 'Thank you, Dr...'

'Foster.'

54

Piper did a double take as Mrs Swanson kept speaking. 'Talk around town says you went to Vandy?'

'Yes. Undergrad and medical school.'

'It's good to have a local boy here to help us.'

'I'll only be here three months until Dr Sheridan gets back.'

Piper's attention moved to the small window in the corner of the room. Her cheeks were too pale for my liking and she rubbed at something on her wrist.

Once I was done chatting with Mrs Swanson, she and Dex left the room and Piper started to follow.

'Hey, can you hold on a second?' I asked.

Her lips thinned into an unhappy line. 'Why?'

'Because I want to talk.'

'About what?' There was a sudden chill to her voice as she kept rubbing at her wrist. No, not rubbing, but tracing the edges of a colorful hummingbird tattoo.

'Don't be upset by this incident. I've seen preteen boys do a lot worse.'

'I'm not upset,' she said, shoving away a loose dark hair near her mouth.

'Are you sure?'

'Please tell me you are not questioning whether or not I know my own feelings.' I didn't like how she went quiet again. 'Can we please not do this?'

'Do what?'

'Pretend like you don't know who I am.'

I held her panicked gaze. 'What do you mean?'

The rest of what color was left in her cheeks drained away. 'You worked at Memorial Springs Hospital, right? I was there right before I went to rehab. My brother said he spoke to a Dr Foster. I was unconscious and you told him to talk to me. That I'd be all right,' she said on a wobbly breath.

Like a blurry image coming into focus, I saw the whole picture. The stillness of her body in the bed. The hunch to her brother's shoulders as he held her too pale hand.

'Let's make a deal.' Her voice turned to iron. 'I'll avoid you while you're here and you avoid me.'

'Why?'

'Because I've worked hard to straighten out my life, even if some people still don't trust me.' Her gaze moved to the door. The way Dex's mom had spoken to her now made sense. 'What I don't need is you skulking around as a constant reminder of that past.' My mouth must have drooped, because she followed up with, 'The broken person you saw in that moment doesn't exist anymore, and that look of pity currently settled into the curves of your face is something I don't want to see every time we pass in the street, and we will, because Ivy Falls is damn small.'

'Pity?' I circled a hand around my face. 'This is not pity.'

'What is it then?' she said with an annoyed huff.

Desire.

Lust.

Want.

Yeah, none of those words were coming out of my mouth while she glared at me like I was an insect she wanted to stomp.

'Look.' I pushed my glasses up the bridge of my nose, taking my time so I didn't screw this up. 'I'm not going to deny that I remember you now from the hospital, but I was only on shift for that one day. I never examined you or had any other interaction with your case. Seeing me is a shock, I get that. But, I swear, I'd never do anything to

56

make you uncomfortable. And from watching you in the bookstore, and just now with Dex, it's clear you're doing well.'

She pulled in a thready breath. 'You don't know a thing about me.'

I couldn't explain it but a raw ache built in my chest. It was like every element in my body was screaming that I should touch her. Offer some kind of reassurance that she was safe with me. She was right though, I didn't know her. But I wanted to. There was still that insistent pull inside me wanting to ask a dozen questions. To know every single little detail about her life. How she got involved in theater. Where all those rings on her fingers came from. Why she frantically rubbed at that tattoo when she was nervous.

'Like you said, you're only here for a few months.' Her firm voice pulled me back from my spiraling thoughts. 'Let's just agree to stay out of each other's way.'

'Wait—' I started to protest.

'Goodbye, Dr Foster.'

She was gone in a flash and I stood alone in the exam room, my thoughts a jumbled mess.

What she'd asked was fair, and I'd respect her wishes. But I was also painfully aware of how hard that task was going to be.

Chapter Seven

PIPER

Make An Impression

Torran raced in the door like her ass was on fire which, to be honest, was usually the only state I saw her in. Her brain was like a freight train, always rushing in one direction with a singular focus. She'd been like that since we were young. Ambitious, determined and unwilling to veer from her goals. It was one of the many reasons why my brother had fallen in love with her.

When I first came back to Ivy Falls, it wasn't a surprise to learn Torran had a flourishing renovation business. Or that a major network wanted to showcase her work.

It made me admire and respect her, but I was also willing to admit it was damn intimidating. I always wondered what it'd be like to have that kind of resolve. To know exactly what you wanted and not be afraid to go after it.

I'd told Dr Catherine during therapy that I needed that same drive. To have a goal. A purpose.

Sadly, I was still searching for what that may be, but volunteering at the theater felt like a step in the right direction.

I may have been a shy kid growing up, but when I walked onstage I became a butterfly emerging from its pupa, ready to take my place in the spotlight. Now, if I could only recreate that same feeling in the drama that was my own life.

'Sorry, sorry.' Torran pulled out a chair at the table. 'Manny and I got caught up in the listing details for the old Thomas Place with Diego.'

Torran and her business partner, Manny, had spent the last few years renovating historic homes in Ivy Falls. Their life was chaos between creating new design plans and tearing down parts of old houses, all while shooting their TV show. Once the filming was over and the project completed, they worked with Diego Morales, a good friend who also owned Gold Star Properties, to help sell the houses.

The lovesick look on my brother's face was too much as he patted Torran's hand. 'It's okay, we just sat down. Is everything straightened out?'

'No, as usual Manny is being a pain in the ass about the price. He keeps telling Diego he wants it to be in a range where someone local can afford it,' she said, pulling the salad bowl toward her. 'I get his point. It'd be nice to sell to an Ivy Falls family, but with the success of the show, the likelihood of that happening is small. Diego said he's had to hire two new agents because interest in properties around town has risen two hundred percent.'

I liked Diego. He was smart, honest and good at keeping secrets. A few months ago, I went to see him without telling Torran and Beck. We'd talked about rental places nearby, and he'd taken me to see a few when I had a rare day off. Yesterday, he'd shown me a newly renovated place in town I loved. He told me I'd need to decide soon as it wouldn't stay available for long.

I'd lived in this house for almost two years. Beck claimed that he'd bought it for me to keep our family's history alive. To remind me of better times. What it felt like to grow up here. At first, that shook me to the core. I didn't know if I could step back into the old memories. Stay here knowing our parents would never walk in the front door again. It took time, and a lot of therapy, to realize this was home. That living with the memory of our parents wouldn't be too difficult. That it could be the perfect space to start over.

A few months after I left rehab, I took a job at Sugar Rush. Then, a year later, I agreed to manage the coffee bar at the P&P when I wasn't working at the café. For years, I'd dreamed of my life being this normal and productive, but one thing was still missing: independence. That meant moving out on my own. All I needed was to find the nerve to tell Torran and Beck that fact.

'It'll work out.' Beck's gaze moved to the engagement ring on Torran's left hand. This house was big but the closer we got to their wedding, the smaller it felt. It was time for me to move on. Neither of them would admit it, but they knew it was true too. 'Let's eat before the food goes cold.' Beck passed around plates as I dished up the fettucine Alfredo I'd prepared. It was the deal I'd made with them when they agreed to let me live here. I'd do the cooking, and most of the cleaning, because they wouldn't let me pay rent.

While I was in rehab at Changing Attitudes, Beck took part in my family therapy sessions. Since our parents died, he'd become overbearing, constantly checking on me and interfering in my life. Not that I could blame him. I'd spent most of my late teens and early twenties out of control. Alcohol and pills my preferred method of blotting out the pain of losing our folks when we were both so young.

Beck stuck by my side through it all, putting all his own hopes and dreams on hold. When I'd finally come back to Ivy Falls, I thought I'd turned a corner. But being back here brought all my grief to the surface, and I ended up making a choice that nearly destroyed this house and almost cost Beck and Torran a future together.

It was at that moment I realized I wasn't only taking a sledgehammer to my own life, but to my brother's too. After that, I resolved to get sober. In therapy, we both discovered how to grieve properly, and Beck learned that his constant hovering only made me more anxious. Dr Catherine told him he should ask fewer questions and listen more. Wait for me to offer information I was willing to share.

It'd taken him a while to loosen the tether he'd held so tightly, but I understood his worry. Loved and appreciated his need to protect me, but life was a tightrope walk. After years in therapy, I'd learned that I needed to inch out to the edge and take that first step. It was the only way I was going to build a life I could be proud of.

'If you're getting ready to list, does that mean the final touches on the house are done?' Beck asked.

'Manny says we'll be finished next week, and Lauren swears they'll be done shooting final B-roll tomorrow. Then we can do a last polish and put it on the market.'

Beck's lips pressed into a thin line whenever he heard Lauren's name. He liked the show's producer, but she'd become a burr in his side due to her meddling over the wedding.

'Did you talk to her about our plans?' he asked.

'I told her we wanted to keep things for the wedding simple, but Hearth and Home is still insisting they be involved.'

'Tor, we talked about this,' Beck grumbled.

'I know but Lauren says they want to show the ceremony at the end of the upcoming season.'

He put his fork down and shook his head. This happened whenever the topic of filming their wedding came up. Beck wanted it to be a private affair – friends and family only. Torran wanted the same thing but felt beholden to the show, which had allowed her and Manny to make a big difference in Ivy Falls after it had struggled for years with financial issues.

Since they'd gotten engaged, they'd agreed on a few things. The date in early October. That Tessa, Torran's sister, would be her maid of honor, and Pete, Beck's business partner and closest friend, would stand up with him. How they'd say their vows underneath the big magnolia in the backyard at dusk with a reception following. Barb and Susan from Sugar Rush insisted on making the cake and, of course, baking a few of Torran's favorite donuts too. But whenever they got into a good planning rhythm, the issue of Hearth and Home reared its ugly head. At some point they'd have to agree one way or another because the clock was ticking.

As their stalemate continued, I glanced toward the stairs wanting to escape the tension that filled the room.

Beck huffed out a rough breath. 'I thought we settled this already. That it was going to be a private ceremony.'

'It's complicated but I understand where the network is coming from. We were part of the focus for Season One. It makes sense they'd want to bring our story full circle.'

'Don't you think it'll take away from the intimacy of it all?' he said, pushing the food around his plate.

'I don't know.' Torran turned her attention to me. 'What do you think?'

'Oh no. I am *not* getting involved.'

'Let's talk about it later.' Torran's voice wavered. 'Give it more thought. There has to be a compromise that would make us both feel comfortable.'

Beck nodded even though he'd been clear about what he wanted.

In a quiet moment after they'd gotten engaged at the P&P, we talked about our parents. About how happy they'd be that we'd both found our way home to Ivy Falls. That they'd be thrilled he was marrying Torran. What went unsaid was how acutely we felt their loss every day. How a part of his reticence about the filming was that it would make the gaping hole they left behind more acute. That their absence would eventually come up via an interview or off-handed comment.

Beck wasn't always against the show's presence. At the beginning, he didn't mind Hearth and Home documenting the restoration of our house. What he hadn't anticipated was the audience's reaction to the show. How it'd turned Torran and Manny into mini celebrities.

Fans started flocking to Ivy Falls after the first few episodes aired. At first, it was wild to see people filming the square. Taking selfies in front of the Dairy Dip and Sugar Rush. It got less amusing when fans started showing up on our doorstep, asking for photos, or to come inside like we lived in a tourist attraction. It freaked me out enough that Torran and Manny talked to Lauren about it. Convinced Hearth and Home to pay for a privacy fence to keep people out.

Even though he didn't say it, I think Beck worried that somehow his wish for a small and quiet wedding would turn into a circus with cameras around.

'How were things at the theater today, Pipe?' Beck asked, eager to change the subject.

'Uh, fine.'

Now I was the one pushing the food around my plate. I wanted to keep what had happened with Dex a secret, but Ivy Falls gossip tended to spread across town in its own kind of tsunami. Beck and Tor would hear about it soon enough.

'The kids were good. They're excited about the show... but there was one small hiccup.'

Beck paused with his fork halfway to his mouth. 'Hiccup?'

'One kid thought it'd be funny to shove a gummy bear into his ear.'

Torran smothered a laugh. 'Why would anyone do that?'

'Preteen boys. Dare them to do anything and they'll make bad choices.' I stared Beck down. 'In fact, I remember you doing a few things that made our mom's hair go gray.'

Torran set her hands on the table. 'Oh, now this is interesting. We've known each other for a long time, Beck. What are you hiding?'

'Piper.' Beck's voice held a thin warning that was all bark and no bite.

'When we were young, we were playing hide-and-seek. Beck thought it'd be funny to climb up into the eaves of the attic to hide, but he got so high that our dad had to use a ladder to get him down.'

'What is it with you and the attic?' Torran teased.

64

When Beck first bought the house after bidding it away from Torran at auction, he acted like an asshole, thinking he could restore it on his own. That was until he put a foot through the floor in the attic and almost fell through. Torran had to show up and save him, which was something I regularly ribbed him about.

'It was a good hiding spot,' he chuckled.

'Like I said,' I gave my brother a smirk, 'preteen boys.'

'What happened with the kid?' Torran said.

I was afraid of this question. The looks of worry I knew would cross their faces. 'I had to take him over to the community health center.'

Torran's eyes narrowed. 'Did you meet the new doctor? My dad says he's a traveling physician. That he recently spent time on a hospital ship in Senegal, but he's originally from Harpeth Manor.'

Harpeth Manor. Huh. I wouldn't have pegged him as the old-money type, but then again, I didn't really want to know much about him. Sure, he was cute in a buttoned-up, nerdy kind of Peter Parker way, and how calmly he put Dex at ease may have sent a shot of heat across my skin, but I was trying to move forward, and Dr Foster being here was a walking, talking reminder of my past.

I played with my napkin, wondering if I should tell Beck he'd already met him at the hospital. All my instincts said to be quiet, but at some point I was sure Beck would run into the guy in this tiny town.

'Yeah, he took care of Dex. Was really good with him.' I hesitated before pushing out, 'You've met him before, Beck.'

The lines in his forehead pinched. 'How?'

'He did a shift at Memorial Springs.'

They both stared at me a little puzzled until they finally got my meaning.

Beck's voice softened. 'How do you feel about that?'

'I only know about your conversation with him. But to put a face with a name,' I shrugged, 'it was a little weird.'

'Piper,' Torran said gently. 'You're doing great. This doctor being here doesn't mean anything. It's not like he knows you.'

'Yes, he was in and out of the room in less than five minutes,' Beck added.

'Well…' I hedged.

Beck sat back and I didn't like the way he clutched his napkin in a death grip.

'Our encounter at the clinic wasn't the first one.'

Creases folded around Torran's eyes as Beck stayed quiet.

'I saw him at the P&P. Kids were running around and I sort of got tripped, and, well, the doc got an iced-latte dousing.'

My mind raced back to the way I'd patted down his pants. The look of amusement in his eyes.

The corner of Beck's mouth twitched and Torran let out a bubbling laugh. 'Oh no.'

It was just what the tense conversation needed. I was tired of them treating me like I was a fragile piece of glass in one of those antique chandeliers Torran loved to put into her houses.

'Yeah, he was dressed up in a blazer and fancy shoes. It was a disaster.'

Beck shook his head, trying not to let out his own laugh. 'That's one way to make an impression.'

I laughed along, the tension finally being sucked from the room. This was good. Us, laughing and joking. It was the perfect opening I needed to talk about my plans.

'Speaking of impressions, Diego has spent some time recently showing me a few rentals around town.'

With only a few words, all that tension was back.

'Pipe, I don't want you to leave. This is your home. You belong here,' Beck insisted.

'No, it's time I stand on my own two feet. Build my own life.'

'And you can take on the financial responsibility?' he pressed.

'Yes. I have the small allowance from my trust, and I've built up a little nest egg for rent.'

It was the first time in my life I'd ever been able to hold on to any kind of money. Not spend it on booze and whatever pills I could get my hands on. It was another victory, and I was damn proud of getting to this point.

'You two will be married in a few months, and I'm sure you'd like some privacy.' My cheeks heated. Even though my room was on the other side of the house, they were embarrassingly loud.

Beck took an uncomfortable gulp. 'There's a lot going on. Let's talk after the wedding.'

There was a plea in his eyes that said he wanted me to stay so he could continue to keep an eye on me, but I couldn't remain in this bubble any longer. My life was waiting for me outside these walls. Was there all sorts of temptation too? Of course. But I'd learned after three stints in rehab, and many long hours in therapy, that I had to accept responsibility for my actions. Acknowledge my struggles and not hide from them. The only way I was going to grow, find my purpose, was to live on my own.

By the set of his jaw, it was clear Beck wasn't going to give in tonight, but I'd keep talking, wear him down, because I needed to move on and he did too. That mantra I kept repeating filled my head again.

Face. Forgive. Forward.

If I wanted to have a new life, he needed to let me go. They both did.

Chapter Eight

FORD

Intimate Secrets

I'd forgotten how running during the peak of a Southern summer was like choking on a wet rag. You couldn't get more than a few paces before your face beaded with sweat. Your clothes stuck as tight to your body as kudzu climbing a tree. The heat of the sun, even at seven a.m., cooked your skin until it was a ripe pink.

I turned the corner past the Dairy Dip and headed toward the limestone fountain in the center of the square. The signs in this town were wild. The marquee for the hardware store read, *We'll help you nail any project*. As I turned the corner, the sandwich board outside the music store said, *We'll make you pitch-perfect. No – not like the movie.*

It was hard not to laugh as an opaque fog clouded my glasses. I kept up my stride, the brick-paved sidewalks growing solid beneath my feet. My body was finally in a normal circadian rhythm after a long bout of jet lag. It always took a while to get used to living on the other side of the world. For my internal clock not to think night was day and day was night.

I wish I could've blamed last night's restless sleep on that issue, but when I closed my eyes all I saw were amber-brown eyes and a beautiful beauty mark that sat above luscious ruby-red lips.

Piper had asked me to keep my distance and I understood why. No one wanted a constant reminder of their past. I, more than anyone, understood that reasoning. It was why I'd decided I wanted to live as far away from my parents as possible. But there was something about her that got under my skin. Made my heart beat faster. I liked how Dex went calm when she looked at him. How the timbre of her voice filled the room with a sweet melody.

I picked up my strides as I barreled toward the edge of town. It didn't make sense to imagine anything between us. In three months I'd be back in Africa, but that didn't ease the ache in my chest.

Pushing my pace, I swung my arms at my sides, my feet slamming against the ground. I'd thought I could erase my feelings with a punishing run, but nothing could chase her from my mind. How she traced that tattoo on her wrist. The way the sunlight filtering into the exam room made her hair the color of rich maple syrup.

I slowed down and walked in a circle, my hands resting on top of my head. When my heart rate returned to normal, I pulled in a few full breaths and headed back toward town. The scent of fried dough and sugar yanked me toward the Sugar Rush Café on the corner.

Donut make sense to come inside?

I couldn't help but laugh at the sign as I followed a group of teenagers through the door. They crowded around the domed glass cases, picking out their choice of donuts and sugary coffee drinks. I swiped at my foggy glasses with the edge of my soaked T-shirt.

'Can I help you, hon?'

A woman with bright burgundy hair gave me a broad smile. An intricate tattoo of a mermaid spanned most of her forearm.

'What would you recommend?' I asked.

'You can't go wrong with anything here. We make all our pastries and donuts fresh every morning.'

A blurry figure moved in the kitchen behind her. I slid on my glasses and a pleasant shock raced down my spine. She worked here too?

Piper wore a pink apron. Her dark hair was braided in a crown around her head. Every time I looked at her it was like I was teetering at the top of a high rollercoaster, my heart in my throat as I waited for the massive drop to come.

'Uhh,' I mumbled like a love-struck teenager.

The woman glanced over her shoulder and then back at me with a knowing look. I was sure I wasn't the only guy who came in here and went speechless when they saw Piper.

'How about a glazed donut and a coffee,' I finally managed to say.

'Take a seat. We'll bring it to you.' Her voice went stern as she took my money and glanced at the growing line behind me.

I stepped out of the way, trying not to be obvious about where my gaze went. The noise in the café was subtle as people sat at the wrought-iron tables swapping conversation. An older couple sitting near the back caught my eye. The sweet way they leaned into each other, holding hands under the table, made me smile.

I found a spot near the door and pulled out my phone. More missed calls and texts from my mom. I'd been meaning to reach out, but every time I thought about how she'd ambushed me at the club, the way she refused to listen to what I wanted, I slid my phone back into my pocket.

A woman with warm brown skin and short curly hair approached my table. She set down my donut and coffee and paused. 'You visiting Ivy Falls?'

'No, I'm here for a while.'

She gave my sweaty running clothes a quick scan. 'Business or pleasure?'

Was everyone this nosey around here?

'I'm working over at the community clinic,' I offered.

Her suspicious gaze morphed into surprise. 'Are you the one filling in for Doc Sheridan?'

People at the tables around us turned and looked in my direction. 'Yes, I'm Dr Crawford Foster. Everyone calls me Ford.'

She reached out and shook my hand excitedly. 'It's good to meet you. Janice has been telling us all about you.'

'Only good things I hope.' I said it as a joke but wasn't sure, considering the clinic's office manager was still a little irritated with me about not spending enough time with the patients. I was used to a quick pace and it was hard for me to slow down once I got going.

'Well, of course!' she gushed. 'I'm Susan.' She cocked her head to the woman at the register. 'That's my wife, Barb. We own this place.'

'Good to meet you.'

Piper moved out of the kitchen and started to clear tables. It was impossible not to track her every move. I was the moth. She was the flame.

'May I?' Susan pointed to the open chair next to me.

I gave a slight nod as my stomach gurgled. After a five-mile run, my stomach needed food and the donut looked and smelled delicious.

She must have heard the grumble because she said, 'Please go ahead.'

'No, it's all right.' I paused as her gaze stayed fixed on me. 'Did you have a question?'

'Well,' she hedged. 'It's not a question. More of a statement.'

I sat back, not expecting that response. Most of the time when people found out I was a physician, the next thing they wanted to do was ask about their headaches or back pain.

Her mouth thinned into a straight line. 'I couldn't help but notice you were looking at our Piper. And, while we hadn't met yet, we did hear about you and...' she stuttered. 'The incident with young Dex at the clinic.'

Wow. Gossip is like a contact sport around here.

'Piper's been through a lot. Maybe more than most,' she went on. 'It'd be nice for her to have some peace for a while if you get my meaning.'

The people in this town seemed to know a lot, but they were missing out on one important fact: I already knew about her past.

'Yes, we've had some interactions, and I can assure you I'm only being friendly.'

She twisted her hands in front of her. 'Barb and I have been together a long time. We never had children, but we consider Piper to be one of our own. All I ask is that you tread lightly there. She's got a tough exterior, but she's, well...' She bit the corner of her lip. 'Still a touch fragile.'

I was quickly learning that while people could be meddlesome in this town, they also cared for one another

73

very much. You only had to watch how kindly people talked to each other in the clinic's waiting room to see that.

'You don't have to worry about a thing, ma'am. I'm only here to fill in for the doc like I promised.'

Piper strode out into the room again and stumbled to a stop when she saw me talking to Susan. She glowered in my direction and I gave a small shrug. I waited, hoping she'd come over to the table, but she turned on her heel and went back to the kitchen.

'I heard you worked in Africa. That must've been interesting.'

'Yes, I loved it. I'm going back there after Dr Sheridan returns.'

'That's good.' The relief in her voice was clear. Her gaze veered to the growing crowd of customers near the register. 'I should get back to it. It was nice to meet you.'

'You too.'

She moved away from the table, and I bit into the donut that melted on my tongue.

Holy shit, that was good.

I started to chew, Susan's voice filling my head. She was right about Piper. I should stay away from her. But there was something about her presence, an invisible string that drew me to her every single time she was near. I shook my head like I could somehow wipe her from my mind.

Focus, Ford. You're here to do a job and then leave.

I pulled out my phone and scrolled through the latest headlines. It was all a ploy to keep my gaze from following Piper as she moved around the room. Customers flooded in and out of the front door. The tables filled with people chatting and drinking their delicious coffee. For such a small town, this place did a brisk business.

As I went through my email, a familiar subject line caught my eye. I opened the file and read through the acceptance of my new contract for *Humanity of the Seas*. I pictured the ship floating in the harbor. The anticipation I felt every morning as patients lined the hallways, waiting for the medical care they desperately needed. Some days it was providing life-saving vaccines. Other times it was doing a general exam before prescribing medication or scheduling a surgery for a cleft palate or a poorly set bone.

My scrolling continued until I was interrupted by a panicked shout. The older man at the back table was on his feet. He patted the cheeks of the woman who was slumped in the chair. The man cried out again. Shook her shoulders.

Piper rushed to the table and squatted down in front of the woman. Not more than a second later, she turned and locked eyes with me. The desperation in her gaze forced me from my chair. I rushed toward her and cocked my head until she inched away, giving me some room.

'Ma'am. Can you hear me?' I bent down and clasped the woman's hands.

'Her name is Mrs Vanderpool,' Piper said in a shaky voice.

'Mrs Vanderpool.' I squeezed her fingers but she didn't react.

'We were gabbing about the day. She said she felt light-headed and then—'

'It's okay, Silvio,' Piper said. 'This is the man filling in for Dr Sheridan. He'll help her.'

Her eyes pleaded with me to act.

'You said she felt light-headed? Does she have any medical conditions?' I asked.

'Uh...' He scratched frantically at the white whiskers on his chin. 'She has arthritis. Sometimes gets headaches.'

I stood and checked her pulse, which was irregular. Called her name again. Her lashes fluttered and she opened her eyes.

'What's happening?' she asked on a shaky breath.

'You fainted, Mrs Vanderpool,' I said.

Her pinched gaze ran the length of me. 'And who are you?'

'He's the new doc over at the clinic,' Silvio said, patting her hand.

She took a thick gulp, her eyes still too unfocused for my liking.

'Have some water.' I pushed a glass on the table toward her. She took several swallows, color seeping back into her cheeks.

The crowd stayed quiet. She noticed the attention, especially Barb and Susan who hovered a few steps away.

'Y'all get back to your breakfast. Just an old woman having a moment here. Nothin' to gawk at.'

Prying eyes turned away and Mrs Vanderpool focused on me.

'Heard quite a few things about you, young man.'

'Have you?' I chuckled. 'Let's put that aside for a minute and talk about *you*.'

'Oh good,' she cooed. 'My favorite subject.'

That got a smile out of Silvio and Piper.

'How is your health? Did you recently start taking any new medications?'

'No siree. I'm nearing eighty-one and fit as a fiddle.'

'Greta.' Silvio made a face and her bravado fell.

'Fine,' she huffed. 'I've been a bit tired lately.'

'And your breathing at night,' Silvio urged.

'Don't you go telling all our intimate secrets.'

Now Silvio was the one with pink cheeks.

'How about we walk over to the clinic? Let me do a short exam to make sure things are all right?' I said.

She waved me off. 'Not necessary. I haven't been sleeping well and it's taking its toll.'

'Honey,' Silvio started. 'Get your sweet behind out of that chair and get movin'. Can't hurt to let the doc give you the once over.'

'Since when did you get so bossy?' she lovingly chided him.

'Where've you been? I've been this saucy since 'round nineteen seventy.'

She huffed out a laugh. I gave a brief glance to Piper, who kept her worried gaze fixed on the ornery woman.

'Young man, mind helping me?' Silvio scooted around the chair and we each took a hand to help Mrs Vanderpool to her feet.

He walked her to the door and I grabbed my keys and wallet off the table. Barb and Susan quickly intercepted me. 'Thank you, Dr Foster.' Their solemn gazes flicked to Mrs Vanderpool. 'Will she be all right?'

'Not sure. I'll know more after I check her over.'

I started to say my goodbyes when Susan reached for my hand. 'You're good people. Glad you're in Ivy Falls.'

'She's right,' Barb added. 'Coffee and donuts on the house the next time you stop in.'

'That's not necessary.'

'Just say yes,' Susan huffed. 'Once my sweetie sets her mind to something, there's no changing it.'

'All right then. See you next time.'

I waded through the crowd. Another tug in my chest had me glancing over my shoulder for one last look at Piper, but she'd already disappeared into the kitchen.

Outside, my lungs filled with another blast of wet air. I followed a few steps behind the older couple, their hands sweetly entwined again.

I tried not to jump to conclusions with a patient, but I'd seen her symptoms before and suspected she needed more specialized care than I could provide in Ivy Falls.

Chapter Nine

PIPER

The Uncomfortable Pause

I did not have to say a word. Barb and Susan rushed behind me into the kitchen and helped loosen the ties on my apron.

'Now don't get in the way,' Barb started. 'When you get to the clinic, stay in the reception area until they come out.'

'She knows, Barbie. Piper can't go in anyway cause old Mrs V won't hear of it. She loves getting into everyone else's business, but when it come to her own privacy that woman is Fort Knox.' Susan grabbed the apron once it was over my head.

'Fine.' Barb sagged against the counter. 'Just be sure to tell Mrs V we're here if she needs anything.'

'Of course.' I grabbed my purse from under the counter and raced out of the café. Tourists took their time ambling along the sidewalks and I quickly skirted around them.

The sun cooked the top of my head as I rushed along the block it took to get to the clinic. My heart shouldn't have been racing, but the minute I saw Mrs Vanderpool go whiter than the half-and-half on the table, slump down like a wet blanket, a breath caught in my chest. She acted like a cranky old bird, but she loved this community with her whole soul. Her getting sick, possibly losing her, would change Ivy Falls forever.

I pushed away the darkness crowding my head. After years in therapy, I'd learned to recognize that even though my mind always went to the worst-case scenario, it was not the only outcome possible.

At the edge of the brick-paved path that led to the clinic's front door, my thoughts went to Ford. When we locked eyes across the café, it was like he could see all the dire endings playing out in my head. As if he knew that I might crumble if Mrs Vanderpool didn't get help. Once he was beside me, he was as calm as a morning ocean. The gentle tone of his voice stilling the panic that zipped through my veins.

Maybe it wasn't so bad to have him around.

When I reached the clinic's door it wouldn't open. Crap. Ford probably locked it behind them. The clinic was closed on Saturdays and I was sure he didn't want anyone wandering in.

I sat on a wrought-iron bench beneath a massive magnolia tree and waited. Cars buzzed through the town's only stoplight. Red, white and blue streamers dangled from light poles. The city workers hadn't taken down the decorations from the town's Fourth of July celebration yet, and they resembled old, tattered flags floating on the breeze.

My nails dug into my palms leaving half-moon shapes. Two years.

Over 740 days since that awful night.

At one time, I would have let the memory overwhelm me. Drag me down into a dark and foreboding hole, but now I viewed the day I destroyed the Huckleberry Lane house like a rope drop at the beginning of a marathon. It was the start of my new life. A path out of a dark and sinister chapter in my short existence.

I'd been to enough recovery meetings to know that I should take it one day at a time, but I saw the broader picture. It wasn't about forgetting the past but embracing it. Remembering how my heart disintegrated when I woke to find Beck at my hospital bedside. How he explained the destruction at the house caused by the partiers I hardly knew. The deep purple smudges beneath his eyes sinking deeper as he told me about the pain I'd caused Torran and Manny. That part of my life was a hell of my own making. In that moment I swore I was never going back, and so far I'd made good on that promise.

As I waited, the wet heat of a Tennessee summer snaked its way around my bare neck, twisting the loose hairs at my shoulders into waves. I closed my eyes. Spoke my short mantra in my head until it was interrupted by the sound of repeated thuds.

Dex rode his skateboard in my direction. When he noticed me, he did a skidding maneuver, coming to a stop a few feet away.

'Hey, Miss Piper. Whatcha doing here?'

Not wanting to add to the Ivy Falls gossip train, I replied, 'Enjoying the morning. How about you?'

He stomped down on the back of his skateboard and caught the tip in his hand. 'My mom was still sleeping when I woke up. Thought I'd let her have some quiet. She's been working a lot lately.'

'Have you been practicing your lines? The choreography for "Step in Time"?'

A flicker of worry flashed behind his eyes. 'Uh. Yeah. Sure.'

'The dance routine can be tricky at first. Do you need more help?'

'No,' he said too quickly.

'All right, but if you need extra practice I'm happy to stay late at the theater any night you want.'

He scrubbed at his messy tangle of brown hair. 'Like I said, I'm good.'

We both knew he wasn't being honest, but I wouldn't push. More times than I cared to count he'd tripped over his own feet while trying to learn the routine. His friends were beginning to razz him about it too.

He flipped the board around in his hands, looking everywhere but at me. A gurgle that sounded too much like the creature from *Alien* came from his stomach.

'Have you eaten?'

He shook his head.

'Head over to Sugar Rush. Go to the counter and tell Barb you need the morning special.'

'I didn't bring any money, and I got in big trouble the last time I was there.'

The guilty look in his eyes made my chest tight. I remembered how hard it was to be his age – not quite a kid but not an adult either. How the ups and down of puberty shifted faster than your growing body could handle. Visions of me towering over seventh-grade boys, them taunting me with phrases like 'Giraffe Girl' and 'Toothpick Legs', weren't memories easily forgotten.

'It's okay. Tell them I sent you.'

He started to argue until the door to the clinic opened and Silvio shuffled out with Old Mrs V on his arm.

'I won't take no for an answer.' He gaped at the couple before I added, 'Dex. Go now.' The firmness in my voice had him dropping his board and skating in the direction of Sugar Rush.

'Piper, what are you doing here?' Mrs Vanderpool's gaze was sharper than the tools Barb used to cut through rough dough.

'I wanted to check and make sure you're all right.'

She let out an agitated huff. 'Like I told the doc, these old bones are doing absolutely fine.'

Dr Foster slid out the door and locked it behind him.

'Doc, tell Little-Miss-Panties-In-A-Twist that I'm okay so she'll stop looking at me like I'm headed for the great playground in the sky.'

'Nope. We're nowhere near that.' His attention went to Silvio. 'I've made a call. They're waiting for you at the ER.'

'I'm gonna dash over to the hardware store and grab my car,' Silvio said.

'What's happening? Why are you going to the hospital?' I said.

Mrs V patted my hand. 'A precaution, sweetie. The doc says my vital signs are stable.'

'If she's stable, why can't she go home?'

He went mute as he looked to Mrs Vanderpool.

'The doc's being cautious,' she said. 'Wants me to have a few tests to make sure my heart is in good shape. No need to worry.'

Silvio pulled up to the curb and Dr Foster escorted her to the passenger door.

She took a few steps and tossed over her shoulder, 'Tell the gossips I'm tougher than the old clock tower. That you're not getting rid of me so easily.'

'Sure you don't want to call and tell them that yourself?' I said.

She gave me the one-finger salute and Dr Foster let out a thick laugh as he helped her into the car.

I waved at them as they drove off. Dr Foster stepped beside me, the scent of antiseptic and soap wafting off his skin. 'That lady is tougher than an army howitzer.'

'Yeah, she is, but that's why everyone loves her.'

When they were out of sight, a sudden pain crowded my chest, forcing the air from my lungs. My legs shook, and my heart took off faster than a horse let loose from its corral. I started to gasp, dark spots clouding my vision.

'Piper?' He grasped my hand and led me to the bench. With a gentle touch, he eased me down beside him.

'Tell me what's going on?'

'Panic attack,' I gasped.

'Close your eyes. Listen to the sound of my voice.'

I did as he said, the blood in my veins stretched and thrummed like it was desperate to burst from my skin.

'Focus on the solid weight of the bench beneath you.'

'Okay,' I said, clamping my fingers around the curve of wrought-iron.

Like Dr Catherine told me, I tried to imagine my favorite spot. What it looked like. Was I near a lake or a mountain? Did I picture the day or night? The problem was I could never settle on a place or time. Ideas were always changing, shifting in my head like the current in a rapidly moving river.

'Tell me where you were born,' he said in a soft voice.

'Fort Myers, Florida.'

My head throbbed. The scratch in my throat drier than desert sand.

Dammit. Why couldn't I ever pick a place?

'How old were you when you moved to Ivy Falls?'

'I was seven.'

My heart slammed against my breastbone like an animal intent on bursting from its cage.

'What is the first thing you remember about that time?'

'The backyard was big. There was all this green grass. My dad hung a tire swing from a thick branch on a magnolia tree.'

'The first time you used the swing, what color was the sky?'

'A deep azure blue,' I said, finally pulling in a solid breath.

'How did it make you feel?'

'Happy. Content. Like if I could pump my legs hard enough, I'd be able to touch the clouds.'

The weight of his hands, the press of his skin, grounded me. I let myself ease into the feel of him. How his voice was a cascade of warm water. His breath a gentle brush against my cheek.

I inched open my eyes to find his solid blue gaze. Whenever the attacks happened I tried to find a quiet corner, a place to hide. It was embarrassing that my mind raged so out of control, but there wasn't a sliver of judgment in his eyes. All I saw was the attention of a man who wanted to ensure I was okay. That I understood he was here to help not hurt me.

'I'm sor—'

'Don't say it,' he offered quietly. 'You were caught off guard by what happened to Mrs Vanderpool. Worried about her. Your reaction is normal.'

I took a thick gulp. 'Wow. That's new. Most people freak out when this happens to me.'

'The brain is a complicated organ. How it reacts to stress is different for everyone.' He pushed up his glasses and gave me a hesitant smile. 'I didn't know you worked at the café. If I did, I would have stayed away. You stated your wishes very clearly in the clinic the other day, and I'd never ignore them.'

The sincerity in his voice loosened all the complicated knots in my stomach. He stared at me with such a naked honesty that I had to take a quick gulp. Get my thoughts straight. 'No. It's all right. Because of you, Mrs V is going to get checked out. Get the treatment she needs. I'm grateful you were at the café.'

'I'm glad I was there too.'

That sweet smile returned and I inched away from him, too tempted to brush back the dark hair hanging across his forehead.

'Can I ask you a question about Mrs Vanderpool? It'll help calm my racing mind.'

He rubbed at the scruff on his jaw. 'There's not much I can say.'

'Can you at least tell me if she's going to be okay? The whole town is going to want to know. If I get out in front of this, you won't get bombarded by every single person in Ivy Falls.'

'Huh. You're doing me favors now?' The tease in his voice made heat rush to my cheeks.

'This is not a favor,' I sputtered. 'It's more like a keeping-you-from-getting-accosted-on-the-street-by-half-the-town situation.'

He relaxed against the bench, giving me the same even-tempered look he'd used with Dex.

How did he do it? Act so calm? Take everything in stride? My personality was more chaotic, like hitting a patch of ice in your car on a January morning and careening across the highway with no way to stop it.

'If I offer up some non-confidential intel, what do I get in return?' He actually wiggled his eyebrows like he knew I needed to laugh. To let go of the piercing ache that crowded my chest.

'You get peace, because I don't think you understand how intrusive people can be in this town when they're worried. One time Barb and Susan closed the café for two days. No one could get a hold of them. They had a damn town meeting about it. For over an hour, people spewed all sorts of theories about where they were. If they were closing for good. Did we need to alert the sheriff? When the ladies roared back into town on their motorcycles the next day, they were shocked by people's attention. Turns out the two of them just wanted a short getaway together.'

He chewed on his lower lip, like he was trying not to smirk at the ridiculousness of this town. 'I would just explain to people what she said. That she needs more tests.'

'That's it?'

His casual shrug said I wasn't getting another word.

'I should be getting back to work. Barb and Susan can't take care of the breakfast rush on their own.'

I glanced down at the bench, recalling the way his voice had encouraged me to feel its weight beneath me. How his soothing words wrested me from the dark tentacles of my PTSD that enjoyed dragging me down into a deep, dark hole.

'Thank you for helping me.' I moved to stand and he followed.

'Try not to worry about Mrs Vanderpool. They'll take good care of her at the hospital.'

'Yeah, right, don't worry. Try telling that to my over-active brain.'

'She'll be all right, Bird.'

The warmth of his voice sent a streak of lightning down my back.

'Did you just call me Bird?'

'Yes, you have that tattoo.' He pointed to my wrist. 'And isn't a piper a kind of bird?'

I rolled my eyes. 'Do you mean a sandpiper?'

His bashful grin was too much.

'Okay, weirdo. I'm gonna go now.' I tried to look perturbed but my traitorous mouth was fighting a smile.

I started in the direction of the café and he was next to me in a few seconds.

'Considering you're good friends with Mrs Vander-pool, can you encourage her to slow down? While I was taking her blood pressure, she rattled off all the committees and groups she's involved in and it's a lot.'

'Slow down?' I laughed. 'That's like telling her to stop meddling in other people's business. She'd rather gnaw off her right arm than agree to change anything about her life.'

He nodded, his toned arms swinging evenly at his side. His running shorts showed off the firm muscles in his legs. I hated to admit that I liked the way he purposefully positioned himself on the outside of me as if I needed protection from the street. How he didn't feel the need to ask me how I was feeling again.

He rubbed nervously at his jaw before he said, 'Is there any way we could agree to be friends? I like that café and would prefer not to be banned because you work there.'

That raw honesty in his voice returned and it shook me to my core. I was so used to men's bullshit. The way they delivered slick lines as if it was second nature to them. But this guy, he was so genuine. That was rare. I had absolutely no clue how to react to him.

88

'If it's too much, I get it,' he said soothingly. 'I guess I don't *need* the Sugar Rush.'

I glanced in his direction and there was a far-off look in his eye I'd seen many times before.

'You had one of the glazed donuts, didn't you?'

His brows bunched together. 'How did you know?'

'People only get that desperate look of want when they've had one of Susan's donuts.'

He chuckled. 'Yeah, I have to admit that damn thing practically melted on my tongue.'

The way he said tongue in that deep Southern drawl set off heat in several parts of my body.

A few kids raced past us on their scooters, calling 'Hi, Miss Piper' as they zoomed by.

'You're a favorite around here,' he said.

'They're kids from the theater.'

'You mentioned that the other day. The bookstore, the café and the theater. Three jobs?'

'The theater is a volunteer position.'

'Still, that's a lot of work.' He slowed his strides to stay beside me. 'What made you want to do that? It looks like you're already pretty busy.'

'There you go again,' I said.

'Go again?'

'Assuming things about me you don't know.'

He scrubbed a hand over his mouth. 'Right. You don't owe me an explanation.'

The contrite tone to his voice had me saying, 'I lived in New York a while back. Made an attempt to be an actress.'

'That's fascinating. I've never met an actress before.'

'Don't get too excited. I was never cast in anything.'

We walked past the Dairy Dip and the P&P. Tessa's colorful array of summertime cookbooks was the perfect display for the front window.

'To put yourself out there, face rejection, that takes guts.'

I was caught off guard by his response. Usually when I told people I was an actress, I could see them mentally rolling their eyes.

'Is that what you studied in college?' he asked.

'No, I only went for a year before I dropped out.'

I waited for the uncomfortable pause. The weighted look of pity and disappointment when I spoke about not completing a degree, but like before, his stare remained firmly on me, his lips twitching like he was eager to ask more questions.

Ahead of us, a crowd formed a line outside Sugar Rush.

'I meant what I said before. It'd be great if we could be friends. I'm only going to be here a short time, so we can at least be cordial.'

'You don't have to stay away from the café or the bookstore,' I said. 'You have just as much right to be there as anyone else, but don't expect any more than a "hello" from me.'

'What about a slight wave too? Would that be acceptable?' he joked.

Even when I was pushing him away, this guy was nice. How was that possible? Most of my life when a man I was dating was met with any kind of rejection, or pushback, he became either defensive or angry. Sometimes both.

The line doubled in size as more tourists filled the square. 'Barb and Susan need me inside. I'll see you around, Dr Foster.'

That megawatt grin lit up his face. 'See ya, Bird.'

He took off in the direction of the fountain, giving me an all-too-good view of his backside.

Friends? Yeah, that was not going to be easy.

Chapter Ten

FORD

Golden Boy

A good thing about the new apartment was how quickly the water got hot. I stepped into the shower and let the sharp stream pummel my back and shoulders. Hot water was the one thing I missed while living on the ship in Senegal. After a while you got used to the lukewarm trickle that barely allowed you to rinse the soap off your body and the shampoo out of your hair.

After I toweled off, pulled on a T-shirt and gym shorts, I made my way toward the couch and my computer. Logging in remotely to the clinic's mainframe, I confirmed that the blood I drew from Mrs Vanderpool would go to the lab as a stat request and confirmed the notes in her file about the results of her EKG.

When I'd walked out of the clinic with Silvio and Mrs Vanderpool, the last person I expected to find was Piper. She stood erect. Hands fisted at her sides. There was something in the way she held herself so tightly, like rope wound securely against a sailing line. It was the same way she'd behaved with Dex. Like she wanted to tug those she cared about close and keep them from harm. When her chest started to heave, hands trembling at her sides, I understood what was happening.

Over the years, I'd witnessed several panic attacks. My reaction to hers was different. Gone were all the clinical directions, the rational response to her fear. Instead, I wanted to surround her in my arms, hold on to her until her body stopped shaking. Whisper that she was safe. That I'd never let anything harm her. It took focus to calm her down. To not sweep a hand over her cheek, cup her face and reassure her that she was going to be all right.

Once her breaths returned to normal, it struck me how she shifted right into caretaker mode, her concern immediately turning to Mrs Vanderpool. It was a rare sight for me.

Growing up in Harpeth Manor people were self-involved. The only issues that mattered were the ones that affected their status or wealth. Sure, they volunteered at charity events, attended fundraiser balls, but that was more about jockeying for position in society rather than caring about the cause. It wasn't until I witnessed the staff on the *Humanity of the Seas* go out of their way to help our patients, comfort them, ensure they had the barest of necessities, that I began to question how I was raised. What I truly valued.

Piper was another reminder of the goodness in the world. She didn't have to say a word. Her concern for the people of Ivy Falls was clear in her actions. The worry etched into the lines around her mouth when she saw Mrs Vanderpool move unsteadily on her feet.

A sharp knock at my door pulled me from my thoughts. When I opened it I was shocked to find Gray on the other side.

'What are you doing here? How did you find me?'

'Made a phone call yesterday. You'd be surprised what a little sweet talk to the woman who answers the phone at your clinic can do.'

Gray stepped inside the small and simple apartment. The way the skin pinched around his eyes said he thought the place was beneath me. This was where the two of us parted as brothers. He loved the indulgences our upbringing provided. Prep school. A new car for his sixteenth birthday. Access to his trust fund at twenty-five. He enjoyed filling his life with things, where I was content with medicine and the way it connected me to people.

He took two strides forward and plopped himself down on the couch. 'Got a beer?'

'It's nine a.m. I am *not* giving you a beer.'

He mumbled something that sounded like, 'Killjoy.'

'To what do I owe the honor of this unexpected visit?'

He crossed his arms over the Prada polo he was wearing. From the unpleasant twitch of his lips, I understood where this was going.

'Stop worrying. I promise I'm going to call Mom.'

He leaned forward and clasped his hands in front of him. 'Can't you give her a break? She means well even if she has a shitty way of showing it.'

I dragged my hands through my wet hair and sank down beside him. 'How long before Mom and Dad let go of this dream that I'm going to come back here, join some fancy practice, and live the country-club life? Since we were kids, I've been telling them I want another path.'

He rubbed a hand over the dark stubble on his chin. 'Ford, you've always been like this.'

'Like what?' Irritation filled my voice. I was tired of having this conversation with him. Tired of my family wanting me to be something I wasn't.

'Stubborn. Unwavering in what you want. There's never been even a flicker of compromise in you.'

'Compromise?' I ground out. 'Just because I'm not happy with a nine-to-five, playing golf on the weekends, sleeping my way through every eligible woman in Harpeth Manor, does not mean I can't compromise.'

He flinched as I spoke. I probably should not have thrown his very existence into his face, but this topic was getting old. It came up every time I returned to Tennessee.

'I'm sorry,' he grumbled. 'It's only that when you leave, Mom and Dad freak out because their "golden boy" is gone and all they have left is me.'

Even though he constantly razzed me as a kid, Gray and I spent a lot of time together when we were young. Our backyard led to an open portion of woods where we'd build forts and pretend we were pirates or explorers. Our parents were always gone at work or committee meetings so we spent a lot of time hiding from the housekeeper or begging her to make us the boxed macaroni and cheese our mother hated. When he went to college in Texas, he made a point of calling me once a week to check in. To make sure that our parents weren't being too overbearing – which they always were.

I took in the white hairs sprouting up around his ears and across his temple. How his sun-worn skin made him look older than thirty-five. Every time I fled home I was doing it to pursue what I wanted, and I didn't think about what I was leaving behind for him.

'That's not true. You know you're the epitome of what they want in a son,' I said.

That puffed-up façade of his wavered. 'I've tried. Went to Rice like they expected. Took the banking job they approved of even though I wanted to be a golf pro. I've looked after them as best I could, but then… after Mom's accident…' A rough breath left his lips. 'They made it very clear that they needed you more. That my opinions and insight didn't matter. It's a good thing you're back to stay this time. It takes the pressure off me.'

I looked at my hands, unable to meet his steady stare.

'You are staying, right?'

How could I tell my brother that Africa felt more like home than the place we were raised? That the staff and crew looked out for each other. How a birthday was never forgotten – or, worse, ignored – but met with gifts and a song during the dinner hour. The way the crew hung white twinkle lights around the ship for the winter holidays. Tethered a massive fourteen-foot tree with colorful ornaments on the bow. The only thing my parents ever did was force us into uncomfortable smiles for a Christmas card that masked years of mutual disdain.

I could offer up a dozen excuses, but he'd never understand what it was like to have the unequivocal trust of a patient who needed your help. That during my time in Senegal, I'd triaged debilitating facial tumors, cataracts that had left people blind for years, and other serious medical issues that required the care of the surgeons on board. What I did wasn't a profession, it was a calling, and no matter how many times I tried to explain it to him or my parents, they never understood.

'I signed up to do another six months. I leave in early October.'

'Dammit, Ford. Why do you keep doing this? Are we so bad to be around?'

'It doesn't have anything to do with you. I go where my skills are needed.'

'And you think you can be of more help in Africa than here?'

'Yes. I'm not only seeing patients, but I'm helping to train future doctors from the country. Those who can stay and help their community.'

He crossed his arms over his chest like he wasn't convinced.

'It's all right, Gray. I've had several conversations with Mom's doctors and physical therapist. She's made a great recovery.'

He flung his hands out in frustration. 'See, that's what I mean. I can't talk to those people. Understand all the medical jargon. And Dad, well, he does as little as possible to show he's interested. That he cares.'

'I understand what you're saying, but you don't want me here. I make every interaction uncomfortable. There will never be a time when I say or do the right thing for them. They hold me to a standard that is unachievable and it's fucking exhausting.'

'How do you think I feel? Being under constant scrutiny? Never reaching the level of success they expect?'

'It's hard, I'd guess.'

'Damn straight,' he huffed, shook his head. 'And this is what you want? What you need to do?'

'Yes. It's important to me.'

'Do they at least appreciate you? Treat you right?' he said with brotherly concern.

'They do. In fact, you should come visit me. The people and the city are beautiful. Maybe if you witnessed what I did, you'd have a better understanding of why I'm so committed.'

He stood and stalked to the sliding glass door, looking out to the square. 'What do you do for excitement around here?'

This was Gray's go-to move when things got uncomfortable. He reverted to the playboy, fun-all-the-time persona, which got grating.

'I don't have much time for fun. If I'm not at the clinic, I'm here eating or sleeping. It's a pretty mundane life and I enjoy it.'

He glanced at his phone, pushed a couple of buttons and a number appeared in my texts.

'I saw Missy at the club yesterday. Even though you disappeared from brunch like some kind of jewel thief, she still wants to catch up with you.'

'That's not going to happen.'

'Why not? How long have you been alone? Call her. Have a drink. Maybe a fun weekend in the sheets. You're leaving again anyway,' he said, unable to mask the bitterness in his voice. 'It's the perfect scenario.'

'Maybe for you, but I don't operate that way.'

I stood and moved to the glass door, my attention snagging on the pink awning over Sugar Rush.

Was Piper still there?

Was she talking to Barb and Susan about me?

I shook my head. Focused back on my brother. 'Besides giving me grief about our parents, was there a reason you drove all the way here from Harpeth Manor?'

'Oh, I almost forgot.' He pulled a red envelope from the back pocket of his golf pants. My name was embossed on the front in thick black ink.

'What's this?'

'Mom and Dad are having a fortieth anniversary party at the club. Cocktails and dinner. Champagne toast. They've asked that we both give a speech.'

I closed my eyes. Dragged a hand down my face. I was not a 'speak in public' kind of guy. Too many eyes narrowed in my direction. Too much expectation for me to be witty, clever and heartfelt all at the same time. I'd rather place twenty catheters than speak to that crowd.

'How about you talk and I'll stand dutifully by your side?' I said.

'Hell no. If I have to be trotted out like some kind of show pony, you do too.'

'Fine,' I said, taking the envelope from him.

He gave a satisfied nod like he was James Bond completing some urgent mission. 'Mom said you should bring a date.'

'Goodbye, Gray.' I yanked him toward the door and threw it open.

He patted me on the head and turned for the hallway. After two steps, he spun back around. 'You need to tell Mom and Dad the truth about going back to Africa.'

'I know,' I said heavily. 'Give me some time.'

He gave a stiff nod. 'Call Missy.'

'You're a menace.'

'Older brothers know best,' he cackled, and continued down the hall.

I closed the door and leaned my head against the wood.

A date? Nope.

The only woman who made my heart race had absolutely zero interest in ever being my plus-one.

Chapter Eleven

PIPER

The Next Chapter

As the saying goes, this town wasn't big enough for the two of us.

Even though we'd agreed to be friends, I still tried to avoid the new doctor. But every time I did an errand, went out into the square, I'd run into him. Most of the time I said very few words as I passed him on the street or in the cereal aisle at Minnie's Market. He was always kind, offering up a soft smile that made my heart flutter against my own will. My plan to ignore him, and those gorgeous blue eyes, for the next few months was going to be about as easy as getting Old Mrs V to slow down.

I wiped the thought of him from my mind and focused on Dex, who stood still as Maisey took measurements for his costume. Since I'd seen him in the square, his attitude had changed. Instead of questioning every revision to a line in the script, where he needed to stand during blocking practice, he eagerly agreed to whatever I told him. Urged other kids to pay attention when I was talking. Who knew a little kindness, and a few free donuts, could elicit loyalty in a twelve-year-old?

Maisey worked her magic, standing the kids in a line and using her tape measure to get all the details right.

When I'd mentioned last week how the theater's wardrobe department was in rough shape, she'd eagerly volunteered to help out.

After college, she'd worked for a few fashion designers in Nashville. Even talked about creating her own ready-to-wear line focused on separates, but when Ada first arrived, and then Jordan came quickly after, she fell in love with being a mother. She never spoke of it, but when we wandered in and out of dress shops, she took her time examining hems. The materials used. When she had time again, I had no doubt she'd go back to designing.

Ferris and Silvio worked on constructing the sets near the rear stage door. They traded their regular barbs until a new voice floated into the mix. I moved around the curtain and came to a stuttered stop. Ford filled most of the doorway with his wide shoulders. A backward baseball cap covered his dark hair. Clutched in his arms was a load of lumber and his biceps flexed under the weight.

'Hey.' The hesitancy in his voice warned he wasn't sure how I'd feel about seeing him.

'Hello. What are you doing here?'

'I saw Silvio and Ferris near the square yesterday. They said they were volunteering to build sets for the show. They needed help, so I offered my services.'

'Services?'

'I am a man of *many* talents, Piper.'

He was *not* giving me that bashful, yet way too cute, smile.

No. This guy was off limits. So why was it that every time he looked at me, my insides burned like I'd swallowed a damn blowtorch?

'Fine. Listen to Ferris and Silvio and don't get in the way. I've already had one trip to the community health center and had to deal with an annoying doctor.'

His booming laugh filled the air and Silvio's head snapped toward us.

'Doc, I thought you were here to work, not flirt!'

I loved that his cheeks went pink as he hitched his thumb and said, 'Duty calls.'

'Okay. Good,' I mumbled like an idiot as I walked back to the kids. As I jogged down the stairs at the side of the stage, Maisey waved me toward her.

'I hear our friend from the P&P is filling in for Doc Sheridan? That's an interesting development.'

'Yes, and just so you know, because everyone runs their mouth around here, he was at Memorial Springs while I was there.'

Her supportive smile said I didn't need to share any more.

The minute I returned to Ivy Falls after rehab, Maisey came to the Huckleberry Lane house. She sat her butt down on the edge of the newly constructed porch and refused to leave. We talked for hours, and not once did she treat me like some wounded animal she needed to fix. Instead, she invited me along for walks with her kids, on ice cream dates and trips to the movies.

Thanks to town gossip, she knew everything that had happened when I'd come home, how royally I'd messed up, but she never pressed me for any kind of explanation. Silently and sweetly she showed up every day, returning to the same supportive friend from my childhood. I was damn lucky to have her and I didn't tell her that enough.

'How are you feeling about that?' she said.

'At first, when we recognized each other, it was weird. But now?' I shrugged.

'Go on,' she pressed.

'According to him, and Beck, he was in and out of the room in a few minutes. I didn't speak to him and he never examined me. And the way he jumped right in to help Mrs V at the café proves he wants to help this town. That can never be a bad thing.'

She tapped her chin. 'If I remember the story right, he told Beck to talk to you. That the doc had been in places where people had severe injuries, been unconscious, and it helped to hear their family talk. Know they were there.'

'Yes. That aligns with what I've been told about his work overseas.'

'Don't you think traveling that far off is interesting? Wouldn't you like to know more?' Maisey was about as subtle as a slap to the back of the head. 'Ooooh!' She beamed like the damn Christmas tree they lit near town hall every year. 'You could be friendly. Invite him to "Music in the Square" next weekend.'

'No way. My plate is too full of other distractions, and the last thing I need to do is encourage the hot doctor.'

'So you do think he's hot?' Her sneaky gaze moved to where Ford was helping Silvio lift another piece of wood, those damn biceps flexing again.

'Don't you have more kids to measure?' I pressed.

'You are zero fun, Piper Townsend. What you need is a little excitement in your life. I think a handsome doctor could be the right medicine.' She giggled at her own joke.

'My life is simple and uncomplicated. I like it that way.'

She must have heard the catch in my voice. 'I shouldn't push. When you're ready, you'll do what's right for you.'

'Thanks, Maise. I do need more time.'

She gave me a distracted smile that said something else was on her mind.

'How are you? Are the kids sleeping any better?'

'A little.'

'But...' I urged.

Her shoulders sank. 'Being here. Working on the costumes. It's reminded me how much I love fashion. That I miss the imagination of it all. Dreaming up new designs in my head. Thinking about the right fabrics and thread.'

'Have you considered going back to work? You've talked a lot about creating your own line.'

'Ada and Jordan are still too young.'

'That doesn't mean you have to stop planning. Thinking about what comes next.'

I let my gaze wander to the stage where the young actors scurried around. How my chest warmed as they worked on their lines. Practiced the basics of the choreography.

'Maybe when the kids go to school full-time.'

'Whenever it is, I'll be here to support you in any way I can.'

She pulled me into a quick hug.

'I can't thank you enough for helping out,' I said.

She inched back and patted my cheek. 'It's my pleasure. Now let's talk about Dex's costume.'

I answered a few questions about hem length, and whether the chimney sweeps needed suspenders. A few minutes later the entry doors to the theater opened. Diego from Gold Star Properties walked down the main aisle and gave me a beckoning wave.

When I reached him he said, 'Do you have a minute?'

'Sure. We can sit at the back of the theater.'

Once we found spots in the upholstered red chairs, he pulled out his phone.

'I got an email this morning from a young couple who live in Atlanta but are interested in moving to Ivy Falls. They were in town a week ago, looked at that apartment you liked several times, and want to sign a lease. You've been wanting to move for a while, and I could tell you liked the space.' He scrubbed a hand over his mouth. 'Don't tell Beck I said this, but I think it'd be a good spot for you. If you want it, you need to make a move. Today.'

Well, crap. That was unexpected. Of all the places I'd seen, the small apartment was the best fit. It was already furnished, and the way golden light streamed in through the sliding glass door in the late afternoon was beautiful. I had already pictured myself sitting out on the balcony and having coffee on cool autumn mornings. It was just two units, so I hoped it would be quiet, peaceful, with only a single neighbor.

Beck said he wanted to talk more about me moving out, but Diego's arrival felt like a subtle push to make a decision. I imagined walking past the building on my way to the P&P or the café, regret crowding my chest because I hadn't jumped at the opportunity to make it my home when I had the chance.

'You're right. Ever since you showed it to me, I've been thinking how perfect it is. I'll take it.'

'Great! Come by the office later this afternoon and we'll sort out the paperwork.'

'Can you… not say anything to my brother for the moment. I want to tell him on my own.'

'Sure. I'm happy you're doing this and,' he gave me a confident nod, 'I'm proud you're taking this step.'

'It took a while, but I'm glad I'm here.'

His smile widened as we shook hands.

My own place.

A chance to start the next chapter.

Excitement zinged through my veins but quickly faded. Now I had to go home and tell Beck what I'd done.

He'd have a hard time letting me go, but no matter how much he wanted me to stay, I was ready to finally be on my own. It was a step I had to take, and I needed him to believe in me this one last time.

—

My work schedule meant I could return to the house on Huckleberry Lane by the late afternoon. It allowed me a few peaceful hours to clean up and start dinner before Torran and Beck came racing in the door from work.

I pulled the veggie lasagna out of the oven and sat at the table like a prisoner waiting to hear their final verdict. The speech I'd composed raced through my head on a constant loop.

It wasn't like Beck could keep me here, but he'd done a lot for me. The last thing I wanted to do was hurt him. That was why I'd created a list of all the reasons why it was a good idea for me to move out.

A few minutes later the front door opened and Torran and Beck's laughter filled the house. The sound of her boots shuffling, some soft murmuring, said she and Beck were sharing one more kiss.

This was another reason why I couldn't stay here. They shouldn't have to hide in the foyer when they wanted to be affectionate.

When they finally stumbled into the dining room, their eyes went wide.

Okay, so maybe I'd overdone it, setting the table with the good dishes and a bouquet I'd picked up at Minnie's Market.

'What's all this?' Beck said.

'Dinner,' I said casually.

He and Torran swapped a measured look before they sat at the table. I tried not to smile at the way Beck wiped at his mouth knowing his lips were still kiss-swollen.

I began spooning food onto plates when Torran said, 'We have some news. It looks like we've come to a compromise with Hearth and Home about the wedding.'

'Oh, what did you all decide?'

'They can take video of us getting ready, but filming of any kind will not happen during the ceremony or the reception,' Torran said.

'And they can post stills on the network and the show's social media that same day, but nothing more,' Beck said, helping himself to a piece of garlic bread.

'That's great. Problem solved,' I said.

'Sort of,' Torran hedged. Shadows smudged the creases under her eyes, and she wore a thick blanket of weariness that wasn't normal. This negotiation had taken a lot out of her. 'We were hoping you'd help out that day with the crew and all. Keep them confined to certain spaces. Make sure they don't try to sneak a video camera in during the ceremony,' she said.

'Would they do that?'

'Hopefully not,' Beck answered. 'But Lauren can get overzealous.'

'So you want me to play bad cop on your wedding day?'

'Yes,' they said at the exact same time.

'You're the perfect person, Pipe,' Beck went on. 'You know all the cameramen who work with Hearth and Home. You can be our eyes and ears that day.'

Torran gave me a pleading look. They'd finally figured out a plan that worked for them. Who was I to get in the way? The more I considered it, the more I realized I could use this to my advantage.

'I'll do it as long as I get something in return.'

Beck cocked his head. 'What do you want?'

I clutched my napkin in my lap and pushed out the next words. 'Your help transporting boxes because I'm moving out.'

Torran went green and Beck's slice of garlic bread hit the table.

'I thought we agreed to talk after the wedding,' he said.

'The apartment I like has a lot of interest. Diego came by the theater and told me if I wanted it, I had to make a deposit and sign the paperwork today.'

Beck dragged his hand down his face. 'You already put money down?'

'First and last month's rent.'

Before he could object, Torran interjected. 'Is this what you want? What you need to do?'

'While I know you both want me here, and I'm so thankful you gave me a home when I needed one, I can't have my own life if I'm living under my older brother's roof.'

'We could give you more space. Anything you need,' Beck insisted.

'That's not the point. With me gone, you and Torran can have privacy. Quiet, intimate dinners. Make those small upgrades to my bathroom you've been talking about. Hell, you could have "naked breakfast" if you wanted.'

'Naked breakfast?' Beck said.

'Yes, after, well, you know…' My gaze flicked to their bedroom upstairs. 'You could eat down here…'

Torran laughed. 'That's an interesting option.'

Beck let out a heavy breath. 'I'm trying hard to listen to you, Piper. If this is what you want, I'm on board, but you have to promise if you need anything you will reach out to us both, no matter the time. Day or night.'

'The apartment is a mile down the road, not in Chattanooga, Beck.'

'Promise me,' he repeated.

'All right. If there's a problem, you'll be my first call.'

He gave a hesitant nod and Torran reached out and squeezed his hand.

I understood this was hard for my brother. For ten years my choices had made his life a nightmare. It felt awful to know I'd caused those feelings in him, but we'd been through years of therapy and he knew deep down it was time to let me go.

'Tor, can we use Sally Mae for the move?' I asked.

Her old truck was a menace, often sputtering and spitting out black exhaust, but it also had ample space in the bed to transport what little I owned to the apartment.

'Of course! After dinner we'll pull the extra boxes we have out of the attic.'

Beck's pained gaze remained on me. I understood the stakes. This new move had to be a success or he'd never let me out of his sight again.

Chapter Twelve

FORD

Earworm

I'd never planned on helping out at the theater. After a long day at the clinic last week, I was headed toward Minnie's Market to pick up a few groceries and passed Silvio and the local handyman, Ferris, sitting on the bench by the fountain. Their voices carried across the square like they were having an argument.

I had every intention of scooting past them when Silvio waved me over and asked if I knew anything about carpentry. A part of me wanted to pretend I hadn't heard him, but then Janice's comments about getting to know the people in town filled my head.

'Just some basics,' I'd answered.

'Ferris keeps insisting that the two of us can build the sets needed for the show at the theater, but I'm pretty damn sure it's too much work for us. Do you have time to help out?'

With the two of them staring at me with a hint of desperation, I'd agreed. Now, two days later, my back still ached, and my hands were covered in new calluses thanks to all the sawing and hammering.

It didn't help that I'd been on my feet for twelve hours today. The clinic was packed with allergy cases, several kids who had hand, foot and mouth, and a wrist that was broken in two places thanks to a loose dog and a bad bounce on a trampoline, according to one of the mothers in town who spent twenty minutes telling me the entire story.

I wouldn't trade my aches and pains for anything though. Being at the theater had given me another chance to be in Piper's orbit. To witness how she easily connected with the kids. When she sat down at the piano and sang 'A Spoonful of Sugar', I nearly dropped the hammer I was holding on my toes. Her voice was what I imagined an angel would sound like: sweet and shimmering like a morning sunrise. Listening to her made that thrum in my chest grow louder, the blood dance in my veins. She'd undersold her talent by a thousand degrees.

With the song playing on a constant loop in my head, I headed down the hallway to Dr Sheridan's office. As the light faded from the windows, I finally got my first break of the day. Unfortunately, my work wasn't done yet. Before she'd left for the day, Janice had reminded me there were reports and case files on my desk that needed to be reviewed.

I sank into the rickety wooden desk chair and thumbed through the paperwork. A report attached to Mrs Vanderpool's file made me stop. Her echocardiogram showed what I expected – atrial fibrillation. The notes from the hospital described the plan of treatment, and the blood thinner prescribed to help with the problem.

My thoughts returned to Piper. Her panic and fear outside the clinic. I couldn't tell her what was happening with her friend, but I hoped Mrs Vanderpool would let her know about her condition when she was ready.

I thumbed through the rest of the reports and came across a Post-it taped to the inside of her file. It noted that Silvio had called twice today with questions.

I picked up the phone and dialed his number. A gruff, male voice barked, 'Hello.'

'Silvio?'

'That you, Doc Foster?'

'Yes, I saw you called twice today. Is there a problem?'

'Hold on a minute.' The phone went muffled and then there was a sharp snick of a door closing. 'Had to go outside cause Greta is in a mood.'

'Tell me what's happening.'

'She's been lying to me.'

'About what?'

'I've been asking if she's taken the prescription the cardiologist prescribed. She said she has but I noticed the bottle today. Doesn't look like a single pill is gone.'

'Did you talk to her about it?'

'She admitted that after the pharmacist gave her the pills she read the side effects and it scared her. Now she's refusing to take them.'

'Put her on the phone.'

'Could we come see you instead? I know Greta. You gotta look her in the eye. Tell her how serious this is.'

From the way everyone watched her at Sugar Rush, it was clear people wanted to know what was going on with her health, and Piper had made that clear with her prodding after Mrs Vanderpool left the clinic. Perhaps a quiet, face-to-face conversation was better.

'All right. I'll wait here for you.'

'Thanks, doc. You're the best.'

A slight knock sounded against the glass door to the clinic. Silvio gave me a brittle smile. Mrs Vanderpool was a different story.

'Why the hell am I being summoned here?'

'Because we need to go over your treatment and care.' I waved them toward the office and got a scowl in return.

Silvio reached for her hand and I followed them down the hall. My gaze lingered on their intertwined fingers.

I couldn't remember the last time I'd seen my parents show any kind of affection toward each other. It was another element of Harpeth Manor I hated. It was like people walked a thin tightrope between being human and what society defined as appropriate. There were too many forced smiles that never wrinkled thanks to Botox. A vacant look in the eyes as if no one could remember the last time they'd experienced any kind of joy. A half-life where every person worried more about their reputation than making genuine connections.

It was a big reason why I never wanted to go back there. I didn't care how many zeros were on a bank statement, living a sterile and loveless existence was a deal with the devil I had no interest in negotiating.

Once Silvio and Mrs Vanderpool were seated in front of my desk, I shuffled through her reports. They sat stiffly, Silvio's hand resting on top of hers. Again, that quiet signal of reassurance was endearing.

'Get on with it, doc,' she demanded.

'Let's start with the good news,' I said, flipping through the paperwork. 'Your cholesterol and creatinine numbers look good. White blood cells in range too.'

'I appreciate the rundown, but you didn't bring me here to blow sunshine up my rear.'

This woman was really full of fire. So much like Piper. Now I got why they were so close.

We had a brief staring contest before I recognized the twitch in her lower lip. A flicker of fear behind her clear blue eyes. She knew what I was about to say.

'Dr Engel at Vanderbilt told you about the atrial fibrillation, right?'

'Yep. My heart's not pumping right.'

'That's correct, and he gave you medication. A blood thinner?'

She nodded.

'Have you been taking it?'

The way her skin paled said she understood the real reason for this impromptu visit.

'This is serious. That medicine will regulate your heart rhythm. If you don't take it, you could faint again. Possibly have a stroke.'

Silvio took a thick gulp. 'Doc, I've been telling her...'

She shot him a traitorous look and he went silent. After shifting uneasily in the chair a few times, she said, 'I've never been too good about taking medicine, doc. Won't even swallow a pill when I have a headache. Something doesn't feel right about putting it in my body. And that paper that came with the medication.' Her voice caught. 'It said I could have nausea, severe stomach pains or confusion.'

'Mrs Vanderpool, this isn't a headache,' I said gently.

'Doc, you're treating me now. Call me Greta,' she huffed.

'All right, *Greta*, you need to do this if you want to go back to a normal life. What do you think people would do around here if you weren't setting them straight and doling out sage advice? Giving them support when they needed it?'

She quirked an eyebrow at my not-so-subtle reference to Piper.

'There are side effects. But worse things can happen besides a nosebleed or stomach cramping if you don't take it.'

Her lower lip trembled as she sank against Silvio.

As a physician you never got used to giving this kind of diagnosis. You fooled yourself into believing that if you practiced long enough you'd build an iron cage around your heart. That you'd become immune to the sadness that comes with the job. But then you had to witness the look of terror like the one currently pinching Silvio's face, and it was like twisting a knife in your gut.

Mrs Vanderpool looked at me for a long beat, her breaths coming in unsteady spurts.

'Sweetie, are you hearing him?' Silvio said.

'Um, of course. Thank you, Dr Foster. I'll start the medicine as soon as I get home,' she said, pushing up from the chair. Silvio snapped out his hand to help her stay steady.

'I advise you to take it easy. Try to rest.'

'I will.'

Silvio shook my hand before helping Greta shuffle out into the hall. I held on to the edge of the desk until the outer door clicked shut behind them.

I collapsed back into my chair. This job was supposed to be a blip. A quick way to make some money before I went back to Africa. I never expected to care about these people so quickly.

One of the last things Dr Sheridan said before he left was that Ivy Falls got into your bones. That the longer you were here, the more you felt at home. I brushed away the comment because nowhere but Africa had really felt like home to me. But now I feared his comment was true, because this place, these people, were becoming important to me, and that was the last thing I'd planned when I took this job.

—

After I'd locked up, I took the long way home. I walked past Minnie's Market. Her sign this week was a zinger: *Don't shop at big box stores. The prices will ketchup with you!* The Pool and Brew's was just as wild. *'Wine. Beer. Whiskey.'* beats *'Live. Love. Laugh.'*

Around the corner, the scent of cheese and garlic floated out of Mimi's Pizza. A few more steps led me to the glass windows that lined the front of the P&P. It took every ounce of self-control not to push inside and see if Piper was working. Instead, I forced my feet in the direction of my apartment.

My phone buzzed in my pocket. These days I was almost afraid to look at the screen. The onslaught of messages from my mother was getting to be too much. I hesitated before tapping in my passcode. When I saw it was from Gray I groaned. He'd been relentless in his quest for me to call Missy. This time he suggested we go on a double date with one of the girls he was currently seeing. That wasn't going to happen.

I pushed through the courtyard gate and walked up the stairs. My body hung heavy with the weight of the day. Once I had the outside door open, the electronic sound of early 90s pop filled the hall. A towering stack of boxes sat outside the door beside mine.

Today of all days a new neighbor had to move in?

I stifled the grumble crowding my throat. All I wanted was to come home to peace and quiet. Now that plan was shot to hell thanks to the new occupant's obsession with a remix of Britney Spears' 'Toxic'.

It took a minute to flip on a few lights in my apartment. I crossed to the freezer and pulled out a pot pie and threw it into the microwave. After I took off my button-down and khakis that reeked of Betadine and rubbing alcohol, I pulled on a Vanderbilt T-shirt and a pair of athletic shorts. The scent of baked pastry and thawed vegetables filled the kitchen.

On the ship there was a hot meal every night. I'd sit in the same spot at the back of the dining hall with my friends, swapping stories about our day and where we planned to travel when we had precious time off. Standing alone in my empty kitchen left a dull ache in my chest. I missed the heated conversations at dinner over our favorite movies or losing sports teams. If the meatloaf or pot roast was the best thing that came out of the kitchen. How the coffee tasted more like you were swallowing grounds than liquid, but we drank it anyway due to our long hours.

I pulled out a chair at the small bistro table and went to work on the pot pie, scrolling through my phone. There were more texts from my mother that I was ignoring. I knew I had to call her, confess about going back to Africa, but I was too exhausted to cross that bridge.

The music continued to throb through the walls, and I switched to my social media to see what my friends had posted online. It was a time suck, but it felt good to stay connected to the *Humanity of the Seas* staff. To know what they were up to while I was gone.

Britney Spears morphed into the low bass beat of Rihanna. The voice was muffled, but my new neighbor knew every single line to the chorus of 'Umbrella'.

Great. Now I'd have that earworm in my head for days.

The music annoyingly banged around inside my head while I demolished the pie. When my plate was clean, I walked to the sink and dumped the remaining crumbs. Thankfully, I'd bought a new carton of mint fudge ice cream from Minnie's Market.

After a few bites, the knots loosened in my shoulders as I sank onto the couch. The low drone of the Atlanta Braves' announcer made my eyes flutter closed.

A crash a few minutes later nearly rolled me off the couch, sending the half-eaten ice cream flying. Several screeches followed by more than a few F-bombs bled through the walls. Instinct had me on my feet and racing outside. I knocked on my neighbor's door several times with no answer.

My heart picked up speed. What if the new tenant had passed out and water flooded the entire floor?

I continued with my insistent knocks until the deadbolt flipped with a clanging snick. The door flew open and I double blinked at the sight in front of me. Wet dark hair and smooth pink skin wrapped in a lavender plastic shower curtain. A trickle of blood dripped from an arched eyebrow.

'What are you doing here?' Piper tugged the plastic around herself tighter.

I stepped back, not wanting to make her uncomfortable. 'I live… next door.'

'What?' she screeched.

'Yes, and you're bleeding. There's a cut on your head.'

She clutched at the curtain wrapped around herself with one hand and used her other hand to touch her face. Her mouth puckered at the blood staining her fingertips. 'My shower rod fell. Must have caught me in the eye.'

I stayed frozen, wanting to help but knowing this was her personal space that I had zero intention of invading.

'Do you want... Can I have a look at that cut?'

She touched the spot again and winced. 'Fine, come in.'

Cardboard boxes and plastic bins sat in a haphazard pile in the center of the room. Her floor plan was the same as mine but the rooms were flipped so we shared the same bedroom wall.

'Medicine kit and a flashlight?' I asked as the puddle grew around her feet, my gaze snagging on the daisy-yellow nail polish on her toes. I forced my attention to the cabinet where she pointed and I grabbed the white metal box. 'Do you want to get a towel? I can wait.'

Her lips pinched into a thin line. 'You think I'd be standing here in a shower curtain if I had a towel?'

God, she is beautiful when she is annoyed.

'You took a shower without a towel?'

She jabbed a finger at me. 'You can leave if all I'm gonna get is judgment. I was hot and sweaty and wanted to rinse off. A towel was the last thing I was thinking about.'

A vision of her in the shower raced through my head. I took a thick gulp and looked away from her ruby-red lips. At the end of the counter was a napkin and I shoved it in her direction.

'Press this to your head and go put on some clothes. When you're ready, I'll take a look at the cut on your head.'

'You're ordering me around now?'

It was hard to keep a straight face with her tugging that curtain around her, the illustrated unicorns at the bottom scrunching together as she moved.

'Yes, because you'll never get your cleaning deposit back if you keep dripping blood on the floor.'

She rolled her eyes and huffed out, 'Yes, Dr Foster.'

Chapter Thirteen

PIPER

Lost In The Dark

I had the shittiest luck in the world. Here I was trying to stay away from this guy and I ended up moving next door to him?

It was my own damn fault. When I was signing the lease, Diego had mentioned that the apartment was occupied, I just hadn't bothered to ask any other questions.

I raced into my bedroom, a stack of moving boxes piled up against one wall. Everything about this day had gone sideways. I'd loaded up Sally Mae to haul my stuff, and Beck, without my knowing, had taken the day off from work at his advertising agency. It took three tries before we finally got the truck to start. Once we were on our way, Beck shot off a round of questions.

Did the kitchen have a fire extinguisher?

Was the stove gas or electric?

If it was gas, did the apartment have carbon-monoxide detectors?

The questions got more ridiculous as we circled the block four times before finding a parking spot. Heat from the bright orange sun beat down on us as we hauled box after box through the gate and up the stairs. When we were finally unloaded, I pushed him out the door, sweat dripping from my brow. With him gone, I'd gotten the brilliant idea to hop in the shower without a towel. That was until the rod crashed down, and I ended up answering the door in nothing but a cheap children's shower curtain only to find the one man in Ivy Falls I was trying to avoid.

I tore open boxes until I found a pair of leggings, a bra that had seen better days and an old concert T-shirt I'd picked up in a vintage store in Brooklyn. With one hand still pressing the napkin to my head, I used the other to peel off the shower curtain. I cringed at the deep lines and marks from where the plastic pressed into my wet skin.

Once I was dressed, I tugged a brush through my hair and stalked back to the living room.

'Sit down and let's take a look.' His voice was hesitant, like he didn't want to do or say the wrong thing. I hated that it was so damn endearing.

I sank onto the couch and he skimmed the beam from the flashlight across my eyes.

'How's your head feeling?'

'I do not have a concussion if that's what you're thinking.'

'You have to be thorough with head injuries.' He flicked that light over my eyes again.

'Head injuries? It's a cut. You're being too dramatic.'

'Dramatic,' he chuckled. 'Who's the one that answered the door wrapped up like a taco in a vinyl shower curtain? Were those dancing pink unicorns I saw?'

'Yes,' I grumbled. 'The curtains in the adult section of the store were boring.'

He did a poor job of hiding a smirk as he reached for the first aid kit and pulled out a vacuum-sealed alcohol pad.

'This may sting a little.' He eased the napkin away from my head and dabbed at the cut. Under his breath he started to hum and it took me a minute to recognize the melody.

'That song gets in your brain and doesn't let go, right?'

He tilted his head before he realized what I meant. 'Yes, but "A Spoonful of Sugar" is kind of a classic.' His focus went back to my head. 'How long have you been playing the piano?'

'Since I could climb on a stool and reach the keys.'

'And the singing?' he said, peeling apart a sterile package and pressing a white, gauzy bandage gently to my head.

I stared at his cornflower-blue eyes. The flecks of gold that danced around the iris. Dammit. He was too gorgeous for words and here I was behaving like a fucking damsel in distress.

'A few lessons when I was a preteen. Some more vocal training when I lived in New York.'

'Right, you mentioned New York.'

'I was one of those starry-eyed girls who goes to the big city with all these dreams. Thought I could be on Broadway. Spent every penny I made waiting tables to see shows like *Six* and *Hadestown*. Memorized the songs. Even the blocking onstage. I spent hours in front of the mirror practicing my dancing. Had this vision that I could be up there one day performing for packed houses.'

His gaze stayed fixed on me like he'd listen to me talk for hours. 'Did you ever audition?'

'Several times for chorus openings in shows like *Moulin Rouge* and *Wicked*. Me and like a thousand other wannabe actors.'

I rarely talked about my time in New York. While I loved the city, how the pace was like a constant stream of caffeine in my veins, other parts of it were bad for me. The loneliness and frequent temptation of alcohol and drugs. How once the sun set behind the skyscrapers, all my demons crawled out of their hiding spaces and took up residence in my head.

He pulled off strips of tape and pressed them against the bandage, mumbling a word under his breath.

'What did you say?'

'Brave. It's like I said the day Mrs V got sick. Putting yourself out there. Sharing your talent with the world knowing you might get rejected. That takes real bravery.'

'Or a hell of a lot of delusion.'

'I disagree. People spend their whole lives thinking about their dreams but never chasing them. Then, when they are at the end of their life, they voice all their regrets. Believe me, I've heard from more than a few patients how they wished they'd taken more chances. You had a goal and went after it. What you did took courage. Never underestimate how powerful it was to make that choice.'

I sat in stunned silence. He barely knew me but he easily cut right to the heart of the matter. There were a lot of things about my past I wasn't proud of, but auditioning for shows, living in New York, was the one glimpse of sunlight in that stormy period of my life.

'Is it weird?' I asked hesitantly.

'Is what weird?'

'Having to take care of me again?'

It was the damn elephant in the room. Might as well get it out in the open.

'If this, if I'm… making you uncomfortable, I can go because that is the last thing I want.'

'No.' I reached out and touched his knee. He focused on where my hand sat and I quickly pulled away.

'Piper, what you battled is a sickness like any other. You were treated and then followed doctor's orders. Committed to recovery, set a new path, which by the looks of things was a damn good choice.'

Behind those beautiful eyes was not a single flicker of judgment. And if he was going to work at the clinic through the summer, he would have heard my whole story anyway because no one in this town could keep their mouth shut.

His steady gaze never wavered even as I said, 'Am I fixed, doc?'

He pressed his lips into a thin line. 'Ford.'

'Excuse me?'

'I want you to call me Ford.' That sweet grin reappeared. 'It feels appropriate now that we're neighbors.'

I muttered, 'Fine.'

'Do you have a headache or any other symptoms?'

'Besides extreme embarrassment, *Ford*? No.'

That got me a full-blown smile. He closed up the first aid kit, set it on the counter and walked straight toward the bathroom. I chased after him and stumbled into the room, bumping into the pedestal sink.

He ran his fingers over the spot where the shower rod was once anchored to the wall. 'Wow. This took some work. Were you hanging on the bar like it was a jungle gym?' he chuckled.

'No, but I may have been dancing a little. Flailed my hands out and hit it.' The way he bit into his lip said he was holding back another smile. 'Yes, Rihanna does make me want to move, but maybe the shower isn't the best place for a dance party.'

He threw back his head and laughed. 'You think?'

As his shoulders shook, I took in this casual side of him. The T-shirt and shorts. How the sheen in his luscious dark hair made me want to reach out and run my fingers through it. And that smile, it was equal parts boyish and sexy, which only made my mind race with thoughts of how his lips would feel brushing across mine, his tongue parting the seam between us.

'I have spackling paste in my apartment that'll patch it,' he said, interrupting my fantasy.

'That's not necessary. My soon-to-be sister-in-law is a contractor. She can fix it.'

'When? Because unless she can come over in the next day or so, you're not getting a shower.'

'There's a tub. I'll take a bath.'

He rubbed at the dark stubble on his chin. 'Are you always this stubborn?'

'Yes,' I admitted.

'Let me help you out, Bird. It's the neighborly thing to do.'

There was that nickname again. I hated that it was sort of growing on me.

He arched an eyebrow, waiting on my answer. If I called Torran, she'd bring Beck. There'd be a dozen questions and then getting my brother to leave again would be an ordeal.

'Okay. Thank you.'

He left and, as soon as I heard the door close, I raced back into my bedroom. In one of these boxes or bins there had to be my towels. My hair was still sopping wet and I didn't want to keep dripping everywhere.

I wrenched open several plastic containers until I found a hand towel mixed in with my perfume and lotions. Quickly I squeezed out most of the water from my hair and tossed it up into a messy bun. When I raced back into the bathroom, Ford was already covering the hole with what looked like children's glue.

'A doctor and a handyman?' I teased.

'You'd be surprised at how basic skills can be helpful around a house.'

'Did your father teach you?'

The lines in his forehead pinched.

Okay. Maybe not a great question.

'My father is more of a hire-someone-to-do-it-for-you kind of guy. I learned about drywall and plumbing from one of the guys on the ship. My cabin had a broken door handle and Kip, who handles all the maintenance, came by to replace it. I asked a bunch of questions and he showed me how to fix it on my own. Whenever he had other jobs to do, and if I wasn't on shift, he'd let me tag along and learn.'

'The next time you see Kip, tell him thank you for me.'

He gave an approving nod and went back to work. It was hard not to watch his biceps flexing up and down, the intense set of his full lips as he concentrated. The question I'd been wanting to ask since last week ping-ponged inside my head. I guess there was no time like the present.

'Any word on Mrs Vanderpool's tests?'

He stopped mid-spackle and pulled in a heavy breath.

Shit. That wasn't good.

'I can't say much besides she's getting the care she needs.' He pushed up those cute Clark Kent glasses. 'You two seem close. Have you been friends a long time?'

'Mrs Vanderpool is one of the weirder twists in my life and I've had some doozies.'

'Really?' That damn grin was back. 'Do tell.'

'When I came back to Ivy Falls, a lot of people weren't sure how to treat me. Mrs Vanderpool always scared me when I was young. Kids at my school even made up stories about how she was a witch. Liked to boil kids in her backyard if a ball was hit on to her lawn.'

'That's damn morbid.'

'For a long time she was our version of the bogeyman. Then I moved away and when I came back…'

I could still see her piercing blue eyes the first time she ran into me and Beck at Minnie's Market. Everyone knew what I'd done to the house on Huckleberry Lane. Whispered about my third trip to rehab. Mrs Vanderpool marched right past the fruit and vegetables, a box of bran cereal tucked under her arm, and said a sentence to me I'll never forget.

It's easy to get lost in the dark. Let Ivy Falls be your light.

It knocked the wind out of me when she pulled me into a massive hug, held on for no more than two breaths, and then turned in her black orthopedic shoes and stomped toward the register. Since that day, she'd given me a smile, a pat on the shoulder, every time she saw me. On that day she could have easily replaced the words *Ivy Falls* with *me*, because she'd been the kindness and understanding I'd needed at the lowest point in my life.

'It was kids being dumb. I know better now. She's become the grandmother I never had.'

'I wish I could tell you more—'

'No, it's okay. Sorry if I made this… weird.'

'You can ask me anything you want, except for confidential patient information. I'm an open book, Piper.'

'No one is an open book, *Ford*.' That earned me another one of those panty-dropping smirks. 'It's easy to say that but when people ask hard questions, even you might find it hard to be honest.'

He tapped at the spackle with a putty knife and said, 'Let's put that theory to the test.'

I leaned a hip against the sink, studying how he continued to work without a single hint of tension in his athletic frame. He was cocky but not in an off-putting way. In his Harpeth Manor world I bet things were always proper. That certain topics were off limits in order to keep up appearances. Maybe it was time to make him uncomfortable. Set him a little off-kilter like I felt when he stared at me with that pale blue gaze.

'How old were you when you lost your virginity and how badly did you screw it up?'

I waited for him to sputter. To take several uncomfortable gulps. What I did not expect was the roar of a laugh that burst from his lips.

'It was bad. I was in the eleventh grade and at my first senior party. There was a girl in my class I liked. No names to protect the innocent,' he said coyly. 'We kissed at first and then went upstairs. I tried to be smooth, kicked off my shoes, lowered her onto the bed.'

Heat snapped through my veins. Dammit, I'd walked right into a trap. My point was to embarrass him, but I was the one getting all pink-cheeked.

'Once we were on the bed, she rolled me over and kissed me. I thought it was a power play, so I rolled again and sent us careening right off the bed. I landed on her with the full force of my weight, knocking the wind out of her.' He shook his head. 'Poor girl gasped for air for like thirty seconds. It was a real shitshow.'

'After all that, did it… still happen?'

God, my cheeks were blazing. So much for being a smart-ass.

'Yes. After she could, you know, actually breathe again.' He let loose another uninhibited laugh, and it was so infectious I found myself giggling along.

How was he doing this? Being so smart. Cute. Honest. Making me smile so wide my face ached. It was easy to see why he was good at being a doctor. He wore empathy like a second skin and I hated to admit it was a goddamn turn on.

He went back to fixing the wall, anchoring the shower rod and humming 'A Spoonful of Sugar' until the doorbell rang.

I froze. Shit. It had to be Beck. Besides my close family, Diego and Maisey – and, well, now Ford – no one else knew I lived here.

My brother's hovering had to end and I was going to tell him that. I started for the door when Ford said, 'That would be the pizza.'

'You ordered pizza? To *my apartment*? Why?'

Chapter Fourteen

FORD

Like A Fortress

Maybe I'd overstepped. The entire time we were on the couch Piper's stomach gurgled like she was hiding a small monster and it was hard to ignore.

When I went next door, I called Mimi's and ordered. The small pot pie I'd eaten hadn't made a dent, and I was still starving. I thought I could pass it off as a 'Welcome to the Neighborhood' type gesture. But the truth was wrapped in a plastic shower curtain, or wearing an old concert T-shirt, Piper was a damn vision and I wanted more time with her.

'Everyone's got to eat, and after the day you've had,' I glanced at the newly spackled wall, 'I'd guess you haven't had food in a while. But if you want me to go, that's okay. I can leave the food here.'

Her mouth thinned and she clucked her tongue. 'What kind of pizza is it?'

'Pepperoni.'

Her jaw twitched. 'I'm a vegetarian.'

Thankfully I'd thought about that possibility when ordering.

'Good thing I got half with only veggies.'

She tapped her fingers on her hipbones. 'I don't eat dairy either.'

Fuck. Didn't think of that.

'All right. Let's order Thai or Chinese. Whatever you want.'

The corners of her mouth twitched. 'I'm kidding. I love cheese too much to be dairy-free.'

I let out a sigh of relief and she smiled like she really enjoyed messing with me.

We walked into the family room and Piper stopped short. 'I have no idea where my plates are in this mess.'

'Took care of that too.'

I opened the door and paid the pizza delivery guy. Piper waited on the couch and I placed the box down in front of her along with a handful of napkins and paper plates.

'Thank you. This was thoughtful,' she said like she might finally be giving in an inch.

We each picked a slice and spent a quiet minute eating. The room was covered in boxes, bins and five suitcases.

'Did your brother help you move in?'

'He insisted, even though I'm sure he had a million things going on at work today.'

'What does he do?'

'He owns an advertising agency in Nashville with his best friend.'

'That's got to keep him busy.'

'It does and he's planning a wedding too.'

'When's the big day?'

'Early October. They're having it in the backyard of the house where I grew up.'

'That must make your parents happy.'

She stopped with the pizza halfway to her mouth.

'It's, uh, only me and my brother. My parents are gone.'
Crap. I need to stop talking.
'I'm sorry,' I said.
'It happened a long time ago,' she said, nibbling on a corner of the crust. 'How Beck and I ended up in the house is a whole other story.'
'I'd love to hear it.'
She went on to tell me how Beck came back to town and bid on the house, stealing it away from his now-fiancée, Torran, at auction. How he was sure he could fix the place, which was in rough shape, until he fell through the floor of the attic. She grew more animated as she explained the way Torran had to save him. The agreement her brother made with Torran and her business partner, Manny, to restore the house, all while filming a show for the Hearth and Home network.
'That explains the crowds in the square taking pictures. I thought they were just tourists, but I did hear whispers in the café about a TV show. Is that why there are all those funny signs around too?'
'No, that's the town contest. The mayor, who happens to be Torran's dad, started it a few years ago. He did it to help tourism, but everyone in this town is so damn competitive it turned into a big deal. Barb and Susan have won the last three years.' She wiped a bit of cheese from her beautiful lips and caught me staring. 'What?' She patted at her shirt. 'Did I spill sauce on me somewhere?'
'No. It's this place. Dr Sheridan mentioned how everyone looks out for each other. Treats one another like family. At first I didn't buy it, but after being here a few weeks I see what he meant. It's...' I paused, trying not to spoil the mood with my thoughts of Harpeth Manor. How all people cared about was how much money

you could accumulate and who got the prized table in the country club's formal dining room. 'Refreshing,' I finished.

She tucked her knees under her, resting her plate on her lap. It was a simple move but she did it gracefully. I pressed a hand to my chest, an ache filling the space around my heart. I barely knew this girl, but there was something about the way she held herself back, the emotions she kept solidly in check, that made me want to get closer. Help loosen the tethers she kept strapped around her heart.

'Are you close to your family? You mentioned you had a brother the other day at the clinic. Any other siblings?' she asked.

'It's only me and Gray.'

'What's he like? Is he a doctor too?'

I smothered a laugh. 'No, he works for a bank, but I swear his real job is professional playboy. He dates a lot. Travels the world. Not sure the guy has a single care.'

'Really? I would have never pictured that.'

'Why?'

'Because you're focused and even-keeled. I expected your brother to be the same.'

'Gray is like the freaking Tasmanian Devil. He's got his hands in a dozen business projects. If he's not working, he's on the golf course, drinking with his friends, or at a concert or parties.'

'And you're not into that?' she asked, taking another nibble of pizza.

'The complete opposite. I like it quiet. Calm. To sit with my own thoughts for a while, especially after I've had a long day. In Senegal, I often saw close to twenty-five cases on a single shift. It's a constant churn, evaluating patients, figuring out the next steps for their care whether it's a follow-up appointment or the need for surgery. The work is rewarding, and I especially love it when a local medical student works with me. It feels good to pass along what I've learned. Know that when their training is done, they'll take care of their community.'

'What's Senegal like? Why did you decide to go there? Do they speak a different language?' She pressed a hand to her lips like she could stop the flow of questions. 'Am I being too nosey? It's sort of an affliction in Ivy Falls.'

'No. I enjoy talking about my work.'

She smiled, waved her hand for me to go on.

'After I finished my family practice residency at Meharry in Nashville, my parents wanted me to work for one of their friends in private practice. Every time I thought about it, I got this knot in the pit of my stomach. One day I was chatting with an international student who told me about the humanity ships. I went home that day, looked it up, and put in an application. A month later, they sent me an email asking when I could start.' I set down my plate, wiped my mouth, which I was convinced was covered in pizza sauce. 'Dakar, the capital, is beautiful. There are all these open-stall markets and the food is amazing. Fresh fish, vegetables and spices. I love taking a day to explore. Practicing my French.'

'Are you fluent?'

'*Oui. Je parle français.*'

The grin she gave me brightened the entire damn room. She stretched out her long, beautiful legs, and I shoved my hands into my pockets. It was the only way to fight my urge to touch her, know how smooth her skin would be under my fingertips. I couldn't help but wonder if I pressed my hands to her waist, would it make her cheeks flame and her breath hitch?

'I bet your parents were proud once you were accepted. That you were going where your skills were needed.'

I stayed quiet.

'I'm pushing again. We can talk about something else.'

'No, it's only that...' I paused because it was hard to frame my response without making my parents look like the villains in my origin story. 'They were... hesitant.'

Her brows pinched together and she winced like she'd forgotten the cut above her eye. 'That doesn't make sense.'

'They had other plans in mind. None of which included me graduating from residency and flying across the world the next day. They especially hated it when a year later I left the ship and went to work in a field hospital with Doctors in Service.'

'Yes.' Her gaze went serious. 'My brother told me about that.'

'It was hard and not a good fit for me. After I was done, I went right back to the ship in Senegal.'

She must have noticed the stress in my voice because she said, 'Tell me more about Africa.'

'It's beautiful and the people are wonderful.' I sighed, a familiar warmth falling over me. 'They're generous and kind. In Senegal, they have this word they use... *Teranga*. It means being human first. That we each have value. That you are welcome the minute you enter the community. The wards on the ship's surgical units are a symbol of that idea. Most of the beds are only a few feet apart. It's much different than in the US. The patients don't mind though. They comfort one another. Encourage each other through treatment. It's life-changing to see.'

'I'm beginning to understand why you enjoy it so much.'

I took another slice to keep my mind off the fact that, if I leaned in closer, I could brush my mouth over hers, taste the fresh basil and mozzarella on her lips.

'And you like living on a ship? I would imagine it gets cramped.'

'My single-berth room is small. There's only space for a bed, a desk and very tiny bathroom. All I really do there is sleep. If I'm not on shift, I'm out exploring.'

She set her slice on her plate and brushed the crumbs off her fingertips. 'It sounds fascinating. Tell me more.'

'There's this spot called La Corniche that's a pathway along the public beaches. In certain places, they have restaurants where they cook fresh fish on outdoor grills. They also serve madd, which is a fruit. Locals mix the pulp with sugar and water and it's delicious. There's also Lake Retba. Also known as Lac Rose. Pink Lake. The algae in it produces a pinkish hue that's stunning. Locals mine it for salt to preserve fish. In the last few years it's become Instagram famous.'

She tilted her head and held me in that gorgeous amber gaze. 'You miss it.'

'I do,' I said, not realizing how much until I had started talking about it. 'That's enough about me. How about you and Beck? Are you alike?'

'A little.' She slid her plate onto the table. 'But I suppose that's because we're bonded through trauma.'

The way she wrapped her arms around herself, protecting her body like a fortress, warned I was stepping into uncomfortable territory for her.

I wanted to say the right thing, insist she could trust me. My mind spun with the ways I could put her at ease until my phone buzzed in my pocket. It was a message from the clinic, requesting I call a patient who had a question about a new medication.

It was for the best. I'd laid a quiet foundation for a friendship with her tonight, and I didn't need to press my luck.

'I should go. That's the after-hours answering service.'

'Sure.'

For a flicker of a second I could have sworn she was disappointed I was leaving.

'Thanks for the pizza.'

'No problem. Don't go hanging on any more shower rods, all right?'

'That's not what happened,' she laughed, swatting at my shoulder.

I caught her hand in midair. We stayed in a smoldering haze, neither of us moving. I took a step closer, her beautiful red lips drawing me in. Her eyes were a stunning blend of gold and brown with small specks of green around the edges. And, fuck, her hair smelled like coffee and vanilla and I wanted to bury myself in the scent of her.

I pushed a lock of hair away from her cheek and her breath caught. Feeling that undeniable pull toward her, I slid my hand behind her neck. She shuttered her eyes as if waiting for me. I leaned in, so close to brushing my mouth over hers, until my phone buzzed again. The shock of it forced me to take a step back, making some space between us.

'I should go.'

Her gentle eyes took me in and I softly ran my thumb over the bandage on her head.

'Goodnight, Bird.'

A soft smile lifted her lips when she said goodbye.

Friends, I reminded myself as I walked to my own door. That's what we agreed. But when I closed my eyes tonight, I suspected the only thing I'd be dreaming about was her.

Chapter Fifteen

PIPER

Muscle Memory

'Pick an outfit before all my beautiful years are gone and I start sprouting white chin hairs!' Maisey groaned as she fell back onto my bed.

'I'm not going because, if you couldn't tell, I have absolutely nothing to wear.'

'It's a good thing your best friend has impeccable taste. Give me a minute to put a few items together.'

She bounced up and stalked to where I was standing in the doorway to my closet. It'd taken nearly a week, but I was finally unpacked. Having all my stuff in one spot made me painfully aware that my wardrobe was lacking. I'd spent the last two years doing exactly two things: going to work and seeing my therapist once a week. My wardrobe of faded jeans and old T-shirts reflected that lifestyle.

Maisey pushed back hanger after hanger. Small, frustrated sighs filled the shoebox-sized closet. At the end of the top rack, her eyes narrowed on a fringed black skirt. She took two small jumps trying to grab it.

'Shit, I hate being short.'

'You're not short. You're fun-sized!' I teased.

She shot me an annoyed stare. 'Not all of us can be supermodel tall!'

I moved around her and lifted off the hanger.

'Show off,' she grumbled before pulling a sparkly silver T-shirt off the lower rack. With another huff she glanced at my pitiful array of shoes, selecting a short pair of black suede booties.

'This is "Music in the Square" not "Night at the Rave",' I protested.

'Put them on. You know you're going to look great in it with those long legs and that damn glossy hair of yours. I saw Janice from the clinic at Minnie's Market earlier today. She said Dr Hottie McHotterson will be there. Once he sees you in that outfit, he won't be able to take his eyes off you.'

'What are you even saying?' I laughed. 'Ford and I are friends.'

Even as I said the words, I knew they were a lie. When he touched me the other night before he left, I desperately wanted him to kiss me. But it was a bad idea. He was leaving, and was a tie to my past, but that didn't still the need that coursed through my veins when he touched me.

'Yeah, and Simone Biles is just a gymnast,' she called me out. 'He helped you out after your shower curtain tragedy, and how many times did he happen to need a book or an iced tea this week?'

'A few,' I admitted.

Since our impromptu pizza meal, Ford had made more than one appearance at the P&P. He swore it was because he wanted new books, or that the summer heat made him thirsty, but Maisey was right. He did make a few excuses to run into me.

I should have used those moments to remind him we were only friends, but the way his mouth softened, how his gaze hungrily traveled the length of me, had me swallowing all my protests.

It was nice to flirt every once in a while. To remember I was a woman who liked attention from a ridiculously attractive guy. And when he laughed, pushed those glasses up the bridge of his nose, there may have been a swoop in my belly I hadn't felt since I had my first crush in high school.

I walked into the bathroom and shut the door so she couldn't press the subject anymore. Having him in town, living next door, it was too much. The last thing I needed was to catch feelings for a guy who was going to turn around and leave in a few months.

I pushed Ford out of my head and tugged on the shirt Maisey picked and the skirt followed.

Dammit. The outfit looked good.

As if she could read my thoughts, she said through the door, 'You look fantastic, right?'

I cracked open the door and the contrite look on my face made her squeal and clap her hands excitedly. She pushed her way inside the bathroom, yanking out my makeup and grabbing my flat iron from a basket next to the sink. More than once her stare moved to the spot where Ford had to spackle the wall and then to the small bandage over my eyebrow.

'What else did you and Ford chat about the other night?' Her smile faded. 'Did he say anything about Old Mrs V?'

'You know he can't give information about a patient.'

She gave a reluctant nod and started to work on my hair, pulling back half and threading it into a fishtail braid.

'He told me a little about his brother. It sounds like he isn't close to his family.'

'Look at you getting all the details about our mysterious town doctor,' she said like she was impressed. 'He wouldn't answer any of my questions, but I also don't have an ass like yours.'

'Maisey!' I shrieked.

All she did was shrug. 'Only facts here, Pipe.'

'You are incorrigible.'

'And that's why you love me.' She combed out the lower section of my hair and wrapped it around the flat iron. 'What else did he say?'

'That Africa is beautiful. He told me about a couple of spots he likes to visit on his days off. Beaches and a place with sand dunes. He's also fluent in French.'

She fanned herself. 'Well, that makes him ten times hotter.'

'You are too much.'

She barked out a laugh. 'What about his job?'

'He didn't say much, but by the way his eyes lit up when he talked about the other staff and the patients, it was easy to see he loves it.'

'When is he going back?'

'Early October.'

She got a glint in her eye but stayed silent, which worried me.

'It's okay to meet a new person,' I said. 'Get to know them and keep things platonic.'

I might have been saying the words, but the way my heart stuttered every time he dragged his hands through his dark hair said my feelings were anything but platonic.

She bit into her lip while she worked the iron through the rest of my hair.

'You think I'm wrong,' I said, needing to break up the silence.

'Piper, it's your choice. All I want is for you to be happy. If being friends with Ford is all you want, then I'm behind you.'

'But…' I urged because she'd always been careful about my feelings. Not pushing me.

She pressed her lips together, pausing for too long.

'Spit it out, Maise.'

'I love you, but I worry that you've fought so hard to get your life back that you're afraid now to take a risk. Rock the boat against the solid life you've built.'

'Is there something wrong with that?' I said, unable to keep the hurt from my voice.

She set the iron on the edge of the sink and turned me to face her.

'You've been through hell and back. Battled nightmares that would knock most people out for the count. But every damn day you get up and prove to this town that you have the heart and soul of a warrior.' She went back to work on my hair. 'What good is all that fighting, getting yourself to a solid spot, if you're not thinking about the future? Any man on this planet would be fucking lucky to call you theirs, Pipe. I wish that you would be willing to take a small chance. It doesn't have to be with Ford. It doesn't have to be right now. I only want you to think about what comes next, because you, my best friend in this world, deserve goddamn rainbows and unicorns-farting-glitter-out-of-their-butts kinds of happiness.'

'Oh, Maisey,' I gasped. Tears tracked down my cheeks and she pulled me into a firm hug.

'Good thing I didn't do your makeup first,' she said, swiping away her own tears and then pressing a tissue to mine.

'Before I got sober, I made terrifyingly bad choices when it came to men. Those choices hurt a lot of people.'

My mind flickered to the moments in New York where I blew through all my money. How I took drinks from strangers. Walked home alone at all hours of the night. I was reckless, dumb and damn lucky I didn't do anything worse to ruin my life.

'I'm afraid if I let myself try, I'm going to say and do the wrong things. Pick another bad guy. Ruin the people I love again.'

'You won't.' She lovingly patted my cheek. 'From what you've shared with me, you know what you need. What you deserve. After all the work you've done to change your life, don't you owe it to yourself to test the waters? It doesn't have to be a commitment. Go on one date. Have coffee with someone. It's like learning to ride a bike. Start slow until you're ready to pedal like hell on wheels.'

I placed my hand over hers. 'I promise I'll think about it.'

'Thank you. Now enough with the love lecture.'

'Good,' I said, patting at my eyes with a tissue. 'Because I have other issues to deal with, like figuring out how I'm going to get Lauren not to be a pain in the ass on Torran and Beck's wedding day.'

'They agreed to let Hearth and Home film it?'

'Just the getting ready part. After that, they can only have access to a few frames of still photography for the show and social media.'

She faced me back to the mirror to finish my hair. Crying always made my eyes and cheeks puffy. She was right. I was glad makeup was last in her devious plan to make me presentable. 'And this concerns you how?'

'They asked that I run interference with the production crew. Make sure they keep their promises. Not film the ceremony. Stay out of the way.'

'So they're making you play defense to a very cagey offense?'

'I have no idea what that means.'

'It's football. Joe has it on from late August to January. You learn a lot through osmosis.'

I laughed. Maisey was like a computer with about a hundred tabs open.

'You're going to have to keep them from making things uncomfortable during the ceremony, basically.'

That sent a chill down my spine. 'Really? That's what you think?'

'Torran and Beck's wedding will be a big marketing boon for the network. The more images and video they have to promote it, the better their numbers. The more viewers they attract.'

'Well, shit. That sounds like a lot of work.'

She gave my shoulder a reassuring squeeze. 'You won't keep the wolves at bay alone. I'll be there to help.'

The stress that had been building in my bones ever since I agreed to help out Beck and Torran started to ease. 'You're the best, Maise.'

She gave me a cheeky wink in the mirror. 'I know.'

—

The square was aglow with hundreds of twinkle lights. Booths flanked the outer perimeter, the scent of kettle corn and burgers filling the air. Children dressed in their

Sunday best chased each other in a game of tag on the lawn in front of town hall. The wondrous green tinge of fireflies danced around them. On the stage set up near the fountain, a five-piece band unloaded their equipment and tuned their guitars.

Maisey locked arms with me and dragged me to a corner near the community bank where Torran stood with Manny. Beck, Torran's dad and Tessa stood a few feet away having a quiet conversation. Tessa's girls and Manny's daughter sat on a picnic bench, licking frantically at melting ice cream cones all in an attempt to keep their frilly lavender dresses clean. Their hair was plaited in elaborate braids courtesy of Manny and his obsession with online hair tutorials.

When we reached them, Torran let out a low whistle and gave a megawatt smile.

'Nice work, Maise. I can't remember the last time I saw Piper dressed up.'

Maisey gave an overdramatic bow and all I could do was shake my head. Flinch at the way they all stared at me in wonder. It wasn't like I dressed in grubby clothes all the time. Sometimes I wore… nice jeans.

I glanced toward the sidewalk, considering what kind of excuse I could make to get out of this night. Beck, sensing my mood change, took my hand and dragged me over to the stand where they were making grilled corn. More than once his stare moved to the small bandage on my head.

'Next time I see the doc, I need to thank him for taking care of you. Tell me again how the shower curtain fell?'

'Beck,' I groaned. 'I. Am. Fine. See, all arms and legs intact.' I held his gaze. 'You're doing it again.'

'Doing what?' he said as if he didn't know where this conversation was headed.

'Dr Catherine told you more than once during our family sessions that it's not healthy to hover.' I made a propeller motion with my finger. 'But here you are doing just that.'

He scrubbed at his hair. 'Yeah, you're right. Sorry.'

'Don't say sorry because that makes me feel bad.' I paused until he looked at me. 'We have a deal. Open communication. If I need you, I swear I'll call. Stop worrying that any time a problem comes up, I'll risk my sobriety.'

'Is that what you think I'm doing?'

'Yes.'

'Shit, Pipe. That is not what this is about. It's only that I loved having you at the house. It was like we were making up for lost time.'

The band ran a couple of scales, tuned their instruments and then greeted the crowd. With a quick strum of his guitar, the lead singer started the first chords of Shania Twain's 'Man! I Feel Like A Woman!', and people made their way to the dance floor.

'I'm literally four blocks from Huckleberry Lane. Calm down and go ask your fiancée to dance. Think about your own life and stop stressing about mine.'

He gave me an apologetic smile. 'All right. I'll leave you in peace.'

'Promise?' I teased.

He laughed and made his way back to Torran.

Once they were on the dance floor, Tessa and Manny quickly joined them along with Torran's dad and his girl-friend, Isabel.

I leaned back against a nearby light pole, loving the scene. The way the air filled with the sound of people's laughter. The pure joy that emanated from the growing crowd. How a cool breeze blew over the grass near the gazebo. A figure moved up its steps and I walked in that direction.

Dex sat on one of the built-in benches inside the gazebo. With his foot, he tapped out the counts in a song. 'Step in Time', the song featuring the chimney sweeps in the show, rang out in that beautiful tenor voice of his. I inched back down a step to give him privacy, but the old wood squeaked under my feet.

Dex jumped up and caught me trying to flee. 'Miss Piper?'

'I didn't mean to interrupt.'

'You weren't,' he said, toeing at a loose board. 'I'm having problems singing and doing all the complicated choreography at the same time.'

'Want some help?'

In the square, the band moved into Travis Tritt's 'T-R-O-U-B-L-E'. The mood kicked up a notch as couples shuffled and spun around the dance floor.

He toed at the ground again. 'Don't you want to be out there with all the adults?'

'What I want to do is make you more comfortable with this scene. You're talented, Dex. All you need to do is take a breath and relax.'

'Maybe you should give Griff or Connor the role. They're much better dancers than me.'

'Miss Cheri picked you for the part because she knows you can do it, and I agree.'

'I keep tripping when I do the choreography. Can't figure out how to sing and move at the same time. I'm a mess.' He trudged to one of the benches and sank down.

More than once I'd been exactly where he was. Too afraid to mess up. Worried I'd let the adults down with my performance. All I could think to say was what I'd been told by one of my own drama teachers. 'Theater is about having fun,' I said, taking the spot beside him. 'You shouldn't be performing for me, or your parents, or your friends. You should be performing for *you*. If you're not enjoying it, what's the point?'

He shrugged, flipping his skateboard over and over with his foot. 'What if I make a fool out of myself? All my friends will laugh. I'll never live it down.'

'You could look at it that way. Or you could think of it as a way to push yourself. Let me ask you this.' I pointed to his skateboard. 'How long did you have to practice before you could do a few tricks?'

'I spent months at the skate park.'

'Did you practice while your friends were around?'

'Yes.'

'And did you fall on your butt more than once?'

He gave me a half-smile. 'I fell a lot.'

'Did they laugh? Point fingers?'

'No, because they were biting it worse than me.'

'That's all performing is… practice. You do it enough and it becomes muscle memory. The song plays and your body knows what to do.'

'That's kind of like an ollie. I plant my back foot on the tail, my front foot in the center. Toes lined up with the edge.' He grabbed his board to show me. 'Then you snap the tail and jump.' He went into motion and I liked the confident way he held his body. He needed that same attitude with this dance. He skated back toward me and said, 'At first the trick is hard, and you fall a lot. But now, I do it all without thinking about it.'

'Exactly.' I tipped my chin to the center of the gazebo. 'Want to give the choreography another try?'

'Only if you do it with me, because I know you've learned the steps too.' He grinned.

Maybe I hadn't been so subtle standing stage right and moving along with the kids.

'Let's go then.'

We stood a few feet apart and I counted off the song. Together we stepped left. Moved right. Did an intricate crossover all while trying to keep up with our singing. More than once we stumbled, tripped over our own feet, but we kept going.

Toward the end of the song, we moved to the center and we spun in a circle until the world started to tilt. He eventually let go of my hands and we both flung out to the far edges of the gazebo. Dex landed on a bench, while I careened directly into a well-built chest.

'Why are people down there when the real show is up here?' Ford said, gripping my waist, his fingers pressing into the thin fabric of my shirt.

'I was… helping Dex with a little bit of choreography,' I said, inching away from his warm touch.

He chuckled and crossed his arms over his chest. Dammit, I hated that my limbs tingled when I looked at him. That with his dark hair brushed back, those glasses sitting perfectly on the bridge of his nose, he was too gorgeous for words.

'Miss Piper is really good at this. She knows all the steps.'

'I bet she does.' He stepped closer, the woody scent of his cologne washing over me. 'Want to head to the dance floor and show me some moves? I could use a teacher too.' The huskiness to his voice, and not-so-subtle innuendo, made my veins electric.

'We still have a little more to go over here.'

Dex was already grabbing his skateboard. 'It's okay, Miss Piper. My mom's expecting me for dinner and I'm already late.'

He grinned like he and Ford were co-conspirators and took off down the steps.

Ford held out his hand, his voice dropping so achingly low that I felt the timbre of it in every part of my body. The musicians transitioned from one quick song to the next, the sweet sound of the fiddle sweeping through the air.

'What do you say, Bird? May I have this dance?'

Chapter Sixteen

FORD

Shoot My Shot

I'd only been in one serious relationship. Sydney was in my medical school class. We shared the same study groups. Struggled with parts of the pharmacology curriculum. Slowly our classmates found other places to study until it was only the two of us quizzing each other and drinking way too much coffee.

It was reassuring to have her around. To know she was tackling the same kinds of stress as me. What we had was safe. Comfortable.

When the time came to talk about where we wanted to do our residencies, she hinted that she wanted to follow me. Thought it was time for more of a commitment. A week before Match Day, when we'd learn about where we'd do our residencies, she asked me point-blank if I was going to marry her. In that moment I clearly saw what a future with her would look like. It was exactly what my parents wanted: children, a dog and a white picket fence.

Having that sobering vision freaked me out. Syd deserved more than I could give her. So instead of a ring, she got an apology and a not so suave breakup.

That cramping in my chest I'd felt with Sydney, I was convinced would happen with every woman I met, but as the music played, Piper's hand tucked into mine, my breaths came easy. I'd even have called them light.

The band moved from a Johnny Cash song to an upbeat Luke Bryan tune. The crowd hooted, hollered and stomped their feet. Skirts spun in colorful chaos. Boots sashayed across the floor in thick, measured steps. I swung Piper out and pulled her in, doing a quick cradle turn before reeling her back into my side.

'Holy crap. You can really dance.'

'I may have had a little practice, but it's no "Step in Time".'

That earned me a laugh that I swore almost shot me straight to the moon.

When Janice first told me about the 'Music in the Square' event it sounded small-town hokey to me. The more I thought about it though, the more I pictured seeing Piper. Asking her to dance. Chances were she'd say no, but that didn't mean I wasn't willing to shoot my shot.

Once I heard the music from my balcony, I walked out to the square. Booths lined the block selling everything from beer to kettle corn to lemonade. Rows of black smokers sat on the sidewalk, people eager to try the local brisket and barbecued pork. Picnic tables covered in bright yellow gingham spread out across the brick-paved street. On an elevated stage near the fountain a five-piece band played one of their first songs.

Every few steps, I got a smile or a hello from a patient. It was wild how I'd only been here five weeks and already knew so many names and faces.

My gaze flicked over the crowd and my heart sank when I couldn't find Piper.

Earlier, I'd heard her and Maisey giggling through the walls. When the conversation stopped, and her door slammed, I waited a half an hour before I made my own exit.

I checked every booth. Scanned the dance floor. Still no Piper.

I moved outside the square and toward town hall. At first, all I heard was Dex's voice singing out.

Man, the kid was good.

I followed the sound and was treated to Piper's own voice a few seconds later. Goosebumps rippled across my skin as her laughter, and encouraging words, floated out of the gazebo. My intention was to stay in the shadows, only watch for a moment. But then she spun straight toward the stairs, and I stepped out to make sure she didn't take a tumble. As I cupped her against my chest, the feel and scent of her sent me on another rollercoaster drop.

'Dex is getting really good. He's going to blow everyone away during the performances,' she said.

'That's a credit to you.'

We followed the crowd around the floor in a quick two-step, changing positions and shifting our bodies in time to the music. The more we moved, the more eyes followed us.

From across the dance floor, Greta watched us curiously. Miss Cheri stood near the gazebo, giving me a pleased-as-punch grin. Barb and Susan passed us more than once. Their lingering and hesitant gazes saying more than they wanted.

The one stare that never wavered belonged to a guy with sandy-brown hair and a determined scowl. When I'd first met Piper's brother in the hospital, the fear he

wore made him appear much older. Now he just looked…
pissed.

'We're drawing attention,' I said, tipping my chin in
Beck's direction.

'So what. Are you having fun?'

Fun. This was more than that. This was an erotic
fantasy come to life. Being able to press my fingers against
her skin. Hold her this close. Yeah, I'd be dreaming about
it for weeks.

'I'm having a blast,' I said.

'Good. Let's ignore everyone else.'

I spun her again, never wanting to let her go. The
upbeat song blended into a quiet ballad a few beats later. I
waited for her to pull away. Make some excuse to step out
of my arms, especially now with the crowd's attention on
us. Instead, she wound her hands around my neck and laid
her head against my shoulder. I couldn't explain the sweep
of relief that passed through my body at that moment, but
I knew one thing to be true. I'd never felt this way about
another woman.

While the fiddle played a gentle melody, I folded her
in closer. Her coffee and vanilla scent was hypnotic. The
brush of her silver shirt against my hands unleashed an
undeniable want. We'd almost kissed the other night in
her apartment, and I'd been thinking about it ever since,
wanting it even more.

She pulled back and stared into my eyes. I slid my hands
down her arms and my fingers skidded over the tattoo on
her wrist. 'I've been meaning to tell you how much I like
your hummingbird.'

A small smile pulled up the corners of her lips. 'Thank
you. It's special.'

There was an ache to her voice that said it had meaning.

'Tell me about it. More than once, I've seen you trace its edges when you're nervous.'

She worried her full bottom lip and paused like she was weighing if she could trust me.

'When I was in rehab there were a lot of outdoor spaces for patients. A community garden became a favorite spot of mine. Every time I took a walk there, a pair of hummingbirds flitted in between the wildflowers. The first few times it happened, I sat and watched them in wonder, thinking that they nested close by. That the garden must be their favorite spot. One day I asked one of my nurses about them. She said she'd worked there for nearly ten years, spent a ton of time in the garden, and had never once seen a pair of hummingbirds. That it was rare because they were usually singular creatures.' She pulled in a shaky breath. 'It felt weird that they only appeared for me, and I took it as a sign.'

'What kind of sign?' I couldn't help but ask, curious for her to share more of herself.

'This may sound ridiculous, but I started thinking they were a symbol of my parents. That they were there watching over me. Letting me know I was going to be okay.' She shook her head, her gaze going to the ground. 'As soon as I started getting better, I wanted that bird tattooed on me as a reminder that my parents are always in my heart. That I want to make them proud.'

She'd mentioned that she and her brother were bonded by trauma, and from town gossip, whispered to me in pieces, I knew her parents had died tragically in a fire. I'd never asked for more details because it felt too much like invading her privacy.

'I don't think it's ridiculous. We have lots of touch-stones in our lives. Ways we want to remember what's important to us.' Softly, I traced over the bird's head and down over its wings and she shivered under my touch. 'I like that you want to feel close to them. Not all of us have that special bond with our parents.'

Her arms tightened around my neck like she wanted me closer. 'I still don't understand your folks. What is it about your choices that bothers them so much? Most people would be proud to have a son who is selfless. Who wants to use his skills and education to help a community in need.'

I pressed my lips together. My parents were not my favorite topic, but the way she watched me with interest, cocking her head slightly, said she wanted to know more. Know me.

'There's a sort of unwritten code, a legacy, that is expected of every kid born into the Harpeth Manor world.'

'What kind of code?'

'You're born there. You're educated there. You return to work and raise a family with other people from that world. If you veer from that path, make your own choices, you're seen as two things: a rebel or a weirdo.'

'And which one are you?'

'Definitely a little of both.'

Her glossy dark hair swayed against her shoulders. The hoops in the tops of her ears glittered in the moonlight. She gave a little smirk and said, 'Funny, I like that combination.'

'Do you?' I inched her closer, hungry for the heat of her.

'Yes, and to be honest, that life sounds boring and sort of incestuous,' she said with a hint of contempt.

God, I liked this woman. She didn't pull any punches. Told it like it was. I needed more people like her in my life.

'I guess it is, and my parents, well, they like the Stepford lifestyle. Their parents accepted it. As did their parents before. Gray and I have broken that mold, and they're not pleased about it.'

'Raising two successful men. Men who are choosing their own path. That is something to be proud of, not to scoff at.' Her eyes went hard. 'Don't ever introduce me to your folks. I might not be pleasant.'

I laughed again and it felt damn good.

'No worries. I promise to keep you far from the lion's den.'

The song ended and the band announced they were taking a fifteen-minute break.

'Want a drink?' I asked.

'Sure.'

She followed me to the booth at the far end of the square where they were selling water bottles, sweet tea and lemonade. When we got close to the front of the line, Piper noticed Greta sitting at a table with Silvio.

It struck me again how sweet the two of them were. Janice at the office told me they'd both been widowed a long time, lived their own quiet lives, until Greta started harassing Silvio about climbing ladders and lifting too heavy boxes at the hardware store. Their bickering turned into coffee dates and then real dates.

As I watched them chat, all I could think was I was glad she had him. That he was encouraging her to take the medicine. Having him steady by her side would make getting used to her new normal a lot easier.

'Do you mind?' Piper tipped her chin to their table. 'I want to check in with Old Mrs V.'

'Not a problem. What do you want?'

'Lemonade, please.' She flashed me a bright smile that made me take a thick gulp. Did she have any idea what that did to my heart?

She moved in the direction of the table and I couldn't help but watch her go.

'You're holding up the line eyeballing my little sister like that.'

Beck stepped up to my side. His expression was a complicated mix of caution and suspicion.

'Oh, sorry,' I said, trying not to act like a busted teenager.

'Saw you two dancing. You look good together.'

'It's all her. I was only following her lead.'

'That's bullshit. I saw you spinning her around. You know what you're doing.'

'Cotillion,' I mumbled.

'What?'

'Forced cotillion classes will do that to a guy.'

'Oh, yeah. You're from Harpeth Manor, right?'

'Yep.'

He nodded like he was sizing me up. 'I'm always leery of anyone who wants to be near Piper. But you...' He sighed. 'You already know the situation.' The fear in his eyes said more than he thought. 'She's asked me a million times not to meddle in her life. Said she's in a good place. I believe her.' His gaze moved to where Piper laughed at whatever Silvio was saying. 'How long are you helping out at the clinic?'

'Until October.'

'Are you headed back to Nashville or Harpeth Manor when you're done?'

'No, I'm going to Senegal to do humanitarian work.'

He scrubbed at his jaw. 'Does Pipe know that?'

'We've discussed it.'

'She's been through a lot of shit. Deserves someone who can be a friend. A partner. Someone…' His dark eyes narrowed. 'Who's going to stick around.'

His meaning was brutally clear. That someone was not me.

'We're friends. Neighbors. That's all.'

The lie stung but I wasn't about to tell him I'd had more than one hot dream featuring his sister.

'Yeah, Diego told me you live in the other apartment above the law office.' His shoulders loosened. 'That explains the bandage over her head that was too perfectly placed. She said something about a falling shower rod?'

'It was a small issue. Not a big deal.'

'I'm glad it's you there,' he mumbled. 'Was a bit worried about who might take that apartment. Since my fiancée's TV show took off, we've had a lot of out-of-towners move in. I didn't want her living next to a stranger.'

I almost said she was in good hands, that I'd look out for her, keep her safe, but suspicion still lingered in his eyes.

The line inched forward and I tried to be subtle as I kept an eye on Piper. By the way Silvio and Greta kept laughing, it was clear neither of them were ready to tell anyone about what was happening with her health.

A tall, bald guy in the booth shouted 'Next!' in my direction.

'I'll let you get to your order,' Beck said. 'Welcome to Ivy Falls, doc. Let us know if you need anything.'

The band returned a few minutes later with another fast song. A woman with reddish-brown hair and several young girls in purple dresses spun in circles on the dance floor. I set the lemonade down next to Piper as she let out a loud whistle, cheering them on. They turned in her direction and the three girls raced toward her. She gave each of them a firm hug while the woman quickly scanned me, eventually turning her interest to Piper.

'Are you going to make introductions?'

'Tessa, I'd bet twenty bucks you already know who this is. And if you don't, I'd say the Ivy Falls gossip train is losing its steam.'

One of the girls who looked to be around thirteen said, 'He's the new doc. Everyone knows that.'

'Thank you, Lou, for proving my point.' Piper winked at her and the girl lit up.

'Hey.' The woman shot out her hand toward me. 'I'm Tessa and these are my girls, Iris and Rose.' The two girls gave me smiles that had more than a few teeth missing. 'And this cutie,' she pointed to the teen girl, 'is my boyfriend Manny's daughter, Lou.'

She gave my hand a firm shake. 'Barb and Susan at Sugar Rush told me you've been to Africa. Have you seen lions or elephants?'

That got the other little girls' attention.

'I've been on a few game reserves. Seen both lions and giraffes.' I lowered my voice. 'Zebras and hyenas too!'

'Oh, that's cool,' Lou said like she was trying not to be impressed.

A big guy with dark hair ambled in our direction. 'What kind of trouble are you all causing over here?'

He reached out and clenched my hand. 'Hey, doc, I'm Manny.'

It still shook me a little that everyone in town knew who I was.

'Pop, he's seen zebras! Like the kind in the wild not at the zoo,' Lou said, that chill façade slipping.

He ran a loving hand over her hair. 'Louisa loves all kinds of animals.'

'I'm gonna be a veterinarian. Take care of all kinds of animals big and small like that Dr Oakley on Nat Geo.'

Piper smiled at Lou like she'd be the first one cheering at her graduation.

The last chord of a song rang through the air and the lead singer announced it was the final song of the night.

'Girls, shall we?' Manny bowed to each one and swung his arm in the direction of the dance floor. Tessa and the girls followed and they joined hands in a circle and swayed back and forth.

I'd never pictured myself with a family but they sure made it look tempting.

Silvio led Greta out to the floor. Most of the town joined them including Maisey and her husband, and Beck and Torran, who continued to shoot curious looks toward our table.

'What do you say, Bird? Want to dance one more time?'

She took my hand as the band played a slow ballad I recognized.

'No one else should sing "Wild Horses" except for the Rolling Stones.'

She scoffed. 'The cover by the UK band The Sundays is much better.'

'Are we about to have our first disagreement?'

She rolled her eyes. 'Just hold me tighter, doc.'

As we moved slowly to the music, the cumulative stares of Ivy Falls were daunting. Instead of being loose in my arms this time, Piper's body was wound tighter than a tourniquet.

'What's wrong?'

'I know I said to ignore them, but that.' She tipped her chin to the crowd. 'Is getting annoying.'

'They'll tire of us soon enough. It's not a big deal.'

'Really? So when you first went to the Sugar Rush, Susan didn't tell you to stay away from me? That I deserved a little peace?'

'How did you know that?'

'It's the same speech she gives any guy that comes into the café and stares at me a little too long.'

'I take it that happens a lot?' I said, even though I wasn't sure I wanted to hear the answer.

Lazily she tapped at her chin. 'What's a lot?'

She loved every minute of making me squirm.

'Barb and Susan aren't a worry now. They like me, and I get free donuts and coffee whenever I want,' I said smugly.

'Uh-oh, watch out. With that kind of treatment, you'll never want to leave Ivy Falls.'

She'd meant it as a joke, but a little part of me wondered what it'd be like to stay. To see if she'd let me be a part of her life.

It made me pull her in closer. Hold on to her for as long as she'd let me.

Chapter Seventeen

PIPER

Training Wheels

After saying a way too long goodbye to my brother and Torran, I let Ford take my hand and lead me back across the square. Even with the sun long set, the summer heat still clung to my skin. Perspiration rolled down between the center of my bra and soaked the thin fabric of my shirt.

When we reached my apartment door, I hesitated. A big part of me wanted him to come inside. See what kind of a kisser he was. Yet that knot that always sat low in my chest weighed heavier tonight. I wasn't quite sure if I was ready for any of this.

'Uh, do you want to come inside?'

Sensing my awkward pause, he said, 'Let me show you something first.'

He led me to an opaque glass door at the end of the hall and pushed it open revealing a circular wrought-iron staircase. I followed him up the steps and out to the roof. The view spilled out all the way to the city line. I'd never seen Ivy Falls from this vantage point. It was such a sweet collection of eclectic storefronts with the fountain at the center of it all, gurgling out its regular tune. Overhead the sky was black velvet with a handful of stars tossed up against it like silvery glitter.

'Diego did not show me this feature of the building,' I said.

'I'm not sure it's a feature. When I first came up here there were old fast-food wrappers, a few broken folding chairs, like no one had used the space in years.'

I walked to the edge of the roof and pulled in a full breath. The air was cooler up here, and it helped that a light breeze moved through the night. Lights in the gazebo and over the stage went out. I wasn't sure I'd ever seen Ivy Falls this quiet.

'Does the town hold events like this a lot?' he asked.

'Yes. We have a fall festival. A Christmas tree lighting. Egg roll in the spring on the lawn in front of town hall. You just missed the big Fourth of July parade and fireworks.'

Mentioning the holiday always made acid rise in my throat. Two years later and the memory of that night still hurt like a wasp's sting.

'It's nice that people want to participate. Spend time together.'

'They don't do that in Harpeth Manor?'

'Only if it revolves around golf or society gatherings like the debutante ball.'

'Debutante? Girls still do that?'

'It's gone from a formal society thing to more of a scholarship event, but they still make escorts wear a tux with tails.'

'I bet you looked good in white tie.'

He grimaced. 'It is really not my best look.'

'Scrubs then?'

'Not even that. Those things can be scratchy if they haven't been properly washed.'

I set my elbows on the roof wall. The glow of the few lights on in the businesses gave the square a golden hue. Ivy Falls was nice during the day but at night it felt magical.

'What was it like growing up here?' he asked.

'I'm not going to lie. It was sort of idyllic. As kids we could roam free. Ride our bikes everywhere. My favorite childhood memories are of hanging out at the P&P. My mom loved the shop and adored Mrs Wright.'

'Tessa and Torran's mom?'

'Yes, she owned it first. Sadly, she passed away a few years back. Left it to Tessa. It was one of the first places we checked out after we moved here. My mom took me to the picture books. Mrs Wright introduced Beck to Torran that day. He swears it was love at first sight.'

'Now they're getting married. That's like a fairy tale.'

'They've been through a lot.' I flipped my hair back, rubbed at my wrist. The knowledge that they almost didn't get their happy ending because of me was always a stab to the heart. 'How are you liking Ivy Falls?' I said, desperate to change the subject.

He didn't respond and I turned to find him giving me a pained kind of stare.

'Was that a bad question to ask?'

'It's not that.' He scrubbed at his hair. Pushed his glasses up his nose. 'Shit, I don't know what to do.'

I stepped in his direction, pulled forward by the ache in his voice. 'Do about what?' I asked softly.

'I came to Ivy Falls to kill time until I go back to Senegal. Not in a million years did I think I'd meet someone like you.' He ran his hand over the back of his neck. 'It's kinda freaking me out.'

'Good freaking out or bad?' I inched closer and he sucked in a thready breath.

'Good,' he hissed as my hand slid into his.

It was like time stopped. Holding us in a place where the only people who existed in the world were the two of us. I tried not to let my body shake. Give away how much this moment was messing with my heart and my head.

I'd sworn that my only focus over these last two years was to get sober. To create a stable life for myself. Dating, intimacy, were never part of the plan, but as I stood in front of Ford while he gave me a look that spoke of quiet kisses and more slow dances, I questioned what I wanted.

Only hours earlier I'd told Maisey I wasn't ready for this, but Ford made it too damn easy. He was sweet, kind and had an instinct for when it was the right time to speak. The right time to be quiet and listen.

He stared at me with gentle eyes and all I could think was that he could be my test case. The bike with training wheels I needed to experiment with before I was ready to get back on the road to dating again. It was almost too perfect. We could be together for the rest of the summer and when Doc Sheridan returned, he'd leave. No worries. No regrets.

Face. Forgive. Forward.

This was forward and if I wanted it I had to let him know.

'Tell me what's spinning through that beautiful brain because your silence is killing me.' He dragged a hand over his mouth like he was keeping himself from saying any more.

I let my fingers walk down his collar and my hand stopped over his heart. Another shaky breath escaped his lips.

'What if we made a deal?' I said, stepping in between his legs. The heat of him pressed against my skirt making my blood freaking sizzle.

'What kind of deal?'

'While you're in Ivy Falls, we go to dinner. Maybe the drive-in. Have a little fun in the dark. Nothing serious. No commitment. When it's time for you to leave, we part as friends.'

'Are you sure?' he said with a stutter.

I curled my fingers into his expertly starched shirt. 'Yes, Ford.'

'Okay, but I need a little clarification about the fun-in-the-dark thing,' he said roughly.

'Do you?' I stood on my tiptoes and planted a kiss on the hollow of his neck, dragging my tongue over the top of his collarbone and chasing that with a line of kisses up to the corner of his ear. 'Am I making things clearer?'

'Repeat your question from earlier.'

I liked how his voice went gritty. 'Ford, do you want to go to my apartment?'

He gave me that boyish smile that set my skin on fire. 'Yes, please.'

Chapter Eighteen

FORD

The Match

We weren't two steps in the door when I spun Piper around and pressed my mouth to hers. She gave a delicious squeak before she melted into me. I had a hard time deciding where I should put my hands because I wanted to touch her everywhere. I settled on her lower back as our kisses deepened.

When I'd gotten ready this evening, I'd thought maybe I'd coax her into a dance. Maybe two. Even though we'd had pizza, shared a bit of our history, she'd still been cagey. Doing her best to avoid me when I went to claim my free coffee and donuts from Sugar Rush. Twice now, I'd casually walked into the bookstore pretending to need a book or a drink. The sly smile she'd given me said she knew exactly why I was there, but I kept a gentle distance between us not wanting to push things.

She ran her nails up and down my back. I loved the way she gripped me like she needed to hold on to me tightly, pull me close, ensure I wasn't going anywhere.

Her kisses were slow and languid as we learned each other's instincts and reactions to small bites and hungry moans.

She tugged the shirt out of the back of my pants and I walked her backward until her knees hit the edge of the couch. Once she sank down, I pulled off my shirt and the way she greedily scanned my body nearly undid me.

She scooted back to make room for me but there was hesitancy in her gaze, a tremor in her lower lip. I didn't need anything more from her than to be in her presence. To listen to the melody of her voice and the soft cadence of her breaths.

'Do me a favor,' I whispered. 'Sit on the floor.'

Her eyes narrowed. 'You want me on the floor?'

'Trust me.'

She ran a shaky hand over her mouth. 'You don't know how hard that is for me.'

I ran a finger along her soft cheek. 'Bird, you could ask me to do a backflip, the Macarena, yodel right now, and I'd oblige.'

'Yodel? Can you yodel?'

There was that smart-ass tone I loved.

'Trust me?' I repeated.

She cocked her head. Everything about her was deliberate. How she talked, dressed, interacted with the people of Ivy Falls. It was like she was weighing every encounter. Making sure she never did or said a word to upset anyone. It had to be a heavy load to carry. For once I wanted her to clear her mind and let go.

After letting out a shaky breath, she sank down onto the rug covering the floor.

I took a spot on the couch behind her and loosened the hairband at the end of her elaborate half-braid.

'What are you...?'

'Hang on,' I whispered against her neck, and I loved the way she shivered.

171

Once I had the band out, I unraveled the braid piece by piece until her hair hung down her back in luminous dark waves. I started at the top of her head and lightly massaged, working my way down to her shoulders. Another shaky breath left her mouth, and the tension she carried like tight cords under her skin melted away. I worked my hands down below her scapula and her triceps, taking my time massaging and kneading.

Her breath stuttered as she said, 'All that time studying anatomy was not wasted, I see.'

'Oh, I know how to handle several parts of the body.'

'I bet you do,' she murmured, which made my pants tighten.

I swept back her curtain of hair, placing my mouth against the tender skin on the base of her neck. I kept working her shoulders, pushing aside the thin silver material of her shirt.

'That feels so good,' she stuttered.

'Which part? My hands or my mouth?'

'I have to choose? Well, that's mean,' she teased.

Without any prompting from me, she pulled off her shirt. I had to bite my tongue. Her skin was like silk under my fingertips. Her bra the softest color pink I'd ever seen.

She turned to face me and pulled my mouth down to hers. I tried not to moan at the way her lips moved over mine – sweet and achingly slow. I gripped the edge of the couch as she climbed onto my lap and we fell backwards. Her hands were in my hair and all I could think about was how much I wanted to unclip that bra and place my mouth over her nipples. I reached for the strap and she put her hand over mine. That hesitancy was back.

'Is it okay if all we do is kiss right now? Take things slow?' she said.

I ran a finger along her arm, still amazed that she was letting me be this close. 'Of course. You set the rules and I'll follow.'

'Thank you.' She gave me a relieved smile that made me pause.

Did she think I would argue? It made me wonder what kind of guys she'd been with in the past. How they were idiots not to treat her like an absolute freaking queen.

She moved off my lap and took the space beside me. 'Why did you want to be a family doctor?'

'Where did that question come from?'

'I enjoy learning about people's backstories. How they decided on their life's path. I'm still not sure what I want to do, so I like hearing how other people became inspired. Decided which direction their life would take.'

The vulnerability in her voice said that if she was going to trust me, she needed to know me. To see the real me, not the doctor mask I often wore for the town.

'The truth is that wasn't my first choice.'

She shot me a look of surprise. 'There's a story there.'

I scooted against the couch's cushions. She wriggled between my legs, and I'm sure she could feel how hard I was but she didn't say a word.

'Orthopedics was my dad's idea. He had these big dreams about me becoming the team doctor for the Nashville Predators or the Tennessee Titans. Thought it'd be a great thing to brag about to his country-club pals.'

'Again, your dad is sounding too much like an asshole.'

'He can be a bit much sometimes.'

She rubbed her hand down my leg as a comfort but it only turned me on more.

'Where does this story take a turn?' she said.

'The Match.'

173

'What's that?'

'In your final year of medical school you start interviewing for residency. After you've visited all the programs who are interested in you, you have to list in order where you would prefer to go. Orthopedics is one of the most competitive specialties.'

The memory of that day was still a bitter pill to swallow.

'On "Match Day" you get an envelope and open it with all the other students in your class. Your family surrounds you and it's supposed to be loud and celebratory. All you hear is ripping paper and shouts and screams. Some tears.'

'And your envelope?'

'It's complicated.'

'Go on,' she said gently.

'Two days before The Match I got a call from the dean's office telling me I didn't get into a residency program.'

She sucked in a quick breath, threaded her fingers through mine.

'I scrambled to find another spot, and a professor I knew well encouraged me to take a family practice opening at Meharry. He insisted I had the skills and disposition for the job. Deep down I knew he was right.'

'What happened after?'

I scrubbed a hand through my hair. 'I applied and was accepted.'

'That had to make your parents happy. You getting a spot. Finding your purpose.'

I loved the confidence in her voice. Too bad her assumptions about my parents were all wrong.

'My dad was livid. Told me I was ruining my life.'

Fire burned in her eyes. 'What the hell is wrong with your folks?'

Sadly, all I could do was shrug. 'They're elitists. Even when you practice medicine, there is a hierarchy to each specialty. With orthopedics, especially if I worked in professional sports, they'd have a reason to one-up all their friends. Family practice, which in my opinion is the mainstay of medicine, was not glamorous enough for them.'

She crossed her arms over her chest. 'Did he ever apologize?'

'No, he just said that when I was ready to grow up, I'd move back to Harpeth Manor. Join a practice and provide his friends at the country club with all the Viagra they could ever want.'

That made her shake her head. 'I'm beginning to understand why you took the job in Senegal.'

I pulled her back into my arms. 'They shame me a lot less these days, but there are still biting comments around the holidays after one too many glasses of wine.'

'And Ivy Falls? Are you glad you decided to fill in for Doc Sheridan?' The anticipation in her eyes was sweet.

I slid a hand around her neck and pulled her in for a slow, deep kiss. 'Best decision I've made in a long time.'

Chapter Nineteen

PIPER

Delicious Friction

It was the first time in over a month I'd had a day off from all my jobs. I glanced around my apartment, my gaze lingering on the spot where Ford and I kissed last night.

He'd surprised me. I thought the minute we were through the door, his hands would be all over me. If I'd made all the guys I'd dated stand in a police lineup, I'd label them pathetic, bad and, of course, utterly chaotic with a dose of potential criminal. Nine times out of ten I went for door number three.

Ford was the complete opposite. He asked what I needed and let me set the pace. At one point when he raked his fingers through my hair, I found myself swallowing down a sob. I'd been dating since I was fifteen and never before had a man been so tender with me. Paid attention to my cues. Listened when I said what I wanted.

The mid-August sun sparkled through my sliding glass door and I got an idea. After taking a quick sip of coffee, I moved into the hall and knocked on Ford's door.

He answered a few seconds later and I had to grip the edge of my pajama top. Ford all buttoned up was swoony. Ford with sleepy eyes, unruly dark hair and a day's worth of stubble was five-alarm fire hot.

'Mornin.' He glanced at the dancing cows in hula skirts on my pajamas and that boyish grin of his made it hard to think pure thoughts.

'I'm curious. How do you feel about lakes?'

He scratched at his hair, making his bedhead even sexier. 'Lakes?'

'Yes. You know, big bodies of water. Usually with trees and a shore around it.'

He laughed. 'Yes, thank you, Miss Wikipedia.'

'Lake Rainer is a short drive away, and I don't have to work today. Are you up for a little swimming? Maybe a picnic? I could ask Barb and Susan to throw in some cookies as an extra enticement.'

He stepped out into the hall, the smell of toothpaste on his breath. 'Bird, are you asking me on a date?'

Date. Who knew a single word could send such a shot of terror down my spine.

'Uh. Maybe,' I said, shrinking back.

He tugged on the drawstring of my shorts and yanked me to his chest. Did that move where he slid his hand behind my neck, cradled my head and gave me a kiss so steamy it nearly made my knees buckle. He pulled away much too quickly and pressed his forehead to mine.

'Sorry. Had to get that out of my system.'

'It's okay,' I stammered, my senses engulfed in his woody scent. 'The lake?' I babbled. 'Sound like fun?'

'Count me in.' He gave me a peck on the cheek and said, 'Come back in half an hour?'

'That'll work.'

He gave me a wide smile before saying, 'Oatmeal raisin.'

'What?'

'You said enticement. Mine comes in the form of oatmeal raisin cookies.'

He turned and closed the door before I could sputter out that no one really liked that flavor of cookie.

-

When we first walked to where Ford's car was parked near the community bank, I had to swallow a laugh. I hadn't pegged him as a station wagon kind of guy.

'Go ahead. Get it out of your system.'

'I did not say a word.' My barely contained laughter gave away my amusement.

'What? It's a classic,' he said like he was a little hurt.

'Ford, exactly how old is this car?'

'It's a nineteen-ninety Mercedes and it runs like a dream.'

'Where did you get it?' I said, handing him our towels, tote bags and picnic lunch to load inside.

'It used to be up at our cabin in the Smoky Mountains. I needed a car and asked my parents to drive it down.'

I shook my head and walked to the passenger seat. 'And who picked the color?'

'It used to be gold but the car was parked in a dilapidated barn. Between the winter cold, and the swampy summer heat, it turned into this.'

'Yes, everyone loves a car that's Creamsicle orange.'

'Hey, it has character.'

'Well, as long as this "character" gets us to the lake and back it's all good.'

He patted the roof like it was a loyal pet. 'It'll get us there perfectly fine.'

The car started with a roar. Damn. Maybe it did drive like a dream.

We pulled away from the curb and left Ivy Falls in the rearview. The way to the lake was all small winding roads shaded by a tight canopy of trees. I'd forgotten how beautiful and green Tennessee could be in the summer. How kudzu climbed the trees resembling a slithering snake. The way the halo of moody sunlight seeped through the broad sway of branches like liquid gold.

More than once he glanced at my hand lying against the seat. By the way he'd behaved like a gentleman last night, it was clear if I wanted his touch I was going to have to make my wishes known. I reached over and threaded my fingers through his and the corner of his mouth happily twitched.

'When was the last time you were at the lake?' he asked.

I focused on the scenery to help control the complicated emotions churning in my chest. 'It's been fifteen years. I haven't been back since I left Ivy Falls with my family.'

He stayed quiet, and I liked how he didn't feel compelled to fill the pauses, but waited for me to share whatever part of my past I was ready to reveal.

When he'd come into the café or P&P, I'd catch glimpses of his interactions with people. He always had an easy smile for Silvio or Barb. Was quick to pull a book down from a high shelf for Miss Marta or Isabel when they asked for help. Even when kids approached him on the street, asked questions, he always took the time to give them a thoughtful answer.

For too many years, I'd lived in a world where men chose cruelty over kindness. I wasn't sure how to handle someone who led with his heart and not the lower half of his body. A part of me remained guarded, but every minute I spent with him slowly melted the carved iron bars that surrounded my heart.

'I was twelve. Beck was sixteen. Our parents had friends with a boat. We went fishing. Swam in the coves. It's a good memory.' I sighed. 'It wasn't until I was much older that I figured out those were the platinum days.'

He gave me a curious glance. 'Platinum?'

'That's what I call the careless times I had with my parents and Beck. To me, they were more precious than gold. Of course, I wouldn't know that until we'd lost them.'

Even now with all the years of therapy I'd been through, grief still drew all the air from my lungs. To this day, there were still times when I wanted to pick up the phone to call my mom. Tell her about a funny story a kid from the theater had told me. Explain to my dad how when I worked on blocking, or wrote dialogue notes on my script, hope bloomed in my chest like one of Ferris Johnson's prize roses. It was as if my body knew before my brain that this was what I was meant to do.

As if he could read my mind, sense the sadness building in my bones, Ford lifted my hand and pressed a kiss to my skin. It was such a gentle touch that it eased the ache in my heart.

The sun danced through the trees in wide, shimmering swaths as the canopy thinned and the lake came into view. It was the same azure color I remembered. Small waves made by passing watercraft lapped against the dirt and sand shore.

Ford guided the car through the entrance gate and parked near a stone footpath that led to the water. Once we had all our gear, he slammed the tailgate and immediately reached for my hand. We walked the long, narrow path. Trees crowded the lane until they stopped at a short set of wooden stairs. My gaze flicked to the west side of the shore. It took me a minute but I found what I was looking for.

'This way,' I said. We passed young couples lying on colorful beach towels. A loud and raucous game of Spikeball was happening a few feet away. Further down the shore, small tents shaded families from the late morning sun.

Ford hitched up our bags on his broad shoulders as we kept walking. 'Where are we going?'

'A special spot.'

We continued our trek until I stopped in front of a beautiful tree with an arched form that looked like nature had made its own umbrella.

'That's very cool.' Ford set down our bags and moved around the tree, examining the thick-barreled trunk and massive swoop of branches.

'This was my dad's favorite spot. When we were little, he used to tell Beck and me this tree was magic. That it only appeared when we set our feet on the shore. For the longest time we believed him until Beck started reading the *Magic Tree House* series in school and figured out that a lot of the lore Dad told us came from those books.'

'I remember those stories. Jack and Annie. They were the coolest. Getting to go to Camelot and on the *Titanic*.'

'I was a little afraid the tree might not be here anymore. Over the years I've learned that no matter how much you want it to happen, nothing stays the same.'

He squeezed my hand. 'Then this can be your reminder that certain things can be tried and true.'

There was such confidence in his voice, and I wondered what it was like to have a normal existence like his. Still have his parents. Sure, his folks acted like jerks, but they were alive.

That pall of darkness I spent a lot of time hiding from crept in from the corners of the lake. The sound of an explosion, roar of flames, played like a movie behind my eyes.

I pulled in a low breath. Reminded myself of where I was. What I'd been through. How I'd learned ways to keep myself calm and steady. I tried to picture that special place again but my mind was a stark black screen so I turned to my senses.

Sand under my feet.

Coconut-scented sunscreen in the air.

And a new and anchoring sound – the careful and steady pattern of Ford's breaths.

'Hey.' He gently wrapped his hands around my waist. 'You okay?'

'Trying to be. The memories of this place are strong.'

'Do you want to leave?'

'No, I want a picture.'

He gave me a puzzled look. 'A picture?'

'Yes, let's take a selfie.'

He patted his pockets and then held up his phone. Quickly his arm went around my shoulder. I expected him to take the picture, but he placed his lips against my cheek, giving me a warm kiss before the camera made a clicking sound.

The image of us smiling relaxed the chaotic beat of my heart. This place was full of old memories, but that didn't mean we couldn't make new ones too.

I kicked off my shoes, followed by my shorts and top.

'Last one in is a rotten egg!' I called as I sprinted to the water. Once my toes hit the lake, I sucked in a breath and dove down. I kicked and swam until my lungs protested and I came up for air. Ford, only a few feet behind, did a perfect freestyle stroke toward me. His cobalt eyes matched the color of the water. Without his glasses, a cute little white tan line arched over the top of his nose.

'Rotten egg.' I splashed water in his direction.

'You cheated!'

He dove down below me. I tried to swim away but he caught me around the waist and came up for air again. The smile he wore said he was forming a devious plan.

'Climb on my back.'

'Um, no. I'll drown you.'

'Bird, climb on.'

He hitched his thumb backward and I did as I was told. The guy was solid as a rock and swam like I was a guppy holding on.

'Go along the shore and around the bend. I want to show you something,' I said.

With solid strokes, he tugged me along. Once we moved around the outer corner of the shore, I let out a small whoop.

I slid off Ford's back and swam to the shore. Once I was on the sand, I took a long leap and jumped onto a tire swing hanging from a thick tree. I used my momentum, swaying back and forth until I got high enough to launch my body up and out into the water, landing with a massive splash.

Ford gave me an amused look from the shore.

'You try it,' I called out.

I didn't have to say it twice. He easily mounted the tire. With his strength and weight, it only took him a few swings before he sailed out across the water. The show-off didn't do a cannonball like me but spread his arms wide and entered the water with barely a splash.

When he broke the surface, he swung his hair, water flailing out everywhere. He was gorgeous in his starched white doctor's coat, but with water dripping off his full lips he was achingly beautiful.

He swam toward me and we treaded water for a few quiet moments. His pale blue eyes never left my face. He reached for my hand and towed me through the water to where the lake had no entry from the shore and was hidden by a patch of tall marsh grass.

'What are we doing over here?' I asked.

He planted his feet in a shallow part of the water. Spun around and slid his hands around my waist. His eyes filled with a hunger. That same need pulsed through me and I swung my legs up around his torso. The thin material of my bikini pressed against the hard edge of him. He waited again. Reminding me that I needed to tell him I was ready for this. Ready for him.

I gave a small nod and the kiss he pressed to my lips was gentle and sweet. As he held me with one hand, his other went to my neck in that gentle caress. I angled my head and took the kiss deeper and he let out a groan. Said my name like a cherished vow. 'You don't know how many times I've dreamed about this.'

I ran my finger down his chest, stopping at the line of dark hair that disappeared into the waistband of his board shorts. 'Dreams? Really? How many times am I the star?'

He purposefully hitched me up like he wanted to see my reaction to the delicious friction. 'All I can say is that sleeping is one of my favorite things to do these days.'

His stare went molten as he slid his hands beneath my ass and tugged me in, the hard line of him pressing against my stomach.

'And what exactly do I do in these dreams?'

'It's more about what I do.'

'Go on,' I urged, heat filling my core.

'I trace my fingers across your silky skin. Drag a line of kisses over your throat. Work my way to your collarbone.' He spoke the words into being as he ran his mouth over me.

A few shuddering breaths escaped my lips and he pulled back.

'If this is too much, you gotta tell me, Bird.'

I placed a hand against his cheek. The honesty and kindness in his eyes stripped away all the fear and worries I had about opening myself up again. The turmoil of my past floated away like a discarded leaf on the waves of the lake.

I moved my lips against the beautiful hollow of his throat. Ground my body against his. I nipped the corners of his mouth and he opened for me, the heat between us building.

My nails raked up and down his back and another sweet moan left his lips. I slid my teeth down his neck, loving the taste of salt on him. His hand moved to the front of my bikini. In slow strokes he ran a finger down my center. This time the air filled with my own moan.

'What you do to me when you make that sound.'

I moved my hand to the outside of his shorts, eager to feel the hard length of him.

'See,' he mumbled into my neck.

He continued his slow stroke and I leaned into his touch, my breaths coming faster, a slow heat burning me from the inside out. His kisses moved down my neck and I arched back. He palmed one of my breasts and all I wanted was his mouth on me. We continued to kiss, finding the perfect rhythm of give and take until the sounds of children's voices near the swing broke our frenzy. The wicked smile he unleashed made me want to climb him like Mount Everest.

'Maybe we shouldn't give the kids a show.'

'True. Not a good choice for a respectable doctor.'

His eyes went electric. 'What I was just thinking… What I want to do to you is anything but respectable.'

Heat filled every inch of my body and I tried not to overthink this moment. That in a few weeks he'd be gone from my life. We'd crossed over into something new now, and as much as those fears about what came next crept into my head, I let myself steep in this moment, holding on to him and leaning in for one more kiss.

Chapter Twenty

FORD

An Instinct To Protect

All the way back to Ivy Falls, Piper slept against my shoulder. There was a sweet, contented set to her face that made my heart swell. Just before her eyes flickered closed, we'd been discussing the validity of oatmeal raisin cookies. I insisted they were delicious. She swore the only reason anyone ever bit into one was because they mistook it for chocolate chip.

It was a completely ridiculous argument and I loved every second of it.

Her breaths continued to be smooth, the gorgeous curves of her face relaxed. I'd never meant for this to happen. To let myself get wrapped up in a relationship. I had every intention of killing time in Ivy Falls, appeasing my parents with a few dinners and then racing back to Senegal as soon as possible.

Now that ache to run was replaced with a different feeling. A need to stay planted. To explore what my life would be like if I decided to remain in one place.

My thoughts went back to my last conversation with Gray. Maybe I did leave him behind to take care of the mess that was our parents, but being in that world was like being lowered into a pot of boiling water, the heat and steam suffocating you until you could no longer breathe. A silent scream the only emotion you could utter.

The highway continued to twist and turn. Piper's contented sighs filled the quiet car. I'd watched her today. How she paid attention to the water, keeping track of the children while they splashed and played, making sure their parents were aware of them too.

It was the same way she focused on the kids at the theater. She had an instinct to protect. To love. It filled me with a sense of wonder and curiosity. My mother had been there for Gray and me, but she'd never looked at us with intense devotion. Like we were her entire world. I didn't doubt her love, but she compartmentalized us. Like we were one of the many things she was in charge of supervising, along with her duties to the local garden club, and her role as secretary for the club's board of directors.

Piper snuggled deeper into my side as I drove past the old town sign. When I reached the street to our apartments, a group was standing outside. I put the car in park, tapped Piper's shoulder and she woke with a start. Her gaze was unfocused until she noticed the group rushing toward the car.

Torran reached my door first. Her skin was the color of milk and I didn't like the pained expression she wore.

'Hey, doc. Why don't you have your phone on?' She blinked when she saw Piper.

'It's Sunday. I'm not on call,' I said.

Piper undid her seatbelt. 'What's wrong, Torran?'

Beck was at her door and swinging it open. His chin went firm as he gave his sister a weighted stare. 'Do you have your phone on silent?'

'I don't know. Why?'

He helped her out of the car and Torran and I met them on the sidewalk. Barb and Susan, Diego, as well as Miss Cheri and a few other townspeople, watched us with worried gazes.

'Doc, Silvio's in a panic. He's called all over town looking for you,' Torran said. 'Old Mrs V fell. He managed to get her into a chair, but he says she doesn't look good.'

'Did he call nine-one-one?'

'No,' Beck chimed in. 'Mrs Vanderpool insists she'll only see you.'

'Okay, can someone tell me where she lives?'

'I'll take you,' Piper offered.

'We'll all go,' Beck said, his stare narrowing on where my hand was clenched with his sister's.

'No. Let Ford go and check her out,' Piper said firmly.

Barb and Susan started to object until I added, 'It's great that you care, but Mrs Vanderpool deserves her privacy.'

They solemnly nodded, traded more whispers of worry, before making their way back across the square.

'How long ago did Silvio call?' I asked Torran, who looked painfully tired.

'About ten minutes.'

'Are you okay?' I asked.

'Yes,' she huffed. 'Just a little worried about Old Mrs V.'

'I'm gonna grab my bag.'

I walked to the back of the car and Beck followed. He stayed quiet but the razor-sharp line of his jaw told me all I needed to know.

'I like your sister.'

'Yeah, I can tell that by the way you look at her.' He scrubbed a hand over his mouth. 'I'm not gonna be one of those dick older brothers that says something stupid like "You break her heart and I'll break your face",' he grumbled. 'I'll just remind you of what I said the other night. She's fragile.'

I swallowed back my protests about that description of her. The woman standing three feet away was a warrior. A force of nature. A goddamn goddess. But I understood why Beck saw her that way. As Piper had explained it, since they'd lost their parents he'd become her protector. He only wanted to keep her safe. Make sure she didn't go back to the dark place she'd told me about.

'She's in good hands with me. I swear it on my medical license.'

He glanced at the black kit dangling from my finger-tips. 'And when you leave? She won't be in good hands then.'

I wasn't going to tell him about our agreement. It was a private deal between Piper and me. 'We're both adults who understand the situation.'

Torran walked toward us and I didn't like the way she swayed unbalanced on her feet.

'Babe, you okay?' Beck asked.

'Don't worry about me.' She leaned her head on his shoulder. 'Right now we need to be thinking about Mrs Vanderpool.' Her gaze narrowed, expecting me to get my ass in gear.

'On my way.'

'Piper, call me later,' Beck said in that older-brother voice.

'I will,' she said, waving off his concern.

I slammed the tailgate shut and joined Piper on the sidewalk.

'Should we drive?' I asked.

'No, it'll take longer to maneuver around the streets than to walk.'

Like she wanted to make a point, she slid her hand into mine and tugged me down the street.

'Your brother is…'

'Burning a hole in your back with an acidic gaze. Ignore him. That's what I do.'

He'd brought up a good point though. It would be easy for Piper and me to get lost in our time together. We'd agreed to this arrangement, but neither of us wanted to get in too deep. Hurt one another. The hard thing was the more time I spent with Piper, the more I needed to be near her. How was that going to work when I'd be gone in October?

Knowing I couldn't solve that issue now, I focused on Piper leading me down the street. We passed expertly trimmed lawns and pastel-colored bungalows with screened-in porches. We turned a corner and a large white house with a widow's walk and a massive wrap-around porch came into view. A black wrought-iron fence circled the property.

'Wow, that house is something.'

'That's where I grew up,' she said casually.

'It's amazing.'

'You can thank Manny and Torran for that. Apparently, it was a shithole when they started on it. The previous renters poured concrete down the drains. Stole the cabinets and appliances.'

'Well, it's beautiful now.'

'They're really good at what they do,' she said proudly.

We hurried past more impressive homes until we reached the cul-de-sac at the end of another street called Maple Lane. The house at the end was a canary-yellow two-story colonial with a wide driveway and what looked like a garage apartment in the back. It was beautifully built and resembled something out of a TV sitcom.

I followed Piper up the wide white steps and she knocked on the door. Silvio appeared right away and invited us in. A small brown-and-black dog barked, turning in circles, as Silvio led us through the house. The poor guy looked like he'd been through the wringer. White tufts of hair sprouted out in every direction and his eyes were rimmed in red.

Piper reached down and scooped up the small dog. 'It's okay, Baby,' she cooed.

'Thanks for coming, doc. I keep telling Greta I need to call an ambulance but she's as stubborn as a bulldog who refuses his walk.'

We found Greta sitting at a dark wood farm table in the kitchen. A pale pink tracksuit hung off her. The kitchen towel she was holding to her chin was soaked in blood.

'Tell me you did not just compare me to a bulldog,' she huffed.

All it took was one look at her to know she was hurting.

Silvio shrugged. 'If the shoe fits, dear.'

Greta grumbled until she gave me the once-over. Her stare moved to Piper and her mouth twitched. 'You two been off doing something fun? Sure smells like it.'

This woman. She was clearly uncomfortable, but still she had to comment on the way the briny scent of the lake wafted off us.

'We're not here to chat about our day,' I said.

I sat next to her and she gave me a weak, 'Hi, doc.'

'If you wanted to see me again, you didn't have to put on such a big show.'

The quicker I got her to relax, the better her blood pressure would be.

'May I?' I nodded to her chin. She relented and I examined the oozing gash. 'Tell me what happened.'

Her gaze went to Piper hovering in the doorway. 'Come in, sit down, and don't look so terrified. I'm gonna be all right, sweet girl.'

Piper took the spot beside Greta. By the fear in her eyes she could see how frail her friend looked too.

'It was dumb. Silvio was making tea in the kitchen. I was wearing socks and when I walked down the hall I slipped and caught my chin on the corner of the antique buffet.'

'Have you been taking the blood thinner like you promised?'

'Yes.' She pointed to Silvio. 'For a small man, he's a really big nag.'

Silvio let out a humph and crossed his arms over his chest. 'Damn straight.'

With a hand at her wrist, I took her pulse. Flashed a pen light over her eyes. I glanced at the wound again and reapplied pressure. 'The medicine inhibits clotting, that's why the bleeding won't stop. I can put in a few stitches here or you can go to the hospital. Whatever makes you feel more comfortable.'

'I'm not going back to the hospital. They kept me for three damn days last time. Do you know how uncomfortable those beds are? And the food?' She practically retched.

'Sweetie, maybe that's for the best,' Silvio suggested.

'No,' she spat out. 'Sew me up here, doc.'

Piper stayed quiet, her cheeks turning sunken and pale. 'Tell me what's happening,' she pleaded. 'Why are you on a blood thinner? How sick are you really, Mrs V?'

'Greta,' I said quietly. 'I can't say a word but you can.'

Her firm shoulders gave a little. 'Honey, don't get all worried. The blood thinner prevents strokes because my heart is out of rhythm.'

The panic in Piper's beautiful amber eyes made my stomach knot. 'What does that mean? Out of rhythm?'

'I have something called atrial fibrillation. They call it AFib.' Greta took a thick gulp. 'Two chambers of my heart are out of rhythm. That day at the café, I fainted because less blood was going to my brain.'

The look Piper gave me was a punch to the gut. Like somehow my keeping the diagnosis from her was a betrayal.

Unable to look at her, I turned to Greta. 'Have you had any episodes since?'

'Well,' she hedged.

'She hasn't fainted, but she has been a little weak.'

'Are you eating? Drinking?' I reached out and pinched a small bit of her forearm skin gently. It stayed tented up in place for a few seconds. 'You're dehydrated. I think you should come to the clinic and let me give you an IV. We'll do the stitches there too.'

I waited for the protest, her stiff upper lip to take hold, but she blew out a shuddering breath and nodded.

With Silvio and Piper flanking her sides, they got her into Silvio's car.

—

At the clinic, we found a vein quickly and got some fluids going. It took three stitches to close the gash on her chin. While Greta relaxed, I went out to the waiting area.

Piper sat slumped in an oversized chair, her cheeks wet. I sat down and she collapsed into me, weeping quietly into my shoulder.

'All that blood. And she's so pale. I can't lose…'

'It's okay, Bird. She's getting the right treatment, but it may take a while to work out the medicine and the care she needs.'

Her sobs continued and I held her tightly. I could have told her more about Mrs V's condition. How Dr Engel at Vanderbilt was one of the best cardiologists in the country. But in this moment all she needed to know was that I was here and she wasn't alone.

Chapter Twenty-One

PIPER

Silenced By Tenderness

I should have known better. In my life, a day that started out wonderful always had a chance to do a complete one-eighty and turn into total and complete shit.

When Ford was sure Old Mrs V was hydrated, he walked her and Silvio out of the clinic. He gave them his private cell number. Told them more than once that if she needed help they should reach out any time, day or night. She thanked him again and let Silvio take her arm and walk her to his car parked on the street.

We headed back to the apartment in silence. Late Sundays in the square were quiet. Peaceful. The shops all closed at three, forcing the tourists out of town. In those precious hours until sunset, it was like the place finally belonged to Ivy Falls again.

Ford held my hand as if he was my anchor. A part of me thought he was worried I was mad at him, but I understood why he couldn't say a word. The feeling bubbling up inside of me wasn't anger – it was terror.

Old Mrs V had become my touchstone, my kick in the pants. On days when I was desperately missing my mother, when that relentless voice in my head insisted things would be easier if I had a drink or a pill, she'd appear with a smile and a kind word. Her confident reassurances insisting I was strong enough to let the feeling pass.

I was staying sober for me, but a big part of my need to remain clean was because I couldn't disappoint her. Not after all the ways she'd stood up for me. How she'd stared down the people who whispered their worries about my role in directing the play. Made a big display of telling anyone who would listen that the show was going to be the best one in years because I had talent and knew what I was doing.

Ford moved closer. 'You can talk to me. Mrs V gave me permission to answer any question you have.'

'I don't even know where to start.'

He gave me a weary smile. 'Ask me about her diagnosis or treatment.'

We reached the hallway to our apartments and he leaned against my doorframe.

'Is she in a lot of pain? Will it get worse?' I closed my eyes, my chest tightening. 'Is she going to die?'

His finger slid under my chin, the scent of lake water and sunscreen wafting off his skin. 'Open your eyes, Bird.'

His solid blue gaze was what I needed. It was focused. Confident. He reached out and placed his hand over my wrist where I was rubbing my tattoo. 'Half the challenge is getting her diagnosed. Making sure she is taking the medication and her body is adjusting.'

'And my last question,' I asked, even though I wasn't sure I wanted to hear the answer.

'No one knows how long we have on this earth. For now, she is getting the best care possible and is responding well.'

He pulled me into a hug and the steady beat of his heart washed over me. 'It's been a long day. Why don't you head inside and get some rest.'

There wasn't anything else I needed right now besides him. How the weight of his arms around me made me feel safe. The rise and fall of his chest calming my own frenzied breaths.

When this moment came I was convinced I'd be terrified. I'd spent years in therapy untangling all the complicated feelings I had about intimacy. The fear that wrapped around my heart like barbed wire when I considered trusting another soul. How in the past I'd made hundreds of wrong choices that ended up dumping me into a dark spiral of despair. But as I stared into Ford's soft eyes, I had a very clear understanding of what I wanted.

I threaded my fingers through his and pulled him through my door. Once it was closed, I pressed my body against his, slid my hand up under his T-shirt, needing to feel him.

'Piper,' he said unsteadily. 'A short time ago you got difficult news about your friend. As much as I love how you touch me, I don't think it's a good idea to do this right now.'

I tilted my head to meet his gaze. 'Ford, I'm a grown woman. For years, I've been fighting to get my life back. Before you got here, I'd walled myself off from all emotion. Too afraid that anything intense would interfere with my recovery. But do you know what I've learned since I started spending time with you?'

He lovingly tucked a hair behind my ear. 'Tell me.'

'That letting myself feel, want,' I held him firmly by the waist, 'desire things, will not send me into a spiral.

If I live my life always being afraid, never taking another chance, it'll be a colorless existence.'

'And with me things are…'

I loved the way his breath hitched as I wound my arms behind his neck. 'Things are very much in color. Electric, shimmering, fucking brilliant neon color.'

The smile he gave me lit up every element in my body. I pressed my mouth to his and was met with a kiss so tender it made my limbs quiver. His hands made a slow trek up my back, until they found my hair. With a gentle tug, he pulled away the elastic band and my hair spilled over my shoulders. He was being gentle, careful, and that was the last thing I wanted.

I ran my hands down over his shirt and tugged at the hem. He took the hint, taking off his glasses and pulling his T-shirt over his head. His gaze scanned the room like he was looking for a spot to place them.

'Leave your glasses on. They're sexy.' I nipped at the corner of his lip and followed it with a soothing, slow kiss.

He steered me backwards until my back hit the wall near the door. His kisses were no longer restrained as his mouth moved down my neck. The edges of his fingers skimmed the side of my tank top before he had it up my sides and over my head. Not waiting a beat, the ties were quickly loose on my bikini top. As soon as the small bit of fabric was in a pool at my feet, his tongue was on me, swirling away the ache in my breasts.

'Is it ridiculous to say that even though I've had lots of thoughts about this moment, it's a thousand times better in person?' he whispered against my skin.

'No,' I stuttered as he worked his mouth over my other nipple and I arched back wanting more. His hand steadied me from behind as he trailed more kisses down my side, over my torso, stopping at the waistband of my cutoff shorts.

'Can I?' The reverence in his voice had me quickly nodding.

He fell to his knees and tugged down my shorts, my bikini bottoms quickly following.

Without knowing it, I started to rub at my wrist. Ford's stare moved to my nervous motion.

'Bird, look at me.'

I gazed down into his beautiful blue eyes.

'You need to tell me if you're okay. That you want this. That you want me.'

This was my chance to stop.

To turn back.

The voices that often told me I wasn't good enough, that the only way I could have a normal life was to be numb through drugs or alcohol, were silenced by the tenderness in his gaze. No man had ever looked at me that way. Like he wanted to take care of me. Wanted to know what was truly in my heart. That whatever I said in the next few moments would be all right with him. There was no pressure or expectation, only the hope of what might be.

I twisted his dark curls between my fingers. 'Yes,' I said with determination. 'I want you to be mine.'

The smile that crossed his face was equal parts joy and hunger and it made me dig my fingers deeper into his hair.

Ever so slowly he ran his hands down my thighs. It was a slow kind of torture that made my core throb. He bent down and kissed my ankles. Ran his tongue up my calves until he returned to my thighs.

There was a reverence to his touch that made a sob crowd my throat. Every sexual experience I'd had was about male want and need. It was a frenzied toss of clothes, two seconds of foreplay, until the guy greedily shoved his way inside me.

Ford touched me like I was precious. A gift he slowly wanted to unwrap. Every look, every sigh, said he wanted to take his time. That my pleasure was as important as his. This wasn't a quick screw for him. It was a slow and treading exploration of my body. A whisper of tenderness, a promise of intimacy, he never wanted me to forget.

His mouth was on me again, and I leaned back and let him bring me to the edge of bliss without a single thought except that I wanted more.

Chapter Twenty-Two

FORD

Piece Of Her Past

The only thing that filled my senses was the feel and touch of Piper. I worked her with my tongue and then my fingers, she moaned my name and shuddered around me, her hand gripping my shoulders like she couldn't get enough.

I held on to her as she found her release and when she finally opened her eyes, she dragged me to my feet, spun me around and pushed me toward her bedroom.

The back of my legs crashed against the bed. Before I could say a word, her hands were tugging down my board shorts. Once they were off, she gave me a wicked grin and pushed me back onto the mattress. I scooted toward the headboard and she crawled toward me. She started to seat herself and I grabbed her waist.

'Wait. Condom?' I said.

She dragged a hand through her hair and it was the sexiest thing I'd ever seen. 'In the bedside table.'

I reached over and opened the drawer, tearing off a foil packet. When I rolled back over a question lingered in her eyes.

'Should we talk about it?'

'If you mean how quickly I can get my hands on you again, then yes.'

'No.' Her pretty red mouth went firm. 'Do you want to know my history? If I've been checked?'

I set the condom package down and pressed my fingers into her luscious hipbones. 'You can tell me whatever you want.'

'My life's been complicated.'

I held on to her, never letting my gaze veer from her eyes. She was confessing to a past I wasn't worried about, but instinct said this was something she needed to do.

'I haven't been with anyone in over two years. And I've been tested.'

'Me too,' I said, moving my hands to her cheeks. 'Anything else you want to say?'

Relief loosened her shoulders and she inched forward, teasing the edge of herself against me.

'Confession,' she said with such a sexy whisper I let loose a groan. 'I very much want your hands on me too.'

She laid a hot kiss against my lips and plucked the foil package from the bed. Once she had me sheathed, she pushed me back against the headboard and climbed on. Her movements were teasing at first, settling herself down and then quickly shifting away. My hands rested on her waist as she moved over me, the ache inside me growing with such a fury that I finally locked my hands down and held her until I was deep inside. We moved as one, her eyes closed, my name a plea on her lips.

'Piper, open your eyes.'

She fluttered her lashes until I saw her warm brown gaze.

'I want you to watch what you do to my body. Witness how my breath changes when you touch me. Everything about you, your gorgeous skin, the way you laugh, makes my pulse race.'

With a tight grip on my shoulders she did as I asked. There was a certainty in her eyes, an acknowledgment that she wanted this as much as I did.

Everything about her was unexpected. The way she challenged me. How she never wanted anything more than my presence.

I'd stumbled into this town a confused and disillusioned mess but she'd brought everything into focus. We'd promised this was only for a few months, but the way my heart raced every time she was in my orbit said this was much more than some casual deal.

Her hair swung behind her as I found a rhythm for us. She held on to me, the rings on her fingers scratching against my skin. I shifted and she let out another moan as I found the spot that made her shudder. While I held on to her hips with one hand, the other pulled her down for a deep kiss. Her breaths quickened, her mouth pressing against my skin like a whispered oath.

She shifted, taking me deeper. 'I'm close.'

'Wait for me, Bird.'

I drove into her, clutching her back, holding her tightly against me.

'Ford, please,' she said with a breathy plea. I moved again, finding the spot that made her toss her head back. 'Yes, there,' she whispered, and with one last thrust we went over the edge together.

She collapsed onto me, her dark hair spilling like ink across my chest. I traced slow circles on her back until our breaths returned to a normal rhythm.

I loved the feel of her cheek against my skin. How she melted into me like we were one being. I reached up and stroked her hair, and she murmured, 'That feels good but you're going to put me to sleep.'

'And you don't want that?'

She shot me a determined look. 'Go clean yourself up but then come back. Quickly.'

The want in her eyes had me jumping off the bed. Once the condom was in the trash, I raced back to her and crawled over the sheets until I was hovering over her. I placed a quick kiss to her lips and felt the smile beneath it.

'Not going to lie. That was the best sex I've ever had.'

I couldn't help but laugh. 'If you're trying to pump up my ego, you're doing a good job.'

'It's the truth. You take your time. You're tender and you care about giving me pleasure too. That's a highly underrated quality when it comes to sex.'

I moved to lie beside her, tucking her gently in my arms. 'Never got that. Giving a woman pleasure gets me off.'

'Oh really,' she cooed. 'That's good to know.'

I plopped a kiss on the top of her head. 'I might have an edge though. When you spend a lot of time studying human anatomy, the pleasure centers, you become pretty adept at learning what makes a woman feel good.'

'Maybe you should give a TED talk about it because I'd guess a lot of men don't know that truth.'

'No one wants to hear me give a TED talk,' I joked. 'Especially when it's a lecture on how bad men are at sex.'

'Sadly, you're probably right.'

She traced her fingers over my biceps and down my chest and I went hard again. But let's be real, all Piper had to do was look at me and I got stiff.

As I held her close, her fingers went back to tracing her tattoo. I worried that now she'd had time to think, maybe she regretted what we'd just done. That this was way past the line of our deal.

'You okay?' I whispered into her hair.

'Yeah, just thinking about the lake today. How I was terrified to go back, too afraid that being there would stir up emotions I've tried years to manage, but with you there it was easier. Like I didn't have to face my demons alone. It was a big risk but I'm glad I went for it. I think my parents would have been proud.'

She pressed her lips to the corner of my shoulder, snuggled in so she fit perfectly into the crook of my arm.

'Do you feel comfortable telling me what happened to them?'

'What? The Ivy Falls gossip hasn't made it to you yet?'

'I've heard a few things,' I admitted. 'But I want to know the real story from you if you're ready to tell me.'

I was pushing against that wall of hers and was unsure of how she'd react. Like she sensed my tension, she pulled in an uneven breath and sank in to me rather than scooting away. I wrapped my arms around her, grateful she was ready to trust me. Share another piece of her past, which I knew wasn't easy.

'My parents moved us away from Ivy Falls when I was twelve. I was angry at first. Beck was too because he was in love with Torran at the time.' Her voice rattled but she went on. 'My dad was very smart. His business developed processors that made computers run faster. After he sold the company, he decided to buy a massive RV and have us travel all over the US for a year while my mom homeschooled us. The first couple of weeks on the trip I was a pain in the ass. Made life really difficult for my parents.'

'Sounds like a typical preteen. I was a real shit for my parents too.'

'Yeah, I was pretty fucking mean,' she said with a hint of shame. 'After about two months of traveling, Beck and I understood that was going to be our life. We settled in and learned to love the ways our mom would make every new place an adventure. At Mount Rushmore she quizzed us about the presidents. In Kentucky, she asked probing questions about President Lincoln's birthplace. When we got to Boston Harbor, she gave us each a small packet of tea, joked we could be like the colonists and spill it into the water. She was clever like that. Always working in historical facts without us realizing she was schooling us.'

'Your mom sounds pretty great.'

'She was,' she offered quietly. 'My dad was too.'

I kept her tucked into my chest as she kept talking.

'When it happened…' She sucked in a heavy breath. 'We were in Northern California at a camping spot. It was winter and there'd recently been a big snowfall. I was being the typical annoying little sister, pestering Beck to throw snowballs with me. Off and on throughout the trip, there'd been issues with the RV's propane tank. While we were chasing each other down by the river, there was an explosion. Beck he… tried to get them out, but in the process was badly burned.' Her voice broke. 'My folks didn't make it.'

Her body shuddered and I held her until she stopped shaking.

'The day started out like a dream and ended in a nightmare. I had a family…' She dipped her head down, her breaths going raspy. 'But for a few hours when they were trying to save Beck, I thought I might be alone with no one left.'

Her confession stunned me. I couldn't imagine what I would do if I thought I'd lost Gray. I rubbed her back in slow circles again, offering her any kind of comfort I could.

'After that, I went numb. Or tried to become numb. First, it was alcohol. When a fifth of whiskey didn't take the edge off, pills entered the picture.'

She brushed back her hair. Pulled in another shaky breath. I wanted to tell her how brave she was for sharing her truth. That after what she'd been through, so much trauma, and most likely PTSD, that getting out the other side wasn't an easy task for anyone. She didn't need to hear any of that from me though. All she needed was someone solid to listen, and I was determined to be that person for her.

'Beck came back to Ivy Falls two years ago. Bought Huckleberry Lane, the home we'd left as kids. In his scrambled brain he believed that if he bought it for me, could fix it, he could mend all my broken parts. Somehow, he convinced Torran to help him repair the house even though he'd crushed her heart years before, which is another long story. During that time I arrived for a surprise visit from New York. He confessed to me what he'd done, and I believed I was strong enough to cope.'

She leaned her head back against the pillow, her eyes wracked with a pain that hit me so solid in the chest it took my breath away.

'As you probably have already guessed, I wasn't. That's how I ended up in Memorial Springs. Made my third trip back to rehab.' She traced her tattoo again. 'I told you I got this because it's a special reminder of my parents, but it's more than that. It's a symbol of rebirth. That there can still be joy and wonder in the world. Any time I get that tingle in my skin, the urge to drink or score a pill, I look at my hummingbird and think about all the good things that can happen when I stay sober.' She ran a finger along the stubble on my chin. 'Good things like you.'

I caught her hand and pressed a warm kiss to her palm. 'I'm sure it wasn't easy, but I appreciate your honesty. Being vulnerable enough to share the truth about your life with me.'

'You're wrong about that.' She gave me a wistful smile. 'Everything is easy with you.'

Having her in my arms felt too right. Too good. We'd shared so much in a short time, and even though we'd agreed that this was temporary, I couldn't imagine not always holding her this way. Not having that warm thrum in my chest when I caught sight of her across a crowded room.

She leaned in and pressed a kiss to the rise of my collarbone. With one quick move, she was straddling me again, pressing hot, hungry kisses to my mouth.

I held on to the coffee and vanilla scent of her, pushing the worries from my mind, even as my heart screamed it was going to be impossible to walk away from this woman once my time in Ivy Falls was over.

Chapter Twenty-Three

PIPER

Have A Little Fun

I'd discovered a new form of torture – trying on a brides-maid's dress in ninety-degree heat.

It wasn't Ms Darcy's fault that the air conditioning was out at Brides and Blooms right off the square, but it made sliding taffeta and lace over my skin a scratchy nightmare.

'Turn around one more time,' Tessa said, spinning her finger in a circle like I needed instructions.

Taking small steps in the ridiculously high heels they made me wear, I moved around the elevated circular platform. Torran, Tessa and Maisey sat in old wooden chairs against a bright pink wall that was covered in framed photos of recent Ivy Falls brides. While Maisey and Tessa tried desperately to fan themselves, Torran's attention stayed on her phone.

Tessa tapped at her chin. 'I told Tor sapphire blue was a good choice. What do you think, Maisey?'

When she'd stopped by the P&P earlier, I'd begged Maisey to come to this appointment. I trusted her fashion sense, and knew she'd tell me if I looked like a bright blue popsicle in the dress Torran had picked out months ago.

As I spun another time in front of the mirror, Ford filled my head.

Did he like blue?

He seemed to like the cobalt-colored thong he tore off with his teeth last night.

We'd gotten into a routine lately. Work. Rehearsals. Dinner. Well, a few bites before we ended up in bed together. It was strange how quickly we melted into one another's lives, but every time he pulled me close, pressed a kiss to my forehead, I had to remind myself that it was temporary. That in a few short weeks he'd be on a plane to Africa. That it was the deal we'd agreed to that night on the rooftop.

Maisey let out a low whistle. 'Hot damn, Pipe. That is some dress! The cut does wonders for your shoulders, and a good push-up bra will really show off your tits!'

'Maisey!' Tessa laughed. 'You are too much.'

'You always gotta pump up your bestie.'

She gave me a quick wink, which made the knots in my stomach loosen. This was why I'd invited her. The wedding was making everyone too damn tense. We needed a little comic relief, and Maise never disappointed in that department.

'Tor? Thoughts?' Tessa nudged her sister's knee.

'Yes. It's good,' she mumbled, still staring at her phone.

'What is so important that you can't pay attention to this?' Tessa asked.

'I have a lot going on at work. Teddy Ray, that restaurant client of Beck's, keeps pestering us about that damn property he wants, but it's tied up in probate. It's a mess.' She gulped uncomfortably.

Tessa nudged her knee again. Tried to get her to focus on my dress, but it was clear Torran's mind was in another place.

Ms Darcy returned to the room with a cherry-red pincushion strapped to her arm. She bent down in front of me, surveying the hem. 'It's only a minor alteration. It'll be done in time for the wedding.' She shot a look to Torran like she expected a response, but Tor kept her nose buried in her phone. Once she was done fixing my dress, Ms Darcy said, 'You're next, bride-to-be.'

Torran tried to give the kind middle-aged woman a smile but it didn't quite reach her lips.

Things were settled with Hearth and Home. The old Thomas Place was on the market. Besides the restaurant account, what else was distracting her? Was it Beck? Were there other issues about the wedding? I didn't live with them anymore so I had no idea what could be making her so damn distracted.

Tessa snatched the phone out of her hand but not before Torran made the screen black.

'Go try on your dress. I'll hold your phone,' Tessa ordered.

'Fine. I'm going.' Ms Darcy raced behind her offering to help.

Once Torran was out of earshot, I stepped down from the platform and sat next to Maisey.

'What is going on with her?' I said. 'You'd think she was having a root canal, not preparing for what is supposed to be the happiest day of her life.'

'I don't know,' Tessa confessed. 'Manny says she's been extra crabby these last weeks. He even admitted she's been disappearing from work when they're supposed to be going over plans for their next season.' She glanced in the direction of the dressing room. 'I've always been able to read her, but recently she's put up a wall between us, and I can't figure out a way to knock it down. It has me 'very worried.' She pressed her lips together as the dressing room door squeaked open.

Torran walked toward us and Maisey reached out and squeezed my hand. Silence filled the room as the corners of my eyes burned. My mom would have loved this.

'Holy shit!' Maisey crowed. 'A satin magnolia ballgown with a basque waist and a Regency-inspired neckline. That's some fucking gown, Tor! Well done.'

It should have been a magical moment, all of us finally seeing the dress she'd selected, but Torran's face contorted in an unhappy pinch.

'What's wrong?' Tessa jumped to her feet.

Torran's shoulders slumped. 'It's too tight.'

Ms Darcy watched her with caution until the phone rang in the other room and she rushed out to get it.

Torran kept moving around the platform looking like a baby deer just finding her balance. She could be grumpy on occasion, strong-minded, but the way her body folded inward said she was miserable.

It had to be Beck. Did she want to call off the wedding?

My mind did that panicked, frenzied thing where it spun out like an EF5 tornado. I grounded myself in this place. Focused on the trickle of perspiration racing down my back. The way the ceiling fan made a grumpy-old-man kind of groan.

With careful strokes, I moved my fingers over the hummingbird's wings. Tracing over the head and then down its green belly. Slowly, my breathing returned to normal.

Ms Darcy rushed back into the room and she wasn't alone. Old Mrs V's white hair was freshly set. Her signature pink lipstick expertly applied. Baby sat tucked under her arm and gave a small bark hello.

According to Ford, he'd seen Old Mrs V earlier this week in the office and she was feeling better after a few weeks of the new medicine. As she approached the platform where Torran stood, her posture went stiff. Her jaw locked in resolve. Yeah, the woman we all loved, and feared a little, was back.

'Mrs V, what are you doing here?' Tessa asked.

'I come by every once in a while to check in on my old business. And a little birdie,' she tipped her chin at Ms Darcy, 'may have whispered that Torran was trying on her dress. Thought I'd come by and see if I could get a sneak peek.' Her attention returned to Torran. She paced in front of her, the set of her shoulders growing tense. After a minute she let out a low huff. 'Sweetheart, I spent twenty years putting the women of Ivy Falls into the perfect wedding dress, so please excuse my frankness, but you look damn unhappy in that gown.'

I thought Ms Darcy might be offended but she nodded in agreement.

What color was left in Torran's cheeks faded. 'Do you all think that?'

We stayed frozen until Tessa said, 'Don't panic. We'll fix it.' She turned to Ms Darcy. 'Can you double-check the paperwork to make sure it's the right size? That might be the issue.'

Torran patted at her hips. Stared at how her boobs spilled out over the white lace on the bodice. She shook her head and hopped off the platform. Instead of returning to the dressing area, she sprinted into the bathroom, the door slamming shut behind her.

With her lower lip trembling, poor Ms Darcy said, 'I'm gonna go look at the order.'

Tess jumped up from the chair. 'I need to find out what's wrong with Tor.'

'Please, let me.' Old Mrs V shoved Baby in my direction and marched toward the bathroom.

Tessa slumped back in the chair, her eyes going watery. 'This is what I mean. Our entire lives she's held her worries and fears close to the chest, but in harder moments she's talked to me.' She flailed her hand in the direction of the bathroom. 'But now I have no idea what is happening.'

'Give her time, Tessa. Torran always does things in her own way.'

She gave me a sad nod as Baby made himself comfortable on my lap.

We all stayed quiet until Maisey said, 'She looks good, doesn't she?'

'Baby?' Tessa said.

'No. Old Mrs V. Barb and Susan say she and Silvio are back to having breakfast at Sugar Rush. That she's getting stronger thanks to the medicine she's taking for her heart.'

'You know about her diagnosis?' I said, fanning myself as the room grew warmer.

'Yes,' Maisey replied. 'She's been slowly telling friends all over town, knowing word would spread like wildfire.'

'Smart woman. Tell a few souls in Ivy Falls and by sundown the whole damn town will know,' Tessa snickered.

'Ford did say she was doing better.'

'Ford, huh?' Tessa grinned. 'You two did look cozy at "Music in the Square".'

'We're spending a little time together.'

Maisey nudged my shoulder. 'Told you so.'

I waved away her gushing. 'It's casual. He'll be gone by October anyway.'

'Training wheels,' Maisey said in a singsong voice only I could hear.

I gave her a playful jab with my elbow and she poked my side.

'Hey, don't make me break you two up like I do my girls,' Tess said, even though her stare stayed fixed on the bathroom.

'Where are Iris and Rose? Aren't they flower girls?' Maisey said like she knew Tessa needed a distraction.

'Their dresses came in last week and fit perfectly. Manny took Lou and the girls to see the horses over at Breyer's farm so I could have this time with Torran.'

She stood like she was ready to go pound on the bathroom door, when it opened. Old Mrs V held on to Torran's arm as they walked our way. Torran's red-rimmed eyes had me squeezing the side of the chair. Shit. I knew it was bad.

'Girls, Torran needs to tell you something.'

Torran rubbed a hand over her mouth. Looked at the floor and pulled in a deep breath. She started to speak when Maisey said, 'Oh fuck. You're pregnant!'

'Maisey!' Old Mrs V squawked. 'You never could hold your tongue.'

Tessa approached Torran. The tentative glance they swapped said Maisey was right.

'How many weeks?' Tessa said in a soft voice.

Torran bit into her lip. 'I don't know. Haven't seen a doctor yet. I took my first test, confirming it last week.'

'Why didn't you tell me?'

'Because I wanted to be sure that it was real, which all the morning sickness is surely proving.'

'Are you happy?' Tessa asked.

Torran's chest heaved up once. She bobbed her head, a tear sliding down her cheek.

Tessa burst into sobs and pulled her into a hug. 'How's Beck doing?'

'He's happier than a pig in mud. In fact, he's mad right now because I told him he had to stay quiet until I was ready to tell everyone.'

Maisey put a hand on my shoulder and squeezed. 'You're getting a new sister *and* becoming an auntie!'

Fat tears soaked into my cheeks too. I shoved Baby at Maisey and went to Torran, who pulled me into her hug with Tessa.

'Well, that explains the big boobs and butt,' Maisey cackled. 'Joe always said that was an added pregnancy bonus!'

Old Mrs V stood back and watched us all. The pleased-as-punch smile she wore made my heart light. Once I slipped away from Torran's hold, I went to her side.

'Another Ivy Falls baby.'

She slid her hand into mine and squeezed. 'Another miracle.'

Ms Darcy flew back into the room and came to a dead stop when she saw all of us rubbing our eyes. 'Honestly, all the paperwork shows I ordered the right size.'

Tessa put an arm around her, trying to reassure the poor woman that we weren't upset. That what Torran had on was indeed the correct gown. She gave a confused nod and mumbled a few words about checking the thermostat again.

'Well, now that you all know, I'm going to put my clothes back on.'

Torran turned and Maisey shoved Baby back in my direction. 'That dress can be let out in a couple of ways. Let me tell you about it.'

She reluctantly agreed and let Maisey follow her back into the dressing room with Tessa chasing after them.

Old Mrs V let out a low breath. Her hand shook in mine as I led her to a nearby chair. 'Getting old really bites the big one.'

It was hard not to laugh at the blunt way she saw the world.

'Ford told me you're adjusting well to the medicine. That's positive.'

She gave me a pleased smile. 'I like that you two are together. It's about time you let a fella treat you nice.' She leaned in and I knew I was in trouble by the mischief in her gaze. 'Somethin' tells me that boy is a good kisser too. Those full lips. Wow!'

'I'm not telling you anything about how he kisses!'

She nudged my shoulder playfully. 'Oh, honey, I'm happy that you're letting yourself have a little fun. He's good for you, and by the way you look at him it's easy to tell things are mutual.'

Since Ford and I had decided on this little agreement of ours, I'd done everything I could to not build it up in my head. Every time he smiled at me, whispered that nickname I'd come to love against my heated skin, I had to remind myself that it wouldn't last. When he kissed my shoulder, collarbone, made me grasp his hair as he pleasured me with his fingers and his mouth, I repeated that the tender way he touched me was fleeting. He'd go back to Africa and I'd return to my solo existence. But in the quiet moments, when my dark room was filled with nothing but the sound of his heartbeat against my ear, I questioned if there could ever be more for us. Whether, if I brought it up, he'd consider staying in contact. Seeing me again once he returned. That idea was quickly squashed by the promise I'd forced him to make. We'd agreed to part as friends and nothing more.

Old Mrs V patted my arm. 'Where'd you go just then?'

'Thinking about how long Maisey is going to pester Tor about the dress.'

That knowing look returned to her gaze. She knew I was lying, but she never pushed me. Always gave me enough space to figure out my problems on my own. In so many ways, she reminded me of my mother. She had an instinct for when I needed a supportive word. A subtle push in the right direction like she'd done with me and the musical. More than once she'd told me that she'd adored my parents. That she felt compelled to look after me and, although at first it felt all kinds of strange, now I couldn't imagine my life without her reassuring presence.

'Your mother confided in me once that she was looking forward to being a grandmother one day.' She pulled Baby from my lap and gave him a gentle pat on the head. 'That she'd spoil your and Beck's children terribly. She said that your father often talked about taking them to the lake. Pushing them out on that old tire swing he loved. They both would have been thrilled with this turn of events.'

'Yes, they would have. Beck has been through so much. He deserves all kinds of happiness.'

Her lips pursed. 'The same could be said for you.'

'Not sure I'm there yet.'

She gave my knee a reassuring pat. 'I think you're closer than you'd like to admit.'

I gave her a forced smile. Happiness was within my grasp for the moment, but my luck had never held on for that long.

Yes, Ford made me smile more than I had in a long time. He also made me laugh at his terrible jokes. Moan with passion when he touched me in his gentle way. Inspired me to chase my dreams in spite of my fears. But he was also a temporary gift. One I'd sadly have to relinquish all too soon.

Chapter Twenty-Four

FORD

I'd Rather Eat Glass

'The patients are very happy with you, Dr Foster. You're taking your time with them. Listening even when they tell the same stories over and over. Just yesterday, Ferris, who is always a bit of a grump, told me he thinks you're a keeper,' Janice chuckled from the doorway to my office.

'He's a nice old guy. Keeps telling me about his prize roses every time he comes in to have his blood pressure checked.'

She gave me a determined look. 'Dr Sheridan has served the people of this town for over thirty years. This trip with his wife was put off at least five times until she threatened him within an inch of his life if he cancelled again.'

'I don't blame her. Traveling the world is exciting.'

'Thirty years is a long time,' she said.

'To be in one place? It sure is.'

'What about you? Ever considered planting roots somewhere?' There was a weight to her voice, a knowing look that said gossip about me and Piper had filtered her way.

'Not right now. I still have a few years before I think about finding a place to stay.'

'What about here?'

'This is a nice spot, sure.'

'So you'd consider coming back? Because once people start filling the doc in on what a good job you've done, I think he'd consider bringing you on full-time.'

For a minute I let myself play with the idea. Of finding a cute place in town. Coming in the door every night to Piper. Having her snuggled up naked next to me in the bed we shared.

I'd be lying if I said I hadn't let my mind wander through that fantasy more than a few times. For right now it could not be my reality. I'd signed a contract, and Piper had made it clear that once it was time for me to leave, we had to let go of whatever this was we'd been doing for the last several weeks.

'That's not in the cards for me right now. When Dr Sheridan returns I'll be on my way back across the world. It's where I'm meant to be.'

She tapped her fingers against her hips. 'Plans can be broken. Think about it. We could use more help in this community. The longer that show of Torran and Manny's goes on, the more people will want to move here. We're already stretched too thin as it is now with one doctor.'

'I understand, but the timing isn't right.'

'Fine,' she said, defeated. 'You almost done with your charts? If so, I'll take them off your hands.'

I stood and handed her a dozen Manila folders. 'You know you all could come into the twenty-first century and go digital.'

She barked out a laugh. 'Can you imagine handing a tablet to Ferris or Mrs V and asking them to figure it out?'

'Good point.'

'Although, if we had a young doctor around to help teach…'

I shook my head and she clutched the folders to her chest, understanding she wasn't going to change my mind.

'We're done for the night. You headed out?'

'Yes. I promised Piper I'd head over to the theater. Help with installing the last of the sets.'

She opened her mouth like she wanted to say more. Offer another convincing reason for me to stay. Instead, she said, 'Have a good evening.'

'You too,' I said, hanging my white coat on a peg attached to the wall. After straightening up the desk, I walked to the door. My phone pinged in my pocket. I glanced at the text from Gray outlining all the information for our parents' wedding anniversary party next weekend. What I should wear. The fact that I was not getting out of giving a toast. The last message made me stop in my tracks:

Bring a date asshole or Mom will find one for you.

Shit. Going to the event at all was going to be an exercise in patience and restraint. Having to swap mindless talk about the stock market, and how much the Titans needed a new stadium, was already creating tension in my jaw. Adding a date to that scenario was a thousand times worse. Of course, my mind went to Piper. How having her by my side would make the night bearable. But every time I thought about bringing it up, considered having

223

to introduce her to that vapid crowd, my throat went dry and my pulse raced.

I could barely stand those people. How could I in good conscience consider making her suffer through it as well? And my parents? They'd be awful to her just because she didn't have an old-money pedigree.

The one time I introduced them to Sydney, I had to grit my teeth through the entire dinner because all they did was ask about her family. What her parents did for a living. By the angry pinch to her mouth after they were done with their interrogation, it was obvious my girlfriend wondered what the hell she was doing with me.

I shoved my phone into my pocket and walked to the front door.

All day long the clinic had been a frenzy. Nurses rushed in and out of rooms. Receptionists and schedulers answered the dizzying number of phone calls. But once we closed for the night, a peaceful calm settled over the space.

I'd never pictured myself in a place like this. Getting to know a community in such an intimate way. If circumstances were different, if I thought I could change Piper's mind, maybe I'd consider coming back. She'd been very clear on the terms of our relationship though, and the last thing I wanted to do was push her into something she never wanted.

—

Chaos was too calm a word for the current scene inside the theater. Teenagers chased each other across the stage, singing songs and trying to follow the accompanying choreography. The kids that weren't onstage filled the first three rows. Various parents scrambled around them, pressing costumes into their hands.

I searched the room for Piper and found her at the piano singing along with the kids. Her dark braid swung behind her as she tipped up her chin, head tracking each of the young actors' movements like she was mentally making notes for what needed to be adjusted. I was so mesmerized by her that I didn't notice Maisey walk to my side.

'Piper's damn talented, don't you think?'

'There are no words for it. She is simply… extraordinary.'

She gave me a pleased smile. 'Ding. Ding. Ding. That is the correct answer.'

'Did you think I'd say anything else?'

She tapped her chin. 'You like her.'

'Of course I do.'

'No.' Her eyes narrowed and she stepped closer. Too close. 'You *like like* her.'

I laughed, looking down my nose at this small and very determined woman. 'What does that mean exactly?'

'That this isn't some small-town fling for you.'

I pressed my lips thin and she didn't bat an eye. 'We're enjoying each other's company,' was all I could offer.

Hell, this woman was Piper's best friend. She knew her better than anyone. If I let it slip that Piper was all I thought about, that I couldn't imagine her not being a part of my life, it might spook Piper into ending things with me right now, and there was no way I was risking that.

'Basically, you're rolling around in the sheets with zero commitment. Sounds like a great deal for you.'

Her voice carried and more than a few parents shot unpleasant gazes in our direction.

'I'm not comfortable saying more,' I said in a low tone. 'This is a private matter between me and Piper.'

'You've been here long enough,' she huffed out. 'So I suspect you've heard why she was in the hospital that night.'

'Honestly, no. I've haven't heard much, which I guess is a credit to how much people care about her.'

'That asshole, that...' She took a gulp. 'There was a dealer she owed money to, and he forced her to tell him about the Huckleberry Lane house. He showed up with a mass of people, made her watch while he and his group destroyed the home that Beck, Torran and Manny had lovingly restored. The place that held the last precious memories of her parents. It nearly killed her.'

The murderous look on her face told me there was much more to the story.

'They tore down the antique lighting. Put holes in the freshly painted walls with sledgehammers. Manny spent weeks restoring the stairs and banister, and those guys destroyed it in minutes,' she spat out. 'Imagine finally getting a piece of your family, your past, back and then having it eviscerated right before your eyes.' Her gaze flicked to where Piper stood. 'That girl has been through a lot of rough shit. If things are casual like you say they are, then walk away when the time comes. But,' her breath hitched, 'if your feelings are more serious, tell her. Piper's traveled a long road. She's done the work to get to this life that she deserves. That life should also be filled with real and true love. If you can't be that guy, make sure she knows that before you leave.'

My mind spun back to the night in Piper's apartment when I asked if she could trust me. How pain and fear flickered across her face. She'd been through hell. Treated like crap. The fact that she'd taken a chance on me said volumes about the person she'd become.

Piper walked up the aisle toward us and for the first time Maisey's tough exterior shook. 'All I'm asking is that you don't hurt her. Promise me you won't.'

Hurt her? I'd rather cut out my own damn heart.

'Maisey, you're a good friend. You have my word that both Piper and I will be honest with each other before I go back to Africa.'

She gave me a nod and hurried back to where the parents were inspecting the costumes. Her voice continued to rattle in my head. She had asked me to be honest, but on the rooftop that night, Piper had been firm about the conditions of our plan and I'd agreed. If I pushed, wouldn't I be like all the other men in her life who never listened to what she wanted?

As soon as she was beside me, Piper gave me a smile that pulled all the air from my chest.

Fuck. How could she do that to me?

'Silvio and Ferris have been pestering me for an hour. They need your help backstage to bring in the admiral's platform for the show's opening scene near the Banks' home on Cherry Tree Lane.'

'Okay, I'll head back there in a second, but there's a question I need to ask first. And please feel free to say no if you want.'

She sat down in the upholstered theater chair and pulled me beside her. 'You sound too serious. What's going on? Is it Old Mrs V?'

I clasped her hand. It always felt perfect against my palm. Everything about being near her felt right. 'Greta is fine.'

'There's an uneasy tone to your voice I don't like.'

'It's not a big deal. I just need to ask if you want to go to a party with me?'

Her brows furrowed. 'A party?'

'It's for my parents. I know I talked about keeping you away from them, but it's their fortieth wedding anniversary. My brother and I have to be there. Give a toast.'

'Ford, it's fine. It sounds like fun.'

I pressed my lips together. 'It won't be.'

'Why?'

'My parents, well, I've told you about them. They can be hard on my friends. And,' I gulped, 'especially tough on women I bring home. I'd rather eat glass than have you anywhere near them, but if I don't take a date, my mother will spend the entire evening throwing eligible women in my direction. It will be a nightmare considering the only thing that will be on my mind is you.'

'Ford.' She inched close until our knees touched. 'One night with your parents can't be that bad.'

'You have no idea, Bird. If you don't want to put yourself through the snobbery, the elitist bullshit that's bound to happen, tell me now and I'll go alone.'

She rolled back her shoulders. Gave me a wicked grin that made my dick twitch. 'So you need someone to have your back if your folks get to be too much?'

'Sadly, yes,' I confessed.

'And there's also a possibility that your date will need to get mysteriously and violently ill, giving you an excuse to leave if things go bad?'

'Oh my God, you are fucking brilliant.'

She laughed and put her hand to my cheek. There was so much light in her eyes it made me want to pull her onto my lap. Kiss her until she was dazed. Most of all, it made me want to confess that I was falling in love with her and didn't think I could stop.

She looked and put her hand to my cheek. There was so much light in her eyes that made me want to pull her into my arms, but maybe she realized. Aware of all it could mean. Instead, my chest warned that I'd need to rely on what I'd learned in therapy to get me and Instead, my chest warned...

Chapter Twenty-Five

PIPER

Tiniest Bit Of Access

Ford's leg bounced nervously the entire forty-five-minute drive to Harpeth Manor, which kept me from telling him about the nauseous churn in my own stomach. It'd been two years since I'd been to a party with alcohol. I knew I was steady. Prepared to take this next step, but that regular cramp in my chest warned that I'd need to rely on what I'd learned in therapy to get through the night.

We passed the time talking about the weather. If I was nervous about the show premiering next Friday. If I thought the kids were ready.

'I think most of them will do all right. The only one I'm worried about is Dex.'

'Why? That kid's got some pipes. I watched him during rehearsal the other day. He knows the moves too.'

'It's his dad,' I said, playing with the lace edge of the little black dress Tessa had loaned me. 'He's promised to come to the show, but Dex's mom pulled me aside yesterday. Told me she's worried he might flake. Apparently, he's got a new girlfriend in Knoxville that takes up a lot of his time.'

Ford white-knuckled the wheel. He'd gotten close to Dex since the gummy bear incident. When he'd been at the theater to help, Dex made it a point to seek him out. I may have eavesdropped on a few of their conversations, which usually covered Dex's love of all things skateboarding and basketball, and his often absent dad.

'That kid,' he said with a heavy breath. 'I see a lot of myself in him. He's driven. Ambitious. But he's also desperate for his father's attention. More than once, he's asked me how he can do better in school. Like if he gets straight As his father will recognize his existence.'

'My heart aches for him,' I confessed. 'And his mom, she's doing her best, but she looks tired all the time, which is not lost on Dex.'

'The best we can do for him is let him know he's not alone. That we're here to talk if he needs us.'

I crossed my arms over my chest. 'It shouldn't have to be that way. Dex should be his dad's first priority.'

'There are a lot of people who can't get out of their own way to be good parents.' There was a scratch to his voice that said he spoke from experience, which made me cautious about meeting his parents tonight.

I reached over and placed my hand over his. In the early twilight, his hair was a rich chocolate color. His pale blue eyes the perfect match to the button-down shirt he wore. When he'd knocked on my door tonight it had been hard not to grip onto his bright yellow tie, drag him in the door and tear the clothing off his body. Press my mouth to every inch of his skin that I found myself craving every single day.

I must not have hidden that desire well, because when he saw me he gave me a kiss so hot it made me think about all the things I wanted to do with him once this night was over.

We continued to hold hands while quiet music floated out of the old car's speakers. At the end of a long, narrow road, we turned and made our way through the wrought-iron gates leading into the Harpeth Manor Country Club. Trimmed topiary lined the white gravel road. A wide swath of green led to a pristinely manicured golf course. Cars that cost more than most houses in Ivy Falls lined the circular driveway. Once we stopped, a red-vested valet was at my door helping me out.

Ford was quickly by my side, a hand around my waist, as we walked up a brick-lined path, past a massive two-tier concrete fountain and into a foyer that was covered in wall-to-wall white marble. Ford wasn't kidding when he said this place was ridiculously over the top.

A tuxedo-clad man stopped us on our way into the main lobby. Flutes of sparkling wine sat on his polished silver tray. The waiter offered me a drink. In the past, a zing would have raced down my back as I eagerly grabbed one, but that instinct was gone. I declined but told Ford he could enjoy a glass if he wanted. He slid his hand into mine and said, 'I'm a club-soda-and-lime kind of guy.'

More couples walked past us. The heady scent of flowers and expensive perfume clung to the air.

'Ready for the lion's den?'

I gave him a convincing smile. 'I'm sure we can find a weapon and a chair somewhere if we need to fight them off.'

He pressed a kiss to my cheek. 'I'm so glad you're here, Bird.'

Once he tucked my hand around his arm like a proper escort, we walked toward the sounds of the party. We weren't five steps into the ballroom when a dark-haired guy who shared the same eyes as Ford buzzed in our direction.

When he reached us he gave Ford a perturbed look. 'You're late.'

'Hi. Good to see you too, Gray. This is my...' He took an uncomfortable gulp. We'd never put a label on what we were, and 'summer fling' probably wasn't appropriate for this scene. 'This is Piper Townsend,' he said.

His brother shot out his hand to shake. As soon as he caught my wrist, he flipped it over and kissed the back of my hand all while dragging his gaze up my body.

Okay, yeah, Ford has his brother pegged. This guy is a total fuckboy.

Another waiter passed us and Gray pulled two crystal flutes off the tray and pushed one in my direction. Ford started to object until I shook my head. 'No, thank you. I don't drink.'

'More for me then.' In two gulps his brother had one glass drained.

I waited for that itch in my throat again, the pull in my stomach. How my brain would run through all the scenarios about how I could have one glass and be fine. But in this moment I felt nothing except for the warmth of Ford's hand against my back. The need to be grounded and one hundred percent present for him tonight.

Once Gray finished the second glass he said, 'Mom and Dad got in a fight before they got here. I guess Dad planned a golfing trip to Scotland with his friends and didn't tell her. The weekend he's gone is the annual Botanical Gardens Ball. Not exactly a great start to an evening that is supposed to be about their "enduring love",' he said with a sarcastic edge.

233

Ford grimaced. 'Let's get through the night in one piece. That's all we need to do. Okay?'

'Agreed, and once the toast is over, I'm going to make the fastest exit possible.' Gray tried to hide the slur in his voice but Ford gripped his shoulder.

'Cool it with the drinking. I have no intention of propping you up during the toast.'

'Fine,' Gray huffed. 'Now, if you'll excuse me I need to hunt down George Bryce. He lost a thousand bucks to me in a poker game last weekend and hasn't paid up.' He turned and gave me a formal bow. 'Nice to meet you, Piper, and a word of warning about our mother...'

'Gray.' Ford gave him a look of warning.

'I'm only offering her a bit of advice.'

'Make it quick,' Ford grumbled.

'I love the matriarch of our family, but she can be a viper. Ignore anything and everything she says tonight, because she can be a tad bit protective when it comes to my little brother.'

'Thanks for the heads-up. I'll try to stay away from her fangs.'

An apologetic smile slid over his lips like his advice still wouldn't be enough to protect me from his mother's vicious bite.

It was okay. In all the chaos I'd had to deal with in my life, one overbearing mother didn't feel like too much of a threat.

Ford grabbed me around the waist. Pressed a gentle kiss to my temple. 'Let's enter the fray. The sooner we make our appearance, endure a bunch of worthless small talk, the quicker we can get out of this place.'

For the next half-hour I shook hands, swapped conversations about the stock market and whatever fast and slow greens were. Ford's charm was ratcheted up to a ten. He was good at remembering people's names. What they did for a living. How many children and grandchildren they had. If I didn't know him, I'd have thought he was a regular member of this crowd.

We were finishing a conversation with a banker and his third wife, when an older woman with pale blonde hair, bright red lips and the most stunning diamond choker I'd ever seen placed her hand on his shoulder. Ford spun and gave her a forced smile.

'Hello, Mother.'

'Sweetheart.' She pressed her lips together as she took him in. 'A yellow tie? For evening? Really, Crawford?'

His hand flew to his neck and I hated the way her caustic tone made him flinch. 'It was all I had that was clean.'

Her steely gaze left her son and focused on me. 'Who is this?'

'Mother, this is Piper Townsend. She's from Ivy Falls where I'm working right now.'

In her white silk gown with a regal tilt to her head, Ford's mother reminded me of the Narnia witch. If I didn't know better, I would have guessed she had ice water in her veins.

'Piper.' Her cool stare moved over the way I had my hair pinned up. How my dress cut across my shoulders. Her slow and torturous survey of me stopped at the tattoo on my wrist. Her lips thinned as she added, 'Pleasure to meet you.'

'You too, Mrs Foster.'

'What is it that you do in Ivy Falls? How did you meet my Crawford?'

'I have several jobs. One of them is directing a musical for our children's theater. A young actor had a minor accident and Ford took care of him.'

'Local theater?' she sniffed. 'That is an interesting profession.'

'I love it. The kids are wonderful. It is very fulfilling,' I said with a little too much force.

'Can't imagine that pays much.'

'It doesn't matter,' Ford interrupted. 'She's damn good at what she does.' He reached out and laced his fingers through mine. 'She sings and plays the piano too.'

His mother continued to level me with a stare that fell somewhere between malevolent and appalled.

'Where's Dad?' Ford said.

'At the bar as usual. He'll come over and say hello in due time.'

'Why don't we go that way now.'

'Missy is here.' She gave me another annoyed glance. 'It would be nice if you said hello, especially after the way you treated her the last time you saw her.'

'Mother.' Ford's voice was like a taut wire. 'We've spoken about this. If you hadn't ambushed me, there would not be an issue.'

That chilly façade of hers crumbled for just a flicker. 'Please, son. Go and speak to her like a gentleman. You owe her that much.'

'Fine, if it will keep the peace.'

She leaned in and pressed a stiff kiss to his cheek. 'Thank you, dear. It means a lot to me that you're here.'

Without another word, she slowly crossed the room and stopped next to a group of women who were also dripping in diamonds.

Frustration pulled at the corners of Ford's mouth. 'I'm sorry.'

'Don't be. That was a grand performance. Your mother missed her calling as an actress. She certainly has a flair for the dramatic.'

He tugged me in and planted a quick kiss on my cheek. 'You are amazing. Have I told you how stunning you look tonight?'

'Thank you,' I said, straightening his perfect yellow tie. 'You look pretty damn good too.'

His gaze went playful as he leaned in and whispered, 'I bet it would take me less than five seconds to get you out of that dress. To press my mouth to every part of you. Make you moan wicked things.'

I laughed. Shook my head. I was sure these people would have been beyond mortified if they'd heard us.

'Promises, promises, *Crawford*.'

His face sobered. 'Call me anything you want except that. It was my grandfather's name and he was cruel. I think that explains why my mother acts like a dragon all the time. She needs to keep herself protected.'

I pressed up on my toes and whispered, 'Tell you what, not only will I let you take my clothes off, but you can also tear my underwear off with your teeth too.' His lips twitched until I said, 'Ooops. I'm not wearing any.'

He tilted his head back and groaned. 'You're killing me, Bird.'

I reached up and messed his perfectly combed hair until he looked like my Ford again.

Shit. *My Ford.* I couldn't let myself think of him that way.

We walked to the bar and Ford made quick introductions to his father. It was clear where he got his high cheekbones and dark mop of hair.

'Thank you for coming. This kind of thing means a lot to your mother.'

'Of course,' Ford said.

'Can I get you two a drink?'

'Piper?' Ford said.

'Club soda with lime, please.'

'Make that two,' Ford added.

'That's not a drink that's a palate cleanser,' Mr Foster grumbled.

'Dad.' Ford kept his voice low and tight. 'Please order it.'

With a rude flick of his hand, he waved down the bartender. While we waited, dozens of older couples moved around the room. I'd never seen so many rubies and Rolexes in my life. I'd heard stories about the wealth in Harpeth Manor, but all of this was too much.

As his father handed us our drinks, a man with cropped white hair at the end of the bar waved in our direction.

'That's Guy Sorenson,' his father bit out. 'One of his partners recently retired. They're looking to hire a new doctor for their practice. I mentioned you were looking.'

'Dad.' Ford sighed. 'We've talked about this. I'm not going to work in Harpeth Manor.'

'You're thirty-two, Crawford. When are you going to grow up? Stop gallivanting around the world and get a real damn job.' His fingers tightened around the thick crystal glass. 'I'm growing tired of you and your brother disappointing me. This family has a good name to uphold and you boys are making a mockery of it.'

'All the guilt-tripping in the world won't change my mind,' Ford shot back.

'Guilt? No, this isn't guilt. This is truth.' He took another swig of his drink. 'Your mother and I have supported you and your brother through your ridiculous little forays, but it is time to man up. Face your responsibilities.'

His father's menacing growl drew more than a few stares. Ford had explained how overbearing his family could be, but the condescending and patronizing way his father spoke to him was too much.

'Ford has a good job,' I snapped. 'The people in Senegal, on *Humanity of the Seas*, will be damn lucky to have him when he returns in October.'

The older man's eyes bulged. Ford shook his head and pulled in a heavy breath.

Oh shit. I've said the wrong thing.

'You promised your mother you were done with that nonsense.' His father's voice bordered on incensed.

Ford tipped up his chin. Looked his father in the eye. 'I'm going back. Signed another six-month contract.'

'Why do you keep disappointing us?' Mr Foster slammed his glass down onto the bar, whiskey spilling out into a brown puddle.

The dry, nutty scent of it washed over me. I'd been here too many times. At the precipice of want and need. The ache to be numb so overwhelming it made me gasp. I grounded my feet to the floor. Listened to the rapid thud of my heartbeat, reminding myself that a few hours of being mindless never made the pain in my life disappear, it only blurred the edges until I was dumped back into reality again.

I turned to Ford. Pain rippled across his face, and that hollow claw of need was replaced with an angry heat.

This beautiful man cared for Old Mrs V with a gentle kindness that was beyond his duties. Spent time with Dex, who needed an adult to reassure him that he was worthy of time and attention. He knew my past, what I'd been through, but never hesitated to listen. Asked the right questions and never judged my answers. Mr Foster was lucky to be a part of his son's life. To get to watch him grow and use his skills to help others.

A wall of grief punched against my chest. What I would have given to have my parents alive. To have them see how far I'd come. To be present at Beck's wedding as he married the love of his life.

As much as I knew I should let Ford fight his own battles, I couldn't stand here quietly and listen to his father spew his rage and ignorance all over him.

I stepped closer to Mr Foster. 'Sir, you're way out of line.'

The veins in the older man's temple bulged.

'Piper, no,' Ford said with a quiet plea.

'I'm sorry but I can't listen to this.' I lowered my voice but kept it hard as ice. 'Every single day your brilliant son gives himself to his job. The people in Ivy Falls are a hard group to impress, but they adore Ford. Think he's one of the best things that has ever happened to our community. And the work he's doing in Africa, how he's using his skills to help people in need, is a fact to be admired, not treated like some kind of poor and uninformed choice you and your wife are ashamed of.'

His father glared at me with the heat of a thousand suns, and I shot him the same unflinching look.

What the actual fuck is wrong with these people?

'You're right, Ford *is* thirty-two. You should stop forcing your own hopes and dreams on to him like he's a rudderless child. Be grateful he's got direction. That he's adding some good back into this shitty world. Your amazing and brilliant son is standing right in front of you, telling you what makes him happy. Do you know what a gift that is? Some parents never get to see their children grow up.' I swallowed back a sob. 'To witness their contributions to their community. How they change the lives of the people around them. You should be damn glad you're given even the tiniest bit of access to his life considering the way you've treated him.'

The sound of a knife clinking against glass filled the room as Beck's brother tried to gather everyone in for the toast.

'This is none of your business,' Mr Foster barked at me before jabbing a stubby finger into his son's chest. 'We're not done talking about this,' he spat out before stomping toward the table where his wife stood.

I started to apologize but Ford shook his head, made the slow walk to the front of the room where his brother and the rest of the party were waiting.

Chapter Twenty-Six

FORD

Defend My Choices

It was a three-minute toast but it felt like three hours. Gray and I were supposed to say a few words and then dinner was to be served, but as soon as we were done speaking, every blowhard in the room wanted to share their two cents about how they'd somehow added to the joy of our parents' long marriage.

For the entire toast, my father stayed iron-jawed, never bothering to look at me. I didn't care. Piper had done me a favor by spilling my secret about Africa. I only wished I'd been brave enough to take him on the way she had.

When the waiters entered the room with the first course, I dashed out into the hall. Piper wasn't in the bathrooms or waiting in the lobby. I checked the back lawn and upstairs in the ladies' locker room. Like a ghost, she'd vanished. Panic filled my throat as I dialed her number. It went straight to voicemail every time. I rushed down the stairs and collided with a woman at the bottom.

'Ford,' Missy said with a wide smile. 'It's good to see you.'

'Look, I'm in kind of a hurry, but I wanted to apologize for that day. That situation at brunch.'

She waved me off. 'I swear I did not know that was a setup from your mom. Thought it was only supposed to be a short hello.'

My frantic gaze continued to sweep the area for Piper. 'I really do wish you the best, and it was good to see you, but I need to go.'

'Do you have to run off? I wanted you to meet my girlfriend. It's the first time I've brought her to something like this and it's, well, a lot. Thought it might be nice to introduce her to at least one person here I don't think is a total douchebag.'

'I… I would love to but there's this girl…'

'The stunning brunette?'

'Yeah, she is my…' I took a rough swallow. We didn't have a name for what we were doing, but if I had my choice I would call her my… everything. 'She sort of had it out with my dad and now I can't find her.'

Her eyes lit up. 'Wow. Brave girl. I like her already.'

'Me too,' I gushed. 'But I'm afraid I screwed it up and that she's taken off.'

She made a shooing motion. 'Go. If I see your mother, I'll say you had a patient you needed to see.'

'You're the best! Text me when you're free. Come to Ivy Falls with your girlfriend. I'd love to meet her. Show you around town.'

'We will.' She made that shooing motion again.

I raced out the doors of the club and skidded to a stop in front of the valet. 'My date. Tall brunette?'

'The one in the black dress with those hot legs?'

'Yes,' I said, biting back my jealousy.

'She took off in a ride-share fifteen minutes ago.'

I shoved my ticket and a twenty-dollar bill at him. 'There's twenty more for you if you have my car here in two minutes.'

He took off at a sprint and I dialed Piper's number again.

No answer.

Shit. I had a lot of explaining to do and I hoped she'd give me the time to listen.

–

I knocked twice. Three times.

Panic pressed against the walls of my chest.

What if she wasn't here? What if she'd gone to her brother's?

The walk to their house ran through my head. I turned and took two steps before the door slowly opened.

'What are you doing here?' There was a tentative edge to Piper's voice I didn't like.

'Why did you take off?'

She pulled the door all the way open. Gone was the sultry black dress. Instead an old T-shirt hung from her shoulders. Worn-out jeans with holes in the knees covered her gorgeous legs. 'I didn't think me hanging around was a good idea, considering I yelled at one of the guests of honor.'

'Can I come in?'

The way she shook her head punched the air from my lungs. 'Tonight was a lot. You were right about it being exhausting. I should have listened. That crowd... All the alcohol... What I said to your father.' Her chin quivered. 'Maybe we should let things end now. You go back to your life and I'll return to mine.'

'No,' I said on a frenzied breath. 'Please do not think for a second that I'm upset with you. That I want this to end. Who I'm really pissed at is me. I should not have exposed you to any of it. I should have stood up to my dad.' I scrubbed a hand over my mouth. 'Better yet, I shouldn't have gone at all.'

'No. You needed to be there for your brother. He's a piece of work, but it was clear he did not want to do the toast on his own.'

'Please give me a minute. I want to explain a few things.'

She worried her luscious bottom lip before she took a step back and let me inside.

I walked to the kitchen island and set my coat down. She hovered a few steps away and all I wanted was to pull her into my arms. Breathe in that coffee and sweet vanilla scent of hers, and let my heart go back to a normal rhythm. But before any of that happened, she deserved the truth.

'Things are complicated with my parents. My mom, she had a major car accident a year ago and broke most of the bones in her leg. It freaked out Gray to the point where he was calling me every few hours, begging me to come back, but I couldn't leave because we were down three doctors on the ship at the time.' I clasped my fingers together, not wanting to remember the terror in my brother's voice that day. 'Over the phone, and through online chats, I stayed in touch with my mom's doctors. Made sure she got the best care. When she was out of surgery and recovering, I made a promise to Gray and my parents that after my latest contract was up I'd come home. That's why I took the job here in Ivy Falls.'

'And the new contract?' she prompted.

'When I got back from Africa, I stayed at my parents' house. It was hell. The constant nitpicking, the judgment, it all reminded me of why I'd left in the first place. I couldn't get back to my boss on the *Humanity of the Seas* quick enough to ask for another contract.'

'Why didn't you tell them?'

I sank down onto the stool at the counter. 'I should have, but it's always the same argument, and I'm tired of having to defend my choices.' I tented my hands on the counter, the image of my dad's red face tonight playing through my head. 'My father keeps trying to set up interviews at local practices. And tonight, I couldn't get the words out to tell him, or deal with seeing the disappointment on his face again.' A stilted breath slowly filled my lungs. 'I don't want to hurt my mom either. She's not always the kindest person, but in the end she is my mom.' I rubbed at my tired eyes. 'That terrible scene was all on me, and I'm damn sorry you got caught up in it.'

Her feet padded toward me and when she put her hands on my cheeks, the tension in my jaw went slack. 'It's okay.'

I closed my eyes, too ashamed that I hadn't defended myself. That she'd been drawn into the ridiculous drama with my parents. She already had so much going on in her life and here I was dragging her into my own problems. Exposing her to shit that I had no right to. It was the last thing she needed and I wondered if she regretted making this deal with me.

'You were incredible tonight, Bird,' I whispered. 'Much braver than I could ever be.'

'Ford, look at me.'

When I finally opened my eyes all I saw was her loving gaze. It made me want to tell her that I was falling for her.

That every minute she wasn't with me, I was thinking of holding her hand, winding my fingers through her gorgeous hair. How when she laughed it sounded like a sweet melody. The pure bliss I felt when I gazed at her face every morning knowing that waking up beside her was a damn gift. To me this was much more than a fling. I wanted more time. More touches. More kisses. But she'd made our deal clear, so instead of confessing how I really felt, I bit the inside of my cheek and let her talk.

'The reason I spoke up tonight was because I couldn't listen to your father talk badly about you. What I said to him was true. You've come into this town and earned everyone's admiration and respect. There has not been a moment when you've hesitated when someone has asked for your help. Old Mrs V. Silvio and Ferris. Dex. And for me.' She pulled in a shaky breath. 'You've taught me to trust myself. Shown me that I can build a real connection with someone without screwing it up.' Her hands moved to cup my jaw. 'Your time in Ivy Falls has changed all of us. You've grown relationships here. Made friends. That's a fact none of us will ever forget. And as far as your parents,' she huffed, 'you don't need their approval. If they're too dumb to get out of their own way, to see what an amazing man you are, that's one thousand percent their fucking fault.'

She bent down and brushed her lips over mine, her loose hair falling in a dark curtain around us. I tugged her hips closer and deepened the kiss.

The way she spoke like I was already gone sent a crack through my heart. She'd meant what she said about parting as friends, and the thought of it sent an ache so deep through me that it rattled my bones. I pushed the pain away and settled into the here and now. The feel of her soft skin under my hands. How the pulse of her body thrummed against mine. This was what I wanted, what I needed right now – her and nothing else.

My hands moved around her waist, tugging at her shirt. She wrenched it over her head and then went to work on unbuttoning mine. My pants followed and she reached inside my boxer briefs and cupped my erection. I smiled into the next kiss she planted on my lips, lifted her up onto my waist and walked straight back into her bedroom. It didn't take more than a minute for us to be naked. She climbed onto my lap, making me forget everything about tonight except for the way she held me, and how I loved it when my name ripped from her lips.

Chapter Twenty-Seven

PIPER

Small Hiccups

I'd fallen back into one bad pattern. For almost an hour, I paced backstage before the curtain rose on opening night. Even though I tried to focus my mind elsewhere, I kept coming back to all the ways the show could go wrong. Scenarios like the lighting not working, the musical score glitching, even how the kids might forget every single one of their lines.

Like she could sense my unraveling, Maisey found me falling to pieces in the wings. She grabbed my hand and tugged me to a quiet corner.

'Pipe, you've got this. You've run through the tech half a dozen times. These kids are prepared. Ford, Silvio and Ferris have a team loading the sets in and out. The costumes fit everyone perfectly.' She grinned. 'Tessa and Manny are on hair and makeup. And to add to all that, the entire town is filling up the seats. It's a sellout.'

'What you're saying makes sense, but I can't keep my mind from racing.'

She narrowed her gaze, the corners of her mouth twitching. 'This is about more than the show, isn't it?'

Out of the corner of my eye, I caught Ford and Dex in a huddle. They were talking and doing some handshake with slaps and snaps that looked overly complicated but made both of them laugh.

'It's going to be hard to say goodbye,' Maisey said in a soft voice.

'Why did I think I could do this? Have an easy fling and be over it?'

Maisey stayed quiet, which was always a bad sign.

'Say what you want, Maise.'

'You're not the same person anymore. These past years you've fought so damn hard to build a good life for your-self. To steady your feet on the ground. I don't think you have it in you to do anything casually anymore.' Her chin dipped. 'I'm sorry if my shitty advice led you here.'

'You were right to push me. To encourage me to take a chance. I don't regret a moment I've spent with him.'

'You don't think he'd stay if you asked?'

'I can't. He signed a contract. The people on his ship are waiting for him. That's more important than what's happening between us.'

'Don't you at least want to ask? See what he has to say?'

'I don't want to complicate things for him. We agreed to part as friends and that's what we're going to do.'

She inched back. 'I want to argue, but I'm going to be a good best friend and mind my own damn business.'

'Thank you.'

A few kids called to her from the wings, pointed to their loose suspenders, and she raced to help them. I looked for Ford once more, wanting another glimpse of him, but he'd disappeared into the wings again.

–

Mary Poppins lost her umbrella. The dry-ice smoke didn't work in the admiral's cannon, and during the 'Step in

Time' dance number a chimney sweep kicked her shoe straight into the audience where Diego quickly caught it before it hit anyone. Besides those small hiccups, the performance was perfection.

It'd been a huge undertaking, getting the kids to practice, organizing the music, lights, costumes, but this job had also stoked a fire within me. Made me think about what I wanted to do next.

In a quiet moment last week while Ford was snoozing beside me, I pulled out my laptop and did an hour of research. The local community college offered a few courses on theater direction. Working on the show had reminded me that I only felt whole when I was being creative. Going back to take a few classes would be a small start, but a start I desperately wanted.

After the final curtain call, I waited for the cast backstage. They swarmed me in a massive hug, cheered my name and presented me with the biggest bouquet I'd ever seen. Dex made a point of telling me he'd picked them out with Ford. The way his voice scratched said I wasn't the only one thinking about Ford's imminent departure.

Kids wandered back to the dressing area to change out of their costumes, and I walked to the front of the stage to make sure nothing was left behind. A rush of footsteps came from the wings as Miss Cheri raced toward me. Her bright green-and-purple dress swirled out around her, and before I could say a word, she had me wrapped in the tightest hug. 'I knew you could do it. You were meant for this work.'

She pulled back and pressed her hands against my cheeks. 'All those little ad libs you encouraged the kids to do. How you let them lean into the new choreography, making it their own, was genius. And Dex's performance,' she said with sunshiny glee. 'I'm going to guess that was because of your loving support. When that kid first got here, he wanted nothing to do with this show, but, tonight, he was a consummate pro. I am so proud of you I could burst!'

'This would have never happened if you hadn't agreed to let me take this on. I can never thank you enough for trusting me, even when you had every reason not to.'

'Oh, Piper, sweetie, you've had a rough go of it, but I'm happy that you came back to where you belong. That you've allowed the people here to witness the hard work you've done. To applaud how far you've come. You are just one of the many reasons why Ivy Falls is special.'

She pulled me into another embrace as Old Mrs V appeared and said, 'Let the rest of us show our appreciation too!'

Miss Cheri gave a flippant wave at her friend and backed up so Old Mrs V and Silvio could give me their own hugs. Mrs V's skin was still too pale for my liking, but Ford did say it would take time for her to feel better. Tessa and Manny and the girls were next in line. They handed me another bouquet and gushed about the show. Lou even mentioned she might try out for the next one, which made Manny beam. Beck and Torran waited eagerly behind them.

'That was seriously the best children's performance this town has ever had!' Beck crowed.

Torran gave me a smile but she still looked a little green. According to Beck, the morning sickness was now afternoon and evening sickness too.

'Pipe, you never cease to amaze me. What you did with that show. With the kids. Pure brilliance.' The way my brother beamed at me with pride shook the last of my fears away. For years I'd wanted him to give me that kind of look. The one that said I'd made him proud. Achieved something that made him want to tell everyone I was his sister. As if he could sense my emotion, he plopped a kiss on the top of my head and whispered, 'Mom and Dad would be thrilled.'

That did it. The tears streaked down my cheeks and Torran playfully swiped at his shoulder. 'This is her big night. Don't make her cry.'

'They're good tears,' I said through a choked laugh.

A line built up behind them, and they reminded me I'd agreed to come to the house next week for dinner. Once they were gone, Barb and Susan gushed about how Autumn was the perfect Mary Poppins. How her voice was angelic. The rest of the town filtered through until a single person was left waiting.

Ford looked at me with such awe that I almost burst into tears again. He stalked straight for me, lifting me up and spinning in a circle.

'That show was pure fucking magic. The kids were having so much fun... and Dex.' He shook his head. 'That kid is going places.'

'I hope he keeps pursuing theater. He really does have stage presence.' I waited a beat, too afraid to ask my question but I had to. 'Did his father show up?'

'No.' He couldn't hide the steel in his voice. 'I sat with Rachel. Before the curtain fell, she was texting him. He made an excuse about not having money for gas to get here. Told her to pass along a message to Dex that he was sorry.'

'Dammit,' I bit out. 'That kid deserves better.'

Ford linked his fingers with mine. 'He does but taking on this role boosted his confidence. We've talked a lot

253

about him doing the thing he loves. That his father's choices should not affect how he lives his life. Which is a subject I know something about.'

I gave him a sad smile and he shrugged.

Near the bottom of the stage stairs stood a group of preteen girls, whispering and staring into the wings.

'Wonder what that's about?' I said.

'They're waiting for Dex. I overheard them saying how cute he was.'

I pressed a hand to my mouth, stifling a laugh. 'He's going to love that.'

'Yeah, he is.' Ford lifted my hand and pressed a kiss to my skin. 'What else is there to do besides clean up?'

'Maisey probably needs help with the costumes.'

He pulled me in for a hug and his woody scent washed over me. I wanted to hold on to this moment, knowing we wouldn't have many more.

As we clung to each other, a person in the audience cleared their throat.

Ford spun around and took a step back. 'Mom? What are you doing here?'

In a silky white blouse and navy-blue pantsuit, Mrs Foster was dressed more for a power lunch than a children's theater performance.

'Your friend here said she was directing a show. Thought I'd come and watch.'

His gaze darted around the theater. 'Is Dad with you?'

'No. It's poker night at the club,' she said with a snip. She took two bold strides forward and stopped below the stage. 'Miss Townsend, I've seen theater in New York, London, Montreal, even in Paris.' She sniffed. 'Tonight, I expected to be wholly underwhelmed, but those children…' She pressed her lips thin as if suppressing a smile.

'They were magnificent, and I would assume that's a credit to you.'

'Thank you, ma'am.'

'I was wondering if I could steal my son away for a minute?'

'Oh, sure,' I replied, still stunned she'd offered me a genuine compliment. 'I need to go backstage and help with the costumes. Ford, I'll see you in the square later?'

'Yes, you will.' He kissed my cheek and made his way down the side stairs.

I had no idea why Mrs Foster was here, but the way she walked with the posture of a military commander said it wasn't for a reason that could be good.

Chapter Twenty-Eight

FORD

Hairline Fracture

My mother looked out of place amongst the colorful booths, bounce houses and food vendors lining the square. With her hair pulled back in a tight bun, her high heels clacking against the brick-paved sidewalks, she blended in about as well as a crow in a snow bank.

I didn't know why she was here but her silence made the knots in my shoulders tighten. When Claudia Cannon Beloit Foster showed up anywhere unannounced it meant things were seriously wrong.

'How is your leg feeling? Are you still going to physical therapy?' I said, needing to break the tension.

'I still have a little achiness, some tightness, but the PT helps with those issues.'

'What about the cane?'

She shot me a deadly look. 'I'm too young to be using a damn cane.'

'If it helps with your balance.' I gave an annoyed look at her heels. 'You should use it.'

Her lips stayed tight as we passed the P&P and the Dairy Dip. More than once people stopped me, shook my hand, thanked me for taking care of their child's fever, their wife's cold or a friend's rash. Each time it happened, the lines in my mother's forehead bunched together.

By the time we reached the end of the street, the reason for her unexpected trip to Ivy Falls gnawing at me, I pulled her down onto a wrought-iron bench in front of the hardware store.

'Mother, you did not come all this way to see Piper's show. What do you want? Do you need me to say I'm sorry for not telling you about my new contract? Because I do feel bad for keeping it from you, but I'm not going to apologize for following my passion. For going where my skills are needed.'

She was about to answer when Greta and Silvio turned the corner. Greta made a beeline straight for me with Silvio hot on her heels.

'Doc,' she said, giving me a quick wave. 'Didn't our girl do a bang-up job tonight?'

'She did.'

Greta's gaze flicked to my mother. 'I know most of the folks in Ivy Falls, but you're a new face.'

'I'm Ford's mother,' she said with a brittle smile.

Greta lit up like a Fourth of July rocket. 'Well, how do you do?' She reached for Mom's hand, pumping it up and down. 'You've got to be real proud of your son. He's taken care of this town like a pro. Most of us old folks around here don't do well with change, but Ford's kindness, generosity, has won us all over.'

'It's true.' Silvio gently extricated Greta's hand from my mother's. 'When my sweetie here got sick a while back, Ford stepped right in. Made sure she got the best care. Ever since, he's been to our place regularly, making sure she's improved.' He gave Greta a weighted look. 'Taking her medicine. There aren't enough words to say how grateful we are for having him here for a short time in Ivy Falls.'

'You're being too generous. All I'm doing is my job.'

'No siree, mister,' Greta objected. 'You've got a keen eye.' She turned to Mom. 'Just by doing a few tests, he had an idea of what was wrong with me. Sent me right off to the emergency room at Vanderbilt. Connected me to a world-renowned cardiologist there. Your son is truly something special.'

My mother's lower lip trembled, the steely façade she always wore like an expensive suit cracking with a hairline fracture.

Mayor Wright stepped into the square and called to Silvio about needing more trash bags from the hardware store.

'Duty calls.' Silvio smiled. Greta gave Mom's hand one more firm pump, before she walked to a bench where Isabel and Tessa were sitting.

The screech of kids, sweet scent of cotton candy and grilled hot dogs tinged the air. Every time there was an event to celebrate, Ivy Falls sure knew how to put on a show.

'This place is charming,' Mom said quietly.

'It is, but I'm not letting you change the subject. You never answered my question. Why are you here?'

She scrubbed her hands up and down her pants. 'Your father and I had a fight after the anniversary party.' Her head swiveled to where a group of boys from the show were cheering each other on as they shoveled hot dogs into their mouths. 'They remind me of you and Gray,' she said wistfully.

'The argument,' I said quietly. 'Was that because of me?'

'Yes, but that isn't your fault. It only brought to a head problems that have been brewing for a long time.' Her gaze returned to the pack of boys. 'Since you were young, your father and I have been at odds about parenting. I wanted you boys to have a chance to run a little wild. To have fun, make mistakes, all without the pall of the Foster name weighing on you.' She shook her head in defeat. 'My father was not a kind man. Whenever I made even the smallest mistake, brought home the wrong grade, didn't get picked as valedictorian, missed graduating summa cum laude by a few points in college, he was quick to berate me. In the stiffest, coldest voice he'd say I'd sullied the Beloit name. It was too much for me. Made me insecure. Second-guess every choice I'd made in my life.' She sucked in a heavy breath. 'I never wanted that for you and Gray.'

'What happened then? Why did you always go along with Dad?'

'He bulldozed over me in his tyrannical way. My own father was cruel, and sadly, I ended up marrying a man exactly like him' She patted stiffly at her hair. 'I'm sixty-one years old and tired of living by your father's rules. It's time I break this ridiculous cycle of expectations. And,' she gave me a determined look, 'you and Gray don't need to live by them anymore either.' She tilted her chin down. Clasped her hands firmly in her lap. 'I asked your father to leave. Told him the only way he could return is if he changes. Starts respecting the choices his sons make. I've stood by for too long and let this nonsense go on.'

Miss Cheri and Miss Marta from the elementary school passed by and gave me big waves.

A pained smile crossed my mother's lips. 'They really do love you here, don't they?'

'It's mutual,' I said.

'That young woman, Piper. I heard she let your dad have it at the party.'

'Yeah, she did. I just wish I'd spoken up sooner so she didn't have to go off on him. That's a mistake I won't make again.'

Mom surveyed me for a long beat. 'She means a lot to you.'

'Yes,' I said without hesitation.

'By the guarded way she looks at me, I'm going to assume Gray told her I was a viper.'

I gave her the side-eye and she laughed.

'He's not far off sometimes. Even I know I can be over the top.'

The sounds of children's laughter, the whoosh and hum of the air compressors running the bounce houses, filled the air. All the intensity in my mother's posture faded.

'Your father isn't the only one who needs to change. I don't want to lose you or your brother because I'm too tied to the past. To the rules of a society that don't matter anymore. In time, I hope you'll see that I do love you, and I'm proud of what you've done with your life.' Her lower lip quivered again. 'It's hard to accept you being thousands of miles away for another long period of time, but I can see by this town's reaction to you that you're good at what you do. That your skills are needed in important places.'

'Thank you. I'm glad you're seeing how much my work means to me.'

She waited a beat before saying, 'Have you told Piper how you feel about her?'

'Is it that obvious?'

Her answer was a soft smile I hadn't seen since I was very young.

'It's complicated. She lives here. I need to go back to Senegal.'

'I know I'm years too late to give you advice, but if you'll indulge me this one time?'

'Go ahead.'

'Happiness is a dream we often spend a lifetime chasing. When you find it, you should hold on tightly with both hands and never let go.' She held my gaze. 'If she owns a part of your heart, tell her.' She reached out and patted my cheek. 'Do you understand me, Crawford?'

'Yes, Mom. I do.'

'Good. Now, I smell brisket.' She stood and turned her head toward the food booths. 'Why don't we grab a bite to eat and you can introduce me to the place you've been calling home.'

I held out my arm and she took my offer of support. All of this was hard for her, but I had to give her credit for showing up, for telling me how she felt. The question was could I find that same strength to confess my feelings to Piper?

Chapter Twenty-Nine

PIPER

What Comes Next

After we made sure all the kids had returned their costumes, Maisey and I walked out to the square. A cool breeze swept over the sidewalks. Soon, they'd be covered in hay bales and pumpkins. Ivy Falls coming alive for yet another holiday.

For weeks, Tessa's girls had been discussing their Halloween costumes. They were coordinating with Manny and Lou. The last time I heard them talk, they were all going as characters from *Alice in Wonderland* with Lou insisting she wanted to be the Queen of Hearts so she could yell, 'Off with their heads!'

Maisey stayed quiet beside me, which was unusual. I gripped her hand, pulling her to a stop. 'You okay?'

She let her tiny shoulders sink. 'I think I'm finally ready to admit that I miss designing. That I want to figure out a way to go back to it.'

'I'll help you in any way I can. If you want a few hours to work every week, I can watch Ada and Jordan. Take them to the park or for ice cream. You were there for me at a time when I needed a friend. I want to be that same support for you now.'

She yanked me into a hug. 'Thank you. I'm scared but I'm ready to move on to what's next. Watching you this last year, how you've fought to change your life, has inspired me.'

I pulled back and looked her in the eye. 'None of that would have been possible without you.' A small sob escaped her lips as she pulled me in for another tight hug. We stayed like that, the chaos of the square milling around us until her son's voice called out to her.

'Mommy! Daddy bought us cotton candy!'

Maisey's husband, Joe, pushed a stroller toward us. It was hard not to laugh at the sticky pink fluff staining most of Ada and Jordan's cheeks and mouth.

'Oh lord, my kids are never going to sleep tonight,' Maisey sighed.

'Let them have a little fun. You should do the same!' I said, urging her toward them.

She squeezed my shoulder, whispered that she loved me and raced off in the direction of her sweet family.

I took a moment to observe the square, enjoying the way the town turned out in droves to celebrate the last gasps of summer. I wandered past colorful booths and food vendors, spotting a familiar face in the distance. When Dex saw me he gave an enthusiastic wave, jumped on his skateboard and glided toward me.

'Hey, Miss Piper.'

'Dex, you and I need to have a word.'

His face crumpled. 'That last spin in "Supercalifragilisticexpialidocious" was too fast and I lost my spot. I'm sorry.'

'No,' I laughed to let him off the hook. 'That's *not* what we need to discuss.'

His brows bunched together.

'They have a good drama department at Ivy Falls Junior High. In fact, I heard they're doing *Grease* for their winter musical. I think you should try out.'

He kicked at the ground. 'This was fun and all but from what Autumn says those kids are really good.'

'So are you.'

He shook his head, not convinced.

'Dex, your dad not coming to the show tonight has nothing to do with you. Adults can forget their priorities. Let important moments slip away from them. It's no reflection on who you are as a son. The kind of attention you deserve.'

'Yeah, Doc Foster said the same thing.'

'He's right.'

'Are you two...?' His cheeks went pink. 'You're together, right?'

'Yes,' I said, caught off guard by the turn in the conversation.

'Good.' He grinned. 'Because you deserve some attention too.'

God, this kid knows how to get to the heart of things.

'Dexy!' His mom waved to him from the corner. 'You've got more fans over here who want to talk to you.'

He gave a dramatic roll of his eyes. 'My mom is taking all of this a little too seriously.'

'If you keep performing, I'm sure the adoration will continue, especially from the girls.'

'Really?' His brows perked up. 'Maybe I will give that show at school a shot.'

I waved him off with another laugh as he skated away.

I continued to scan the square for Ford. As I walked, people stopped and congratulated me on the success of the show. Asking if I was going to take over the director role permanently. That wasn't a question I was ready to answer at the moment, but the experience had taught me that theater was in my blood. That in some shape or form it would continue to be a part of my life.

Not far from the fountain, I found Ford sitting on a wrought-iron bench. I let my gaze wander over his riot of dark curls. Those full lips. How his glasses sat perfectly perched on the bridge of his nose. An ache crowded my chest, making it hard to pull in any air.

How was I going to say goodbye to him? Agree that once he was gone we'd only be friends? I'd done a lot of stupid things in my life but making him promise that we'd be nothing more than a summer fling might have been one of the dumbest.

He must have felt my stare because he turned and locked eyes with me. Gave me that sweet little wave.

I strode toward him and sank down onto the bench. 'Where's your mom?'

'She left a few minutes ago.'

'It was nice what she said about the show, but I have a feeling she did not drive all the way from Harpeth Manor to watch a bunch of kids dance and sing.'

He stretched his arm out behind me and tugged my body toward him. I'd never get over the way my bones went to jelly when he touched me.

'You're not going to believe this, but she came to apologize.'

'For what?'

'Years of not standing up to my dad. In her words, for not letting Gray and me run wild. Not allowing us to figure out who we wanted to be.'

I couldn't hide my shock. 'That's a one-eighty turn.'

He pressed a kiss to my hair. 'She also confessed that she kicked my dad out.'

I reached for his hand and squeezed. 'I'm sorry.'

'It's been a long time coming.'

'Do you think it'll be permanent?'

'I don't know. She says he has to prove he's changed first.'

'Can he?'

'That's like wondering if a bear can stop hunting fish in a stream. My dad has no other frame of reference than Harpeth Manor society. He'd have to change his whole way of thinking, and, sadly,' he scrubbed at his chin, 'I don't see him being able to view his world in anything but black and white.'

He pulled me closer and we stayed quiet, letting the joy of the evening wash over us.

'I wanted to uh, talk about something.' He pulled away, took my hands in his. 'My mother asked me a question tonight, and it's made me consider a few things.'

'What was the question?'

He pushed back a loose hair from my cheek. 'I wanted to tell you…'

'Well, this is an unexpected surprise!' A deep voice boomed from behind us.

I froze in place. That voice had been a part of my life since the first day he handed me a lollipop after a checkup.

We both turned to find Dr Sheridan smirking at us. His white beard hung far below his chin. A chic purple-and-yellow silk scarf covered his wife Sylvie's gray hair. A pair of battered black suitcases sat beside them on the brick-paved sidewalk.

Ford jumped to his feet. 'What are you doing back so early?'

'That's a fine welcome,' Dr Sheridan chuckled.

'We were homesick for Ivy Falls. There are only so many Gothic churches and green rolling hills one person can see in a lifetime,' Sylvie said.

As happens in Ivy Falls, word spread quickly in the square and the couple were surrounded two heartbeats later. There were hugs and rounds of questions that would most likely go on for hours.

Ford's demeanor deflated like an old balloon, and I recognized exactly what he was feeling. We were supposed to have more time, but now with Doc Sheridan back neither of us knew what would come next.

Chapter Thirty

FORD

A Little Restraint

Three days later Dr Sheridan still wore that knowing smirk. More than once he'd complimented my handling of the clinic. How everyone he'd spoken to, including Janice, said I'd been a nice addition to the town. He stayed silent about Piper, but his perma-grin told me his feelings about that situation.

He sipped his coffee slowly before setting his mug down on the desk. 'Hard to get a good cup a joe in some of those European towns. Sure, espresso is fine, but I like plain old coffee sometimes.' He leaned forward and tented his hands on the desk. 'Although the way Janice makes it, it can taste a little like tar.'

I smiled because I'd grown used to the strong brew she made. There were a lot of things around Ivy Falls that had grown on me. The gossipy whispers of the office staff when they spotted a cute new tourist in town. How they were all anticipating fall and the return of Barb and Susan's traditional pumpkin spice cinnamon rolls. What kind of booth the office would set up in the square for the festival at the end of October.

An ache swelled in my chest. I'd miss all of it once I was gone.

'Bring me up to date. What's happened in my little town since I've been gone?'

'It's all written down in the charts. Janice was very clear about how I was supposed to keep up so there'd be a smooth transition when you returned.'

'She can be a drill sergeant, but this place would be lost without her.'

'I agree.'

His lips pinched together as he leaned forward. 'Now, tell me the specifics of what is *not* in the charts.'

'Sir?' I said, not sure what kind of information he was expecting.

He sat back and crossed his arms over his chest. 'For instance, how is Greta Vanderpool doing? I got an earful about her fainting spell at Sugar Rush. Is it true you rushed to her care?'

I scrubbed at my chin. 'I forget how quickly information spreads around here.'

'This is Ivy Falls. The minute people finished saying "Welcome home" they told me about her.' He let out a weary breath. 'I'm shocked nobody texted me. Maybe this town is learning a little restraint, or, better yet, they've learned to trust you.'

'Not so sure about that, but they do know my every move. The other day I walked into the market and Minnie handed me the ground coffee I like without me asking for it.'

'People around here are special.' His eyes twinkled. 'But I see you've already learned that considering the time you're spending with Piper Townsend.'

My cheeks went hot. Shit. I was a grown man. I should not be blushing.

'Things are good—' I cut off, not knowing what else to say about the woman who had flipped my entire existence upside down. I was still kicking myself that I didn't tell her how I felt in the square.

'Any chance things might be permanent there?'

I hesitated because I'd asked myself that same question too many times to count. 'Back to Mrs Vanderpool,' I said, not wanting to explain the complications of Piper with him. 'She's in treatment with a mentor of mine at Vanderbilt. I put all of his contact details in her file. I plan to follow up and let him know you've returned and will check in with him periodically.'

He gave a thoughtful nod and I tried not to stare at the psychedelic array of camels spread across his shirt. How his shoulder-length white hair was tucked into a low ponytail.

'Can you stay until the end of our agreement? I'd love to have your help until I get up to speed.'

'Sure, that's not a problem,' I said with relief because I wasn't ready to say goodbye to Piper yet.

With Dr Sheridan's surprising return, Piper and I had been dancing around the subject of my departure. You could feel the tension in our kisses though. How when she touched me it was more tentative, hesitant, like she wanted to remember every single minute we spent skin-to-skin.

Things for me weren't any different. Every time I put my mouth on her, brought her to the edge of pleasure, moaned her name in the way she loved, I held on to it for a beat longer. Wanted to remember the heady thrum of my pulse, the thrill of anticipation as she climbed toward me on the bed, her hair messy, her lips kiss-swollen. Those were the moments I'd hold on to when I was alone in Africa.

'I was engaged before I met my Sylvie,' Dr Sheridan said, bringing me back to the conversation. 'My fiancée, Nora, was my high-school sweetheart. Six months before our wedding, I did an away rotation in Knoxville. I was having a beer at a local restaurant with some other residents and this blonde beauty walked in with some friends. I'm not lying when I say I swear Sylvie had this glow of light around her. Some of her pals knew the guys we were with, and they ended up sitting at our table. Every word out of her mouth, her dreams and aspirations, aligned perfectly with mine.' His eyes glazed over like he was recalling the sweet memory. 'I returned to Nashville after that, but I couldn't get her out of my head. Even in my dreams she made regular appearances.' He gave me a devilish grin.

Yeah, I knew what he meant.

'No matter how hard I tried to forget Sylvie, I couldn't. It was like my heart understood better than my brain what was right for me.'

I nodded again. Piper had been unexpected when I came here, but everything within me screamed we were meant to be together.

'As soon as I returned to Ivy Falls, Nora knew there was something off about me. We had a serious talk about what we wanted for our futures and agreed we were headed in different directions.' He smiled. 'Sylvie and I were engaged a year later.'

'That's a nice story,' I said.

'Ford, I'm not your father or your mentor, maybe not even your friend, but I hope you'll let me tell you one thing about life from my experience.'

'Could I stop you?' I chuckled.

He gave me that smirk again. 'For thirty years, I've taken care of the citizens of Ivy Falls. Some of them have had long and beautiful lives like Greta Vanderpool. But I've also had to give some devastating diagnoses. Seen some young lives sadly cut short.' His voice went quiet. 'You have all these important plans and commitments, which I admire, but along the way you need to consider if those plans are fulfilling enough. If all those achievements are worth celebrating alone.' His gaze flicked to all the frames on his shelves. 'I can tell you from experience that none of my triumphs would have been as meaningful if I didn't have Sylvie by my side.'

'But what if,' I scrubbed at my pulsing temples, 'she's made it clear she wants something else?'

'Has she?'

'When we first started spending time together, that's what she told me.'

'Like you, do you think her feelings have changed?'

'Not sure.'

A sharp knock on the door kept me from saying any more. Janice stuck her head in the room and let out an irritated huff. 'While I'm sure you are both enjoying your bonding time, we have an overflowing waiting room of patients who need to be seen.'

'All right. Thank you for keeping us on the straight and narrow,' Dr Sheridan chuckled.

'It's what you pay me for,' she said with a sharp chirp.

She was a drill sergeant, but a drill sergeant we respected.

'Well,' she grumbled. 'You two are still sitting!'

We moved from our chairs and Dr Sheridan slapped a hand on my shoulder. 'Let's go take care of our town, shall we?'

Our town. The words lodged in my throat like a dry piece of meat. I'd never expected to feel connected to this place. To these people. Now I wasn't sure how I would ever say goodbye.

I started for the door when my phone buzzed with a text. The throbbing in my temples morphed into hammers banging against my skull.

'Problem?' Dr Sheridan asked.

'Yes, sir. It looks like I won't be able to stay after all.'

Chapter Thirty-One

PIPER

Beyond Fierce

Candles flickered in the dark room. Ford sat against the headboard, his arms wrapped around me as I laid against his bare chest. We'd tried to have dinner but only got past the salad. This time we didn't rush taking off each other's clothes. It was a slow dance of kisses, touches and sighs, like we were trying to stretch out our last hours together.

'Have you spoken to your parents?' I asked.

'To my mom, briefly. My father is still pouting like a little boy.'

Ford showed up at the P&P right after his meeting with Dr Sheridan. In a few short sentences, he told me the director of the *Humanity of the Seas* had asked him to come back early. That another doctor had to leave due to a family emergency, and being down one physician made the daily clinic chaos.

'What did she say about you leaving tomorrow?'

'She's sad but she understands this is what I need to do.'

I turned and put a hand on his cheek. 'I'm glad you two are finally talking.'

'Me too.' He pressed a kiss to my palm.

I rested my head on his chest once more. This was the last time I'd get to do this. Be this close to him. Touch his warm skin. Relax in the feel of his arms. A sob filled my throat and I forced it down.

'Dex came to the café today. He said you promised to email him and call regularly to check in. By the wide smile he gave me, it was clear that meant a lot to him.'

'He's a good kid. I want to make sure he stays on the right path. Focuses on his grades. The way his dad has treated him has left a mark. I hope that by staying in touch, he'll be reminded he has another person in his corner.'

I didn't share the rest of my conversation with Dex in the café. How he'd pleaded with me to get Ford to stay. He wasn't the only one. Since Dr Sheridan had returned early, more than a few people had tracked me down at the P&P or Sugar Rush and asked how we could get Ford to stick around.

Yesterday morning, Barb and Susan cornered me in the kitchen as the last of the donuts were rising. I'd played off that things were nothing but casual between Ford and me, but they weren't buying it.

'Honey, keeping your feelings inside hurts no one but you,' Barb huffed. Susan gave me her sad eyes and nodded along. I explained to them that things weren't that simple. That Ford had obligations, commitments he'd made, and that he was a solid enough man to keep his word. It was another one of the reasons I'd fallen for him so quickly.

Did I want him to stay in Ivy Falls? Of course, but that was selfish. Over these past weeks, I'd watched him spark to life when he spoke about his work in Senegal. How committed he was to the program and the people. The way it gave his life purpose. And with the latest text from the program's director, it was clear he needed to be in Africa.

The pain that flooded my chest when I thought about saying goodbye was visceral, but he had people counting on him and I refused to get in the way of his purpose.

'Tell me about the wedding.' Ford's voice halted my spiraling thoughts. 'You met with Torran and Tessa today, right?'

'Yes, and Lauren, the show's producer. That woman I swear has more damn energy than a teenager who's downed a few Red Bulls.'

'She's agreed to stick to the deal about the cameras?'

More than once, I'd confided in him that I was worried that once the ceremony got under way, Lauren and some of the crew would try to sneak some footage.

'Yes, but I've made it clear that I'll be watching every person involved with the show like a hawk. If I see a digital camera, a GoPro, anything that looks like it can record or film, it's mine.'

His chest bobbed up and down behind me as he laughed. 'You are the last person I'd want to go up against, Bird. When it comes to the people you love, you're beyond fierce.'

'Not fierce but...' I chewed on my bottom lip considering the scenario where I'd have to wrestle a camera away from one of the crew who usually weighed at least a hundred pounds more than me. 'Yeah, fine. I'll accept fierce.'

He slid a hand over my hair. Tucked it back so he could kiss my neck. 'How is Torran feeling?'

After he'd confirmed her pregnancy with a simple blood test, he'd suggested a few obstetricians. Torran had seen a female physician in Nashville last week who estimated an early March due date.

'She threw up twice during the meeting.'

'The first trimester is rough. After she gets past the twelfth week, her hormones will balance out and she won't be so nauseous.'

'I hope you're right because at the moment she looks like she hasn't eaten or slept in weeks.'

He held me tighter to his chest, and I wanted to stay in this moment where there weren't any outside forces pulling us away from each other.

'I had an idea I wanted to run past you.'

'All right,' he said with a halting breath.

'The success of the musical has made me do a lot of thinking about what I want to do next.'

He kept softly combing my hair the way he had the first night we were together. It made me want to go back there. Freeze that place in time and never let it go.

'I'm considering going back to community college to finish my basic credits. When they're completed, I can transfer to Middle Tennessee State and get a degree in theater with an emphasis on directing.'

He shifted back, turning me to face him. 'That's perfect. You are damn talented, and whatever you set your mind to you can achieve. When would you start? How many credits would you take? What does the curriculum look like?'

'Slow down.' I gave him a quick kiss. 'Those are all items I have to look into, but your enthusiasm makes me feel better. I'm glad I had the courage to say it out loud. Make sure it didn't sound ridiculous.'

'Dreams are never ridiculous. I believe in you, Bird. Whatever you set your heart on, you'll make it happen.'

There was a tenderness to his voice that almost had me begging him to stay. To confess all the ways he made me felt seen. Loved. Instead, I let the air still between us, the fading candles casting long shadows across the bedroom walls.

'What time is your flight?' I asked when I finally found my voice again.

'Noon.' His breath hitched as he held me closer. 'Can I ask you to do something for me?'

'What do you need?'

'If I call or FaceTime, please pick up.'

I swallowed back the swell in my throat. 'Ford, we agreed this would be over when you leave.'

'I know, but friends still talk. And I want an update on the wedding and Torran's pregnancy.'

There was that flash of torment in his voice and it took every ounce of strength not to break down. I reached for his hand, kissed each knuckle. Maybe staying in touch was the next best thing to having him close. A small bit of contact every once in a while so I could know he was okay.

'That sounds like a good plan.'

He pressed another kiss to the top of my head, the steady beat of his heart thrumming in my ear.

When he'd arrived in Ivy Falls, I'd seen him as yet another way of my former life haunting me, but his presence had been a sweet surprise. It reminded me that my past did not have to be a legacy for my future. That I could make good connections, trust my own judgment. It'd been a risk to do this with him, but I couldn't imagine a better partner leading me over that bridge to a new life.

I held on to his hand. His breath went steady and more than once I had to reassure myself that I was doing a good thing, the right thing, by letting him go without confessing how hard I'd fallen for him.

'You sleepy?' he asked in a rough growl, his hand moving under the sheets.

I turned over and kissed him, moving his hands to the places I wanted him to touch me. He worshipped my body in a way no other man had, his tongue painting a canvas across my skin, over my nipples, between my legs.

Words like *love* and *stay* played on repeat in my head as my body shook and writhed beneath him. I could have said all those words, but I stayed quiet as stars exploded behind my eyes and my heart shattered into a thousand pieces.

Chapter Thirty-Two

FORD

Under My Skin

No matter how often I made this trip, the jet lag was always a killer. It didn't help that every time I closed my eyes on the plane, Piper's luscious lips, the tangle of her dark hair sliding through my fingertips, filled my head.

She wouldn't let us have a long goodbye. I held on to her hands like a lifeline. Asked her if she wanted to tell me anything, hoping she'd open up, or at least give me a hint that she felt the same way I did. Instead, she boomeranged the question back at me and I lost my nerve. She let me hold her for a while longer and when my phone buzzed, notifying me that my ride-share was waiting, she gave me a quick peck on the cheek and disappeared into her apartment.

I stared at her door for a long time, reliving the moment I knocked on it only to find her bloody and wrapped in that ridiculous dancing unicorn shower curtain. The moment I was sure I'd fallen in love with her.

Several times last night the truth played against my lips, but the way she spoke about my commitment to the program, how she'd easily walked away when we said goodbye, said that deep in her heart she'd already let me go. That realization was a fucking jab to the heart I still couldn't shake.

'Ford!'

My pal, Kip, walked down the ship's narrow hallway. His boots thudded against the yellow linoleum, his deep voice echoing off the sterile white walls. I stumbled toward him, forgetting how it took a while to get your balance settled on a bobbing ship.

'How long have you been back, man?' His huge mitt of a hand slapped against mine in a friendly handshake.

'A few hours.'

'You look like shit.'

'Damn, Kip. Don't sugarcoat things for me.'

He gave a simple shrug like that'd never be his way. 'Your cabin is all set up. Made sure your Wi-Fi is in good working order. That leak is gone from your sink too.'

'Thank you. That constant drip before was maddening.'

'How was the States? Do anything interesting on your time off?' Now it was my turn to shrug but I did a bad job because he said, 'There's a story there, and I'm off shift. Looks like you could use a cup of coffee.'

What I could really use was sleep, but in order to get my body on the right time I had to stay up until at least the sun went down. 'Good idea. Let's go.'

We ambled down the corridor, passing cabins and offices. I'd forgotten the constant frenetic pace on board the ship. How the crew and hospital staff were always in motion. The place was like a floating city that never slept.

In his typical booming voice, Kip filled me in on what I'd missed while I was gone. 'The doctor who replaced you was good but distracted. Could have guessed he'd never finish his contract. Apparently his mom had been sick for a while. Heart issues.'

My thoughts went to Mrs Vanderpool. I knew she was in good hands with Doc Sheridan, but there was still a twinge in my chest when I considered her treatment. How they were waiting to see if the medication would work before deciding if she needed a pacemaker.

Thinking of her led to Silvio, Dex and the rest of the town. I'd been convinced when I took the job at the clinic that it was simply that: a job. Not in my wildest dreams would I have imagined that the people, the place, would work its way under my skin. Hell, I'd been gone less than twenty-four hours and I already missed it.

When we stepped over the framed entry to the dining hall, the scent of fried eggs and burnt toast hit me. The wide-open space was just as sterile as the hallway walls. Over two dozen picnic-style benches covered the room. In one corner sat the glass and metal serving area. Beyond it was a bank of machines housing water, ice and soft drinks. Only a few members of the staff and crew sat at the tables as it was well past breakfast.

I took a seat on one of the long benches while Kip grabbed us some coffee. He started filling the mugs until a woman with red hair stepped beside him. They swapped a few words before she lifted the steel carafe off the counter and carried it back into the kitchen.

Kip made his way back and sat across from me.

'Who was that you were talking to?'

'That's Vivienne. She's the one I told you about.' He leaned his head back and looked at the ceiling like he was contemplating the meaning of life. 'Dude, she makes these little quiches with ham and Swiss cheese.' He put his hands to his lips and made a loud kissing noise. 'Total fucking perfection.'

'Have you asked her out again?'

He beamed at me. 'Yes. Last week I took her to brunch at that five-star ocean-view hotel that lets you see all the way to Gorée Island.'

I nudged him with my elbow. 'Look at you going all out.'

'It's probably one of the best dates I've ever been on.'

'And have you made another date?'

'She's busy this week, but we agreed to get drinks at the lighthouse soon.' He took a sip of coffee, his eyes narrowing on me. 'Speaking of women, 'fess up. I can tell by your hangdog look that you met someone.'

I scratched a hand through my hair, took a sip of coffee and made an uncomfortable gulp. 'Gah, that's bad. You can't really drink it if you've had the good stuff.'

'Good stuff? This from the guy who swore the only kind of good coffee was black.'

'Things change,' I murmured, pushing the cup away.

'Does coffee have something to do with the girl?'

I clasped my hands on the table and spilled the entire story about Piper. Showed him the selfie we'd taken at the lake. Told him about our first 'sticky' encounter. The way she'd not wanted anything to do with me at first. How the small town had made it impossible to avoid each other.

He drained his cup and set his hulking elbows on the table. 'How'd you leave it?'

'Said we'd talk. Maybe FaceTime.'

'That's it?'

'She made it clear that when I left we could only be friends.'

'That was after you told her how you felt?'

283

My body sank as I laid my head on the table in defeat. 'No,' I mumbled.

'Ford, you're a smart guy. Since I met you a few years ago, you've had tunnel vision. Married to nothing but medicine. Finally you meet the perfect girl and you don't tell her how you feel? Sounds like a cop-out, man.'

'I was doing what she wanted,' I said in my own defense.

'What about what you want? Even if she turned you down, at least you would have gotten your truth out there. You'll never know how she felt because you were too much of a frightened ass to be honest.'

The telltale signs of jet lag – a throbbing headache, blurry eyes – descended. I sat up and said, 'I need to go lie down.'

'The great thing about living in the modern world is that we can make phone calls, send texts, do FaceTime, Zoom, any time we want,' he said ignoring me. 'You won't feel right until you tell her your true feelings. Take care of it now before you get too wrapped up in your duties here.'

'When did you get so damn smart about women?'

He gave me a weighted look. 'Some a-hole told me I shouldn't give up. That I should practice my French.'

I laughed, told him I'd see him later, and headed back to my cabin. My balance grew more unsteady as I passed the crew's sleeping quarters, the maintenance offices and the section of the ship where they sorted the mail.

More than once, I was stopped in the hallways by nurses, techs, some of the deck crew, who shook my hand and welcomed me back. My wandering led me to my door but for some reason, even though my head was pounding, I continued to the end of the hall and pushed out the door leading to the deck.

Senegal was finally in its dry season and the temperatures hovered around the low eighties. I took in a breath of fresh air. This was what I needed to clear my mind, stop my temples from throbbing.

Laughter and singing pulled me to the starboard side of the ship. On the deck below sat the program's school.

One of the best things about *Humanity of the Seas* was that they allowed families of the staff to live on board, which meant the ship needed a school. I leaned my arms over the railing, glancing down at the kids sitting in a circle. A teacher sat in the center with an acoustic guitar laid across her lap. She whispered to the kids before picking up the instrument and strumming out the first note. The children swayed along until they began singing the sweetest melody.

Piper would have loved this. How the kids sang in unison, clapping their hands along to the beat. The way the teacher beamed at them, nodding her head in an encouraging way.

Since I'd walked on to the ship, I'd waited for the familiar feeling of relief. The comforting sense that I was home, but only a hollow ache filled my chest. My pulse lacking its regular hum of anticipation. It didn't take long for me to figure out what was wrong. Why being here felt like a big mistake. This place wasn't Ivy Falls.

There wouldn't be any more free donuts and unsolicited advice from Barb and Susan, or constant waves and phone calls from Silvio and Old Mrs V. The elated smile from Dex when we did our secret handshake.

Piper made me swear things would end with us once my time in Ivy Falls was over, and I'd let her set the rules because I needed to be with her. But in that frenzy of want, I'd ignored what my life needed. What my mind and heart had been screaming since I'd gotten on the plane. That Ivy Falls was where I was meant to be. That Piper was my home.

The sad part was I couldn't go back. She was thousands of miles away. I was here.

There was no changing that fact now, no matter how much I wanted to make things different.

Chapter Thirty-Three

PIPER

Church-On-Sunday Silent

Rain pounded against the roof of my apartment like someone was dropping bricks from the sky. Wind screamed through the sliding glass door as I grabbed my waterproof coat and raced down the hallway and outside.

The P&P was only a block away, but my T-shirt and jeans were plastered to my body by the time I swept in the door a few minutes before we were due to open for the day. Tessa rushed toward me with one of the towels we used at the coffee bar. 'Here, it's clean.'

I ran it down the length of my dripping ponytail. A loud boom of thunder shook the windows.

'Shit,' Tess shrieked.

'The sky is a pissed-off shade of black,' I said. 'That storm is growing angrier by the minute. As I was rushing here, the chalkboard sign in front of Followes Music got carried away in the wind, and the trees in front of the town hall were bent sideways.'

'The store should be quiet today. No one wants to be out in this.'

I ran the towel down my hair again. A second later, Torran burst through the door. A black umbrella dangled from her fingertips, its frame snapped like an old skeleton.

'Where have you been?' I asked.

'At the bridal shop.' Torran shook out her wet hair and slumped into an oversized armchair. I handed her my towel and Tessa grimaced like she was sure her sister was going to soak straight through the upholstery.

'Final fitting before the wedding this weekend, or should I say reconstruction considering this little nugget.'

The way she lovingly patted her stomach made me smile.

'How about some hot tea to warm you up?'

I walked across the room to the coffee bar. Along the counter sat eight oversized glass jars containing various types of tea. Next to them were four large industrial coffee servers, one of which was always reserved for hot water.

'I'll make you peppermint,' I said, sliding one of the glass containers across the antique hutch Manny had restored specifically for Tessa. It struck me what an incredible act of love it was. How before they'd gotten together, he showed her how he felt in small but thoughtful ways. It was hard not to think about Ford. How he'd been so gentle with me the day I'd had my panic attack on the bench outside the clinic.

If I closed my eyes, I could still sense the press of his fingertips against my back. The way his soft voice soothed the beat of my raging heart. His smile when he called me that ridiculous nickname that I now loved more than I could have ever imagined.

'No, I want Earl Grey,' Torran called out.

'Ford told me you should lay off the caffeine.'

She shot me a look that said if I didn't give her what she wanted, she'd stomp behind the bar and do it herself.

'Speaking of Ford.' Tessa sat on a leather stool at the counter. 'He's been gone for what, three weeks now? How's he settling back in?'

I focused on the tea steeping in front of me. He'd texted me once to let me know he'd arrived safely. We'd tried to schedule calls or FaceTime but with our work hours and the time difference we kept missing each other.

'Pipe, did you hear me? Everything all right with you?' Tessa had a way of dipping her voice in a motherly way, which made it impossible to lie to her.

'No, dammit,' I said as more of a hiss than an answer.

She quirked a reddish-brown brow at me. Torran pushed off the chair and scrambled toward us. 'This I want to hear.'

The wind continued to bellow outside, shearing burnt-orange leaves from the trees. Rain smacked against the windows in thick, repetitive thuds.

The two of them stared at me, waiting for an answer. May as well tell them what a dumbass I'd been.

'Ford and I are complicated. When we started seeing each other, I made him agree to an iron-clad deal.'

'What kind of deal?' Torran said, awkwardly sliding her body onto the stool next to Tessa.

'I made him promise we'd have an easy fling without any strings attached. That once his time in Ivy Falls was over, he'd go back to Africa and we'd part as friends and nothing more.'

'And you made him promise this because?' Torran pressed.

'You know why. Up until a few years ago my life was a shitshow. I thought I'd never be steady enough to have a regular, committed relationship. In Maisey's words, Ford could be my training wheels. The test spin I needed to find out if I was ready for a real relationship.'

'Training wheels?' Tessa grumbled. 'Where does Maisey come up with these ideas?'

'Her heart was in the right place when we talked about it. At the time it made sense.'

'What about now?' Torran said.

'I've come to the realization that I'm a total idiot.' I picked up a rag and swiped at a dried spot of coffee on the counter.

'There's more,' Torran pressed.

'When we were saying goodbye,' I scrubbed at the spot harder, 'he sort of gave me an opening. Asked if I wanted to tell him anything.'

Torran pulled her tea toward her, took a sip and groaned at the rush of caffeine filling her veins. 'And you said "no"?'

'I didn't say "no" but I deflected. Sort of turned the question around on him. In my defense, he didn't offer up how he felt either.'

'The miscommunication trope.' Tessa pretended to bang her head on the counter.

'The what trope?' Torran said.

'Miscommunication. In romance novels, it's what readers hate. How the couple would never break up in the third act if they were honest with each other.' She pointed an accusing finger at me. 'When a simple conversation would solve all their problems.'

'Tessa, this is real life. People are messy,' Torran said. 'Things get complicated when feelings are on the line. As humans, we usually favor self-preservation over the chance of being rejected.'

'Did you think he was going to reject you?' There was Tessa's soft motherly voice once more.

'No. Yes.' I threw up my hands. 'None of that matters because I had to let him go. He has a contract and they need him there. It wasn't like I could spill my guts and expect him to stay. That's not fair to the people he's committed to serve.'

'How long is the contract?' Tessa asked.

'Six months.'

'And his plans after?' Tessa pressed.

I gave a weary shrug.

'Six months can go by in a flash, Pipe. It'd be easy for him to finish his contract and come back here.' Torran paused. 'If that's what you want.'

I went back to scrubbing the stains on the counter. 'What if he doesn't want it? Want me?'

Torran reached over and pressed her hand to mine. 'One thing I learned with your brother is that not knowing is a thousand times more painful than the truth. Reach out to Ford. Tell him how you feel. That's all you can do.'

I squeezed her hand back and her cheeks went pale. She jumped off the stool and raced for the bathroom.

'You should have listened about the tea,' Tessa called.

'Should I go back to peppermint?'

She gave a weary smile. 'Make it two.'

I turned to grab the glass mugs with the P&P logo when my phone went off with a siren noise more jarring than a train whistle. A second later Tessa's phone made the same frantic sound.

'Oh shit.' Tessa gulped and turned her screen to me.

I set the mugs onto the back counter and followed Tessa to the bathroom. She pounded on the door until Torran yanked it open, wiping her mouth with a paper towel.

'What the hell, Tess?'

'Tornado emergency. Get back against the wall. This bathroom is closest to the center of the building.'

I pushed in behind her and sat next to Torran on the floor.

'Tessa, where are Manny and the girls?' Torran's voice edged on panic.

'At home. He'll get them into that secure little closet we have.' Her shaky voice rattled me.

'And Beck?' I traced the outline of my tattoo, trying my best to stay calm. At least I knew Ford was safe a world away.

Torran glanced at her phone. 'He's at work. If the storm moves toward Nashville, their building has a basement.'

A loud boom blasted overhead followed by a screech of wind that sounded like Satan's fingernails clawing against the roof. Tessa scooted in closer and the three of us huddled together.

The building shook like it was on rollers. Outside the bathroom the crash of glass, thud of books, echoed against the walls.

'Tessa, you okay?' Torran held out her hand and her sister grabbed it.

'I have insurance. Right now I'm worried about the other folks in Ivy Falls.'

The storm continued to rattle the building. Monstrous groans overhead warned the P&P's roof was losing shingles. The ground shook like an eighteen-wheeler was barreling through the center of town.

That slow creep of terror did a maddening waltz up my spine. Black dots crept into the corners of my vision like ink splatters. My heart rapped against my chest, and I gasped, chasing the next inhale of breath.

I closed my eyes and searched for that elusive place I could never quite picture. My bones went icy starting with my toes and spreading up my legs. I begged for any kind of relief until one vision slowed the throttle on my racing mind. Ford squeezing my fingers, whispering reassurances, anchoring me to the earth while we sat outside the clinic, stood on the shore of the lake.

It wasn't a place I needed to picture but a person. Him.

I let my mind play like a movie in slow motion, recalling every laugh, smile, kiss. How he gently threaded my hair between his fingers. Whispered intimate promises against my bare skin. Spoke so lovingly to my anxious brain.

Once my breaths slowed and my heart stopped pounding like it wanted to rocket out of my chest, I reached out and gripped on to these two women who had become my family. Who had seen me at my lowest and still believed in me. Still loved me. I'd been through hell and back but it was times like these I was reminded how lucky I was to have them. To have all of Ivy Falls behind me.

The storm continued its blood-curdling scream for another minute and then everything went church-on-Sunday silent. A few breaths later another blare sounded on our phones, making us jump.

We helped Torran to her feet and walked into the bookstore. A jagged branch jutted through a small window. Dozens of books were strewn across the floor.

The sky was a neon shade of green that reminded me of too many creepy science-fiction movies. As if some angry giant had marched through town, wrought-iron benches from the square laid in pieces across the street. One even dangled from a nearby tree. Canopies on more than a few businesses resembled shredded paper.

Tessa pulled out her phone to check on Manny and the girls. She let out a panicked squeak and turned the screen toward me and Torran showing it had no service.

'The storm must have disrupted the cell towers,' I said.

'I should go and check on them.' Tess started toward her office until the front door flew open and Mr Wright shot toward us.

'Oh, thank goodness you're all okay. I was trapped in town hall and they wouldn't let me leave.' He rushed toward all three of us and gave us a broad bear hug. As soon as he let go, he focused on Torran. 'You okay? The baby?'

'Cool your jets, Grandpa. We're all in one piece,' Torran said even as she smoothed a hand sweetly down his arm.

'How's the rest of town? Any injuries?' I said.

'Not that I know of, but we got word that all the local cell towers are damaged.' He pointed to the walkie-talkie clipped to his belt. 'Deputy Ben is supposed to contact me if there are any issues.'

'Is Isabel okay?' Torran asked.

'Yes, my staff checked in with her. Everyone at the bank went into the vault.'

I walked back to the coffee bar to survey the damage. In my rush to get to the bathroom, I set the glass mugs too close to the edge of the counter. With the bookstore shaking, they must have tumbled to the ground.

'Dad, how are the roads? I need to check on the girls and Manny,' Tessa said.

'And I have to get a hold of Beck,' Torran added.

'Trees are down all over town. Let me reach out to Deputy Ben. See if he can get over there. I'll ask him to check on Nashville too.'

Tessa gave an absent nod and I handed her a dustpan, encouraging her to help me clear up the glass from the broken window. When we were finished, I suggested making tea again.

Mr Wright inspected the rest of the bookstore while Torran went back to her stool.

'Peppermint this time. No arguments,' I said.

'If you insist,' she grumbled.

The crackling static of the walkie-talkie moved through the P&P. Mr Wright walked toward us as Deputy Ben confirmed that Manny and the girls were safe. That the storm didn't hit Nashville.

Ben's voice warbled in and out, and Mr Wright walked outside for better reception. He paced outside for a few minutes before pushing back through the front door. I didn't like the worry pinching the corners of his eyes.

'Dad,' Torran said. 'What was that about? Is someone hurt?'

'No. Ben was telling me about Huckleberry Lane.'

'What's wrong at the house?' I gasped.

He scrubbed a hand over the white whiskers on his jaw. 'That massive magnolia in the backyard is uprooted and lying in the middle of the street. There's dirt everywhere and it's taken out the entire back fence.'

'Beck loves that tree.' Torran's voice shook. 'We were supposed… to get married under it.'

'I'm sorry, honey. Ben says it's bad. That it's probably going to take a few days before a crew can come in and clear away the debris.'

'But the wedding!' Torran cried.

'Everything will be all right. We'll figure out another plan.' He wrapped an arm around her trembling shoulders while Tessa shot me a devastated look.

Four days until the wedding.

There was no time left for another plan.

Chapter Thirty-Four

PIPER

No Room For Negotiation

It'd taken some maneuvering but Tessa and I got around the yellow caution tape, multiple severed tree limbs, and more than a few crumpled roof shingles, before we reached the front door of Huckleberry Lane. We found Beck and Torran pacing inside the living room, their gazes darting more than once to the disaster area that surrounded their home.

A day after the tornado and everything in and around Ivy Falls was chaos. The storm had cut us off from all utilities: water, power, phone and internet. More than once, the fire chief had suggested to Mr Wright that in his capacity as mayor he should evacuate certain parts of town, but when he broached the subject everyone in Ivy Falls refused to leave.

'Tor. Beck,' Tessa started. 'Piper and I have something we want to discuss with you.'

'Whatever it is, can it wait?' Torran said. 'The foreman from the first cleanup crew is supposed to stop by and tell us how long it'll be before they can get people here to clear the yard.'

Tessa gave me a weighted look. This conversation had to happen now if our plan was going to work.

'No, because we need to make some decisions,' I said.

Beck furrowed his brow. 'Decisions about what?'

I gave another hesitant glance in Tessa's direction. 'The wedding.'

Torran gave an ugly snort and rubbed at her stomach. 'There isn't going to be a wedding.' Like she knew how that might hit Beck, she quickly added, 'I mean not right now.'

It was clear from their tense shoulders, the way worry colored their eyes, that they'd already given up on the chance of a ceremony anytime soon.

'This tornado has clearly thrown a wrench into things,' Tessa started.

Torran let out a caustic laugh. 'A wrench? It's more like a twenty-foot tree.'

'Let's all sit,' I suggested, hoping to keep things calm.

Torran and Beck slouched down onto the dark leather couch, while Tessa and I found spots in the matching armchairs.

Tessa pulled in a full breath and said, 'We don't want you to cancel the wedding.'

'There's not much choice considering the state of our backyard right now,' Beck said.

'What if there was a choice?' I said.

Beck looked at me with a defeated look that made my heart ache. 'I don't see how.'

'We hold the ceremony in the square.' I paused. 'And we ask the town to help.'

Torran set her jaw. 'Absolutely not. Everyone is dealing with their own issues with this tornado. None of the shops near the square have power. Half the roof on Minnie's Market is gone. We can't ask people to help us when they have their own problems and families to worry about.'

298

'Don't be upset,' Tessa said hesitantly. 'But we've already started floating the idea. There's going to be a town meeting today at three to discuss it.'

I waited for their protests. Instead, Torran turned into Beck's shoulder, letting out small sobs.

'Did we overstep?' I blurted. 'I'm sorry. We only wanted to help. You two have been through a lot, and we don't want to see this day taken away from you.'

Tessa moved out of the chair and knelt in front of her sister. 'Tor, you've done so much for this town. Let them help you and Beck.'

Torran sniffled. 'Dammit. These hormones have turned me into a blubbering mess.' She swiped at her cheeks. 'How could we pull this off in three days?'

'That's what we're going to talk about at the meeting,' I said.

'The wedding will be smaller. More intimate,' Tessa added. 'But none of that matters if we can get the two of you hitched.'

Beck rubbed at his tired eyes and turned to Torran. 'I don't care where, or how, we get married as long as I can slip a ring on your finger and vow to love and protect you for the rest of my life.'

Another tear slid down Torran's cheek. 'That's all I want too.'

A victorious smile lifted the corners of Tessa's lips. 'Then you both agree that if we can put a wedding together, you're in?'

Beck and Torran gave each other such a loving look that I couldn't help but think about Ford. How if he was here he'd be the first person pitching in. Doing whatever he could to help make the day beautiful for the people I loved.

'If you can convince Ivy Falls to help us, we are definitely in,' Beck said before he pulled Torran in for another embrace, her tears quickly falling again.

—

'What the hell is Amos doing?'

Mr Wright paced in the back of the town hall's meeting room, hands shoved into his pockets, shoulders tensed up around his ears.

'He's doing what you asked,' Tessa said. 'You were the one who said you couldn't run the emergency meeting because it was a conflict of interest. That another council member had to be in charge. Amos has been your friend for over twenty years, Dad. He'll handle this.'

He scrubbed a nervous hand over his mouth. 'Maybe this was a bad idea. They've been arguing about excavators for over half an hour now.'

The wood-paneled meeting room was wall-to-wall Ivy Falls residents. Most of the chairs in the twelve narrow rows were occupied by the usual suspects. Ferris sat next to Doc Sheridan and his wife, Sylvie. Behind them was Silvio, Mrs Vanderpool, Miss Cheri and Isabel. To their right was Deputy Ben, Diego and Manny.

All the window shades were open, and Manny brought in a generator for extra light, because the tornado had destroyed many of the power poles around the square.

I hadn't seen this many people attend a town meeting since Silvio swore someone stole the sandwich board outside the hardware store. After a lot of accusatory dialogue, he was reminded that he'd loaned it to Mimi's Pizza for a festival they were doing with their new food truck, which set off a whole other argument about what was the best pizza topping. Ferris nearly lost it when Deputy Ben brought up pineapple, arguing fruit should never be on pizza. Mr Wright had to finally break it up with the promise that they'd do a poll at the end of next month's meeting.

Amos sat in the center of the semicircular table at the front of the room. He'd dressed for the occasion in a starched blue shirt and matching tie, taking his fill-in role for the mayor seriously. His eyes narrowed on the crowd and he banged on the gavel calling the meeting back to order.

'We're not gonna solve how to get three excavators down main street to load up all the trees down near the soccer fields tonight. At this point, we can't even get word from the cell-phone companies about when we can get the towers up and running again.'

Because Ivy Falls was without any kind of cell service or Wi-Fi, everything had been brought to a standstill. Businesses were closed and people wandered the streets aimlessly looking for something to do. More than a few residents mumbled that they felt helpless. Wished they could do more to assist with the cleanup. That's when Tessa had come up with the brilliant idea to put everyone to work on Torran and Beck's wedding.

Amos waved in our direction. 'Tessa, please come to the front and make your presentation.'

Mr Wright squeezed her hand before she moved down the aisle toward where the council sat.

'Hello, everyone. It's good to see you all, and I'm glad everyone is safe.' The piece of lined notebook paper in her hand shook as she spoke. 'I asked that this emergency meeting be called because, as many of you know, Torran and Beck were supposed to be married this Saturday in the backyard of Huckleberry Lane.'

Everyone nodded along.

'I'm sure word has also spread that their big magnolia came down, as well as several other trees, and their fence, in the tornado. Right now their backyard resembles ground zero for the apocalypse.'

Murmurs rose as she went on.

'Torran and Beck are at home right now meeting with a cleanup crew, but we've gotten their permission to have this meeting.' She took a thick gulp and went on. 'This town has always pulled together for the people they love. You rallied around my mother when she was sick. Helped support me when I was struggling with the bookstore. There are countless other ways this community has helped out when you've been called on.' She chewed on her lips nervously. 'I'm here because I'm asking for your help to put on a wedding for them.'

Mrs Vanderpool's hand rose. 'When were you thinking?'

'They've been through a lot. I want them to be able to celebrate on their original day.'

Ferris jumped to his feet. 'You wanna put on a wedding in less than seventy-two hours?'

'Yes,' Tessa said in a voice that insisted there was no room for negotiation.

'Torran's dress is safe, but the flower shop is a mess. My coolers are down and the workspace is torn up,' Ms Darcy said. 'I won't be able to do boutonnières or bouquets.'

'That's all right. We'll use the roses from my garden,' Ferris offered.

'Barbie and I will take care of the cake and the donut tower for Torran, but if our ovens still aren't running we may need to use one in a local home if you have gas,' Susan added.

Isabel and Miss Cheri immediately volunteered.

Mr Wright shot me a hopeful look. When you needed support, this town never let you down.

'The sheriff's office has a tent we use at outreach events. I bet we could get it out of storage. Set it up for the reception,' Deputy Ben called out.

As more people raised their hands, offered their help, Mr Wright rubbed at his eyes.

'You had to know once they were asked, the town would come through,' I said.

'I've been so distracted by the everyday business of Ivy Falls that I've forgotten it's not the paperwork or processes that makes this community function – it's the people. It shouldn't have taken a destructive act of nature to remind me of that fact.'

'It's easy to get caught up in what's going on in our own lives. To forget that we have an incredible support system here if we ask for it.' My gaze darted to where Old Mrs V sat with Silvio. How the ache in my chest reminded me that one important face was missing in this crowd.

Ford would have loved the conversations and wild banter that filled this meeting. The way Silvio teased Ferris about his precious roses. How more than once Isabel glanced over her shoulder to make sure the mayor wasn't pacing too frantically in the back of the room. Old Mrs V's shushing as too many people spoke over each other.

Tessa continued to recruit help. Manny offered to gather a crew to bring in chairs and string more lights in the gazebo. A few people even volunteered to set up their smokers to make brisket or barbecued pork. Others agreed to bring salads and other side dishes to round out the meal for the reception.

Once every task was filled, the space vibrated with the sound of applause. Amos banged the gavel with a little too much fervor and adjourned the meeting.

People filed toward the back of the room and Mr Wright shook every person's hand, thanked them personally for their help. Amos came hustling up the aisle toward us with Tessa following.

'Thought I did pretty good for running my first meeting, don't you agree?'

It was hard not to smile at the self-satisfied look on Amos' face.

'Thanks, pal. You did well,' Mr Wright answered.

'Boy, the power of smacking that gavel is a rush. Maybe I'll run for mayor considering…'

Mr Wright shot Amos a dark look as his old friend pressed his hand over his mouth, shook his head and sped off toward the exit.

'Dad?' Tessa propped her hands on her hips. 'Anything you want to tell us?'

'I was going to speak to you girls after the wedding, but I've decided I'm done being mayor once my term is over. It's time for someone new to lead Ivy Falls. Guide this town into the future.'

'Will you go back to the bank full-time?' Tessa asked.

His gaze flicked to where Isabel was talking to Deputy Ben. 'Part-time. Isabel and I have been talking about traveling. And…' His lips split into a wide grin. 'I'd like to dedicate a lot more time to being a grandpa. Help Torran and Beck out when they need it.' He reached out and squeezed Tessa's hand. 'You and Manny too, because this family is really growing.'

Tessa pressed a kiss to his cheek. 'I'm headed to Huckleberry Lane. You two want to tag along? Help me tell them the news?'

'Yes, I want to see exactly how you're going to convince them this is going to work,' I said.

Mr Wright pulled us both into a hug and said, 'Guess we have a wedding to put on!'

Chapter Thirty-Five

FORD

More Than A Casual Visit

It'd taken three weeks, but I'd finally found my footing on the ship again. My first days back were toddlers-running-the-day-care kinds of chaos. Messages and prescription requests covered the desk in the small clinic office. Half-eaten Pop-Tarts and empty bottles of Gatorade littered the floor. More than once I'd had to wrench my sneakers off the sticky linoleum.

The director had undersold the state of the clinic by a mile. According to several nurses, the last doctor had a great bedside manner, a way to put the patients at ease, but his organization and charting abilities sucked, and apparently he also had the diet of a teenage boy.

'Ford, we can't tell you again how wonderful it is to have you back.' Nancy, one of the head nurses who'd been with *Humanity of the Seas* for over twenty years, gave me a warm smile.

'It's good to be here,' I said as I glanced at the clinic's white board for today's schedule. Nurses moved around the large, sterile white space. Several beds were set up in a line with dark blue cotton curtains available for privacy. At the rear of the clinic, a small door provided access to the operating rooms. On the other side of the surgical unit was another bank of rooms that housed the dental and ophthalmology offices.

Today's schedule left no time for error. I had back-to-back patients until noon, and then a short break for lunch followed by more appointments until six. It'd been this way since I'd returned. Work. Eat. Sleep. Repeat again the next day. More than once at dinner time, Kip asked about Piper. I babbled about time-zone differences and work schedules.

He shook his head like I was an idiot. 'Stay up late. Get up early. Stop being so damn afraid.'

Yeah, I heard that in my sleep now.

All the plastic white chairs in the clinic's waiting room were filled. For a flicker of a second, I thought of Ivy Falls. The way the patients always greeted me with a smile. How I'd slowly learned to love the low bellow of that toy train.

That hollow feeling returned to my chest and I forced myself to look at my first chart. To ignore that incessant ache that swept over me when I thought about everything I was missing by not being there.

I walked back into the clinic, pushing away my feelings and focusing on my first case. The morning flew by as I saw patients new and old. Some were follow-up checkups, while others were preliminary screenings before a surgery was scheduled. As soon as I was finished with my last patient before the lunch break, the intercom sounded in the clinic.

'Dr Foster, please come to the bridge immediately.'

Nancy glanced in my direction. Lifted her brows. I'd been on this ship off and on for over four years and had never been summoned to the bridge.

I checked out with the nurse at the desk and made my way across the decks. The heat of a balmy eighty degrees slid over my skin. Several of the crew worked below me, some straightening out rope lines, others washing the salt and brine off the deck. I pulled in a full breath, taking a minute to gaze at the sweep of the deep-blue Atlantic before heading in the direction of the bow.

Being summoned to the bridge was odd. The hospital staff was friendly with the ship's crew, but we stayed out of each other's way as we all had specific jobs to do.

When I reached the door and opened it, I was greeted by a wide bank of windows and row after row of computers that helped navigate the ship. Captain Alsop was easy to spot with his stark white hair and perfectly waxed handlebar mustache.

'Dr Foster.' He waved me toward him and shook my hand. 'I have a meeting in another part of the ship. Take all the time you need.'

'Captain? What do you mean?'

Instead of replying, he slid out the solid wood door like he was in a rush.

What the hell was going on?

I took two more steps before I got my answer. Leaning against one of the walls, dressed in a starched Lacoste polo and pressed khaki shorts, Gray looked all kinds of out of place.

'Surprise,' he said with a shit-eating grin.

'What are you doing here?'

He pulled a shocked face. 'If I remember correctly, you invited me.'

'I did.' I gaped at the sight of him. 'But you couldn't have called? Given me a word of warning?'

'And give you a chance to blow me off? Hell no!'

'I wouldn't have done that.'

He pulled me into an awkward side hug, glancing around the room at all the whirring machines and the crew performing their late-morning duties.

The bastard had actually done it. Flown halfway across the world to see me.

'Are we gonna hang out here all day or are you going to show me around?'

'Yeah, of course. Come on.'

For the next hour, I gave him a tour of every inch of the ship. We traversed up and down the decks, and his mouth hung open as we walked past the bank, chapel, library, convenience store, gym and swimming pool. Every few minutes, people stopped me along the way, shook hands and smiled as I introduced Gray to not only the medical staff but to the rest of the crew.

He was quiet for the loud-mouthed Gray, and I worried his arrival was about more than a casual visit.

Once the tour was over, I took him into the dining hall. He immediately caught sight of a few nurses near one of the serving bars and went into playboy mode, introducing himself, asking their names and jobs on the ship.

Okay, so maybe he was still Gray.

After we finished eating, I dragged him to the clinic.

Once we passed through the steel door, I guided him around the space, explaining how the hospital portion of the ship had over one hundred acute beds, six ICU beds and fifty self-care beds. We walked through the surgical center, stopping at the teaching areas before moving on to the conference rooms and training simulation labs.

By the time we were finished, I had to go back to seeing patients. Before Gray could leave, Nancy caught sight of him and asked if he wanted to help out. Much to my surprise, he agreed and spent the next several hours restocking shelves with bandages and ointments. He handed out blankets, water and kept the younger nurses in stitches with his terrible flirting and awful jokes.

The afternoon flew by and when the last of the patients were gone, we walked to the back of the ship to see the best view of Senegal's capital city, Dakar. The tall buildings shimmered in the fading evening light. Boats puttered to and from the port. The sky morphed into a riot of color ranging from deep red to vibrant orange.

'Shit, Ford.' He scrubbed at his cropped dark hair. 'You weren't kidding about this place. What you do, how people react to you, it's damn impressive.'

'Better than the country club?' I joked.

He looked out at the darkening water, his gaze going solemn. 'I quit my job.'

'You what? Why?'

'Because of you.'

'Gray, please don't put any choices you make on me. You're a grown-ass man.'

'No, that's not what I meant,' he stammered. 'For years I've watched you push back against expectations, forge your own path. Choose what was right for you. Me,' he huffed. 'I've always been the dutiful eldest son, but in doing that I've ignored every single dream of my own. It didn't hurt that I had a long talk with Mom after she made Dad leave. She told me to go and live my life, and it was the push I needed.'

'What's your plan?'

He scrubbed his hands together. 'I'm moving to Chattanooga. Got a job at a small public golf course as an assistant pro. I'll build up my game, my client base, until I can move to a place where I can be head pro one day.'

'Taking that leap couldn't have been easy. I'm proud of you.'

'I told Mom that once I got settled she should come and visit. It'd be nice to spend some one-on-one time with her.'

'She'd like that.'

He nodded, went back to staring at the ocean. 'How's that girl of yours? Talked to her lately?'

I scrubbed a hand behind my neck. 'No. And she's not really my girl.'

'I'm sorry?' He blinked. 'Why not? She was perfect for you, and the way I heard she handled Dad at the party was damn brave. There are not a lot of people who go toe to toe with Stanford Cantwell Foster and live to tell the tale.'

'To be honest, I fucked it up. Didn't tell her how I felt before I left.'

'There's a simple answer for that. Call her. Grovel. Hell, plan a grand gesture. Whatever you have to do, because I don't think I've ever seen you that happy.'

It was the same lecture I was getting from Kip, and I knew both of them were right.

'Even if you don't want to spill your guts, you should still call and check on her.'

'Why?'

'Do you not read the news here?'

'Gray,' I pressed.

'A major tornado hit Ivy Falls two days ago. It did a lot of damage.'

Before he could say another word, I took off at a sprint. When I reached my cabin, I opened my laptop and searched for Ivy Falls. Pictures of the devastation filled the screen. Parts of trees strewn all over town. Remnants of

311

roofs scattered across the square. My chest pinched at an image of a small window blown out at the P&P.

I scrambled for my phone and dialed Piper's number. My heart sank every time the three flat-toned buzzes rang in my ear and the red message flashed across the screen.

No service. Network unavailable.

Chapter Thirty-Six

PIPER

Fairy-Tale Ending

There was never a doubt in my mind that Ivy Falls was an amazing place, but watching everyone from Ferris to Silvio to Dr Sheridan and Deputy Ben pitch in over the last few days, I had to re-evaluate my opinion of my hometown. This wasn't just a place with a charming square, quaint independent businesses and out-of-this-world food. It was a loving community that always showed up when they were needed.

After rehab, I'd thought it'd be easier to sneak away, to not face the people I'd disappointed, but I was glad I had been brave enough to come back. To be part of a community that was selfless and wanted nothing more than their neighbors to be happy.

Even though Beck and Torran agreed to the wedding, they still worried about how the town was going to pull it off with everything else going on. Tessa finally put an end to her sister's grumbling by pulling the 'Auntie' card, telling her how upset Iris and Rose would be if they didn't get to wear the sparkly pink dresses Torran picked out for them.

'Pipe.' Maisey rushed across the square toward me. The aster-purple, one-shoulder dress she'd made for this occasion was stunning. 'I've been watching the Hearth and Home crew like a dog waiting for someone to drop a morsel on the floor during Thanksgiving dinner. Haven't seen a single camera. Most of the big guys have spent the afternoon helping Manny bring in chairs and setting up the tent for the reception.' She glanced toward the lawn in front of town hall and sighed. 'When we want to pull together, throw a party, Ivy Falls knows how to assemble better than the Avengers.'

She stepped back and gave me the once-over. After Ms Darcy did some alterations, the tea-length sapphire-blue bridesmaid dress Torran had picked out for me was beautiful.

'Give me a spin,' she ordered.

I wobbled on my heels on the uneven pavement. She pulled a small bottle of hairspray and a brush from the pockets of her dress, spritzing and fluffing until she was satisfied.

'You look good, bestie.'

'Thank you.' I gave her the side-eye. 'What else you got in those pockets, Maise?'

She chuckled and pulled out a handful of mints, a tube of red lipstick and some tissues. 'Pockets should be a requirement in dress design. Wish more brands would figure that out.'

'Why don't you do it? Create your own line of formal dresses with pockets. I bet you'd sell out in a minute.'

She tapped at her chin, a slow smile making her face glow. 'That's not a bad idea.'

'I'm here for whatever you need. Just ask.'

She tugged me into a hug. 'You inspire me.'

I pulled back. 'Me? Why?'

'That first day you came back from rehab I was terrified. I sat on the porch at Huckleberry Lane and waited for you to acknowledge I was there. Reluctantly, you came outside and we talked. Over time you let me back into your world, and through our walks, quiet conversations, I learned about what you'd endured over the years. Anyone else would have been completely broken by what you'd been through, but all I saw in you was resolve. A fierce drive to never go back to the place you were before. You've been through so much and you're still fighting. It makes me damn proud to be your friend.'

'Oh, Maise. I wouldn't be in this place without your love and support. I hope you'll let me do the same for you as you go after what you want.'

She squeezed my hand. 'Thank you. I'm definitely going to take you up on that offer.'

Her husband, Joe, called to her from the gazebo where he and Manny were stringing more lights.

'Gotta go help. Come find me if you need any more touch-ups.'

'I won't. My job right now is to hunt down Lauren. Make sure she's behaving.'

She rolled her eyes. 'Good luck with the Energizer Bunny.'

I walked across the street and toward the lawn where the Hearth and Home crew had set up base. Torran was across the street at the P&P getting ready, and Beck was having his nerves calmed at the Sugar Rush with Barb and Susan.

Closer to the entrance to town hall, folding chairs were set up like perfect white soldiers. A runner of cream silk flowed down the aisle. Once we'd convinced Torran and Beck they weren't cancelling, that they could have their wedding near the square, they'd insisted there be a seat for anyone in Ivy Falls who wanted to attend.

Lauren stood at the bottom of the steps by the gazebo, her scarlet-red designer sheath hugging the curves of her body. Her stiff posture, and irritated tap of her stiletto, warned a storm was brewing. As I stepped closer, her voice rose an octave.

'Torran told me I could post photos on the network's website as long as they weren't from the wedding.'

Pete, Beck's business partner and best man, shook his head, a dark lock of hair falling across his forehead. 'Getting ready are the optimal words, Lauren. Taking pictures of Beck having coffee with Barb and Susan, pacing like a madman in the Sugar Rush, does not scream "getting ready",' he put in air quotes.

'Why are you always such a pain in the ass?' she snapped.

He shoved up the sleeves of his white button-down, the ink of his tattoos gleaming in the fading afternoon sunlight. 'And why can't *you* follow simple instructions?'

She threw up her hands, growled 'Pain in the ass' again and stalked off.

His amused grin said he had enjoyed that encounter way too much. From what Torran had told me, he and Lauren had been bickering since they'd started working on a project for a new restaurant being restored near the edge of town. They were an open flame and gasoline, and I did not want to be around when they eventually ignited.

'Causing trouble again?' I said to Pete.

He pulled me in for a quick hug. 'She makes it too easy.'

Beck had always said he wanted a brother, and he'd certainly gotten one in Pete, who was constantly looking out for him.

'Keep a close watch on her and the crew. They have that look in their eyes like they're gonna push the limits on what Torran and Beck said they wanted.'

'I'm on it.'

'There's no doubt in my mind about that.'

He plucked his navy-blue suit coat off the back of a nearby chair. Ferris had already pinned on his boutonnière and it was flipped sideways. I straightened it out as he gave me a serious look.

'You ready for this? A wedding? A niece or nephew?'

'More than ready. Beck and Torran have been through so much crap, they deserve a fairy-tale ending.'

Once the pink rose and baby's breath sat firmly on his lapel, he let loose a low breath. 'You know they're not the only ones who should have good things. Beck told me you met someone. How's that going?'

'He's gone.'

The lines in his forehead bunched. 'Need more than that, Pipe.'

'He was filling in for the vacationing doctor here. When the job was done, he went back to doing humanitarian work in Senegal.'

'That okay with you?'

'Not really, but I'm trying to figure it out.'

He slung an arm around my shoulder and squeezed. The string quartet from Ivy Falls High warmed up as people began to fill the lawn.

'Duty calls.' He started to walk away and then spun back. 'I hope you know you deserve to be happy. To have someone special.'

I put my hands on my hips and laughed at the brotherly intensity in his eyes. 'Right back at you.'

'All right,' he huffed. 'I had that one coming.'

He walked toward the chairs. Without skipping a beat, Barb and Susan appeared at his sides and he led them down the aisle. That was my cue to go and grab Beck.

As the seats filled up, the quartet played one of my favorite Vivaldi pieces. I kept a steady eye on Lauren and her crew. When I was sure they were behaving, I walked in the direction of the café.

Beck stood inside near the domed cases. His blue suit fit his wide shoulders perfectly, and somehow he'd managed to tame his wavy brown hair.

'Do I look okay?' he asked.

All I could manage was a nod.

He took a few strides toward me. 'What's wrong? Is it Tor? Is she throwing up again?'

'You look so much like Dad.' It was impossible to hide the tremor in my voice.

He gave me a sad smile. 'It's weird but I can feel them here. Can you?'

'Yes. On my walk through town this morning, there were two hummingbirds chasing each other across Ferris' rose garden. They buzzed in a circle. Did a little dance like they were performing for me. It was exactly what happened in the garden at rehab, and I know this sounds corny, but it felt like a sign from them.'

He gripped my hand, swiped his thumb over my tattoo. 'That's as good a sign as any.'

'Thank you for never giving up. For seeing a future for me, even when I couldn't imagine one for myself.'

'Oh, Pipe. I should be the one thanking you. Look at what you've done today for me and Tor. The joy you brought to this town with that show. I know I still hover. That I can be annoying at times, but it's only because I love you with my whole heart.'

He pulled me into a hug and I held on to him. That explosion on a cold winter day had changed the course of our lives forever. The weight of our parents' deaths had turned our worlds upside down for too long. We'd been through the darkest times. Both made choices that made our paths rockier. But we'd also worked damn hard to get to this moment, and I wanted to revel in that hard-fought victory for a minute more.

The brass bell jingled as Pete walked through the door and stared at us for a long beat. 'My apologies for inter-rupting, but before we get this party started, I need to tell you something.' He shoved his hands deep into the pockets of his pants, his eyes going solemn. 'You both mean the world to me, and I'm honored to be included in this day.'

'Do not make me cry, Peter! Maisey will never forgive me if my mascara runs.'

'Understood. No crying,' he said on an uneven breath. 'How about we go and get my best friend married instead?'

Pete pushed open the door. Beck held up his arm to escort me, and together we walked out to face all of Ivy Falls.

–

With a fading orange sun setting behind the clock tower, Miss Cheri performed a song from Puccini's *Tosca* while Torran made her way down the aisle. Under the giant magnolia, much like the one they'd lost in their own backyard, Beck waited for her. Once she reached where Mr Wright stood, my brother took her hand and there was a collective sigh from the crowd.

The night music of crickets filled the air as Beck and Torran said their vows. Old Mrs V leaned into Silvio. Manny held on to Lou's hand and beamed at Tessa and her girls, who stood a few feet from the couple.

In the row behind me, Barb and Susan pressed their hands against the tears staining their cheeks. Maisey reached into her pockets more than once and handed them tissues. Even Mr Wright, who was officiating, had a few moments where he had to pause and gulp down his emotions.

On a small white table near the gazebo sat a lit candle. Next to it were pictures of Torran's mom and my parents. A simple way the couple wanted to honor those who couldn't be present.

As a gentle wind danced through the trees, and the town fountain gurgled in the background, Torran and Beck promised to love and trust one another. To be by each other's side, whether their path was easy or difficult. They shared a kiss that made everyone clap and cheer. Lauren, and even the crew, dabbed at their eyes and enjoyed the ceremony without a single camera in hand.

After the couple walked down the aisle under a shower of pink and white rose petals, the party really began. Folks who had their own smokers served up the best barbecue the town had ever seen. Thankfully, electricity had been restored to the town early that morning, allowing Barb and Susan to make a small wedding cake and a donut tower for Torran.

Quiet dinner music morphed into classic rock and there wasn't a single space left on the dance floor. I wasn't sure how'd we done it, but despite the storm of the decade hitting Ivy Falls, we'd managed to get two important people married the way they should be.

The band moved into an old Randy Travis song, and my mind went to the night of 'Music in the Square'. How I'd never expected Ford's touch to shake something loose inside me.

I'd been thinking about the conversation I'd had with Torran and Tessa during the tornado. How miscommunication was born out of people's fear of getting hurt. Torran's comment about not knowing being worse than the truth sat like a rock in my stomach.

During the months I'd been in rehab, my therapist asked me to examine the reasons why I'd turned to pills and alcohol. Why I needed to block my feelings from the world. It all came down to risk and trust. Risk in the sense that I was willing to live my life in a way that embraced both joy and pain. That I understood not every day was going to be balloons and rainbows. But it also wouldn't feel like I was floating on a dark, windswept sea with waves constantly threatening to drown me. It was a balance I had to be willing to accept.

When I'd stepped into Ford's arms that night on the roof, kissed the beautiful hollow at his throat, I was facing the exact risk that had terrified me for too many years. That being vulnerable would expose me to the possibility of loss and grief again, but I knew that if I wanted connection, I had to be open with the people I cared about.

For years I'd had the same nightmare over and over. I was standing in a sterile hallway, my nose assaulted with the scent of antiseptic and death. People moved around me, but when I spoke no one reacted. I raced down hallways, through empty corridors, screaming for the one person who would see me – Beck. But with every door I opened, all I found was an empty bed. Dr Catherine told me it was the trauma from the accident. How for the hours when no one told me about Beck's condition, I was convinced I was all alone in the world.

Since Ford walked into my life, I'd not had the night-mare a single time. He'd become the safe space I'd been searching for my entire life.

Couples continued to sway on the dance floor. At times I could still feel the gentle press of Ford's fingers against my hipbones. How when he kissed me it was if he was placing an oath against my skin. I needed him to be a part of my life, and as soon as things calmed down, I'd call him and say what was in my heart. The possible rejection would hurt, but at least I'd know where I stood with him.

Face. Forgive. Forward.

The mantra had never meant more to me than it did now.

'Miss Piper!' Dex waved to me. He wore a black dress shirt and a purple tie. He pushed away from the table where he was sitting and made a confident strut toward me.

'What's going on, Dex?'

'This is my first wedding. It's pretty cool.'

'And the music?'

'Ugh. Would it kill the band to play something from this decade?'

'They take requests. You should tell them what you want to hear.'

'Maybe.' He kicked the tip of his dress shoe at the grass. 'Speaking of requests, I listened to your advice. Signed up to audition for *Grease*. When you try out you have to sing and dance to a selected song. Any chance you could come over to the gazebo? Let me show you the routine I have planned?'

The party was in full swing and I was finally released from Hearth and Home duty.

'Lead the way.'

Soft candlelight flickered on the tables set up on the grass. The moon was putting on a show tonight, a golden orb dancing against a black velvet sky. It was hard to believe that only a few days ago the lawn had been littered with uprooted trees, jagged branches and more than a few crumpled shingles from nearby roofs.

We walked up the first two steps of the gazebo until Dex came to a stiff halt. 'You've been a real good friend, Miss Piper. I know I didn't make those first days of practice easy for you, especially with the whole gummy bear incident. Thank you for never giving up on me. I'm really sorry I've had to lie to you.'

'Lie?'

He tipped his chin up to the gazebo. 'Don't be too surprised. I think he'd do anything for you.'

'What are you talking about?'

'Go up the stairs and see.'

He jumped off the steps and dashed across the grass to where his mom was sitting. They shared a few words until he pulled her out onto the dance floor, her smile lighting up the night.

I climbed the steps and a breath caught in my chest. Ford stood in the corner, a black suit hugging the outline of his frame. Those twenty-five-hundred-dollar shoes were on his feet, and his dark hair was combed back from his face. As usual, his glasses sat perfectly on the bridge of his nose.

'Hi,' he said, taking a few steps toward me.

'What are you doing here?' I babbled. 'You're supposed to be thousands of miles away!'

'Gray came to visit me in Senegal. He told me about the tornado. I called and couldn't get through. I apologized to my boss, bought the first ticket I could find, and flew back.'

'The cell tower was damaged in the tornado. You could have waited. Tried to call again. That's a long trip.'

He stepped in closer and put his hands on my cheeks. 'See, that's the problem. When it comes to you, I can't wait.'

'Ford, what is going on?'

'That night on the rooftop you made me make a promise, which I convinced myself I could keep. But the more time I spent with you, the harder it was to stay away. To not feel anything for you. What I should have said in the hallway before I left was that I love you, Piper. Coming to this town, finding you, it was all unexpected. For so long I've thought my life only had room for one thing: my career. You've shown me that I need much more. I want this to work between us. How do we make that happen?'

I pulled back and walked to the edge of the gazebo. My breaths came in choking spurts. Tears burned the corners of my eyes. Ford was behind me a heartbeat later. The intoxicating heat of him wrapped around me like a warm hug.

'I know you're scared. That you've been through so much, but I'd rather break my own thumbs than hurt you. I swear that as long as you're with me you'll be loved *tous les jours de ma vie*.'

Even with his uneven breath speaking French, I couldn't move.

'I'm sorry. Was this wrong to do?'

'No, but you have to understand that I never thought I'd get here. To a place where I felt happy. Believed I deserved to have a good life. I've made so many mistakes and shitty choices. When you've plunged to the darkest depths, it's hard to believe you'll ever see the light again.' I turned and found those beautiful blue eyes. 'Spending time with you has felt like the biggest gift I've been handed in this life, and I don't want to give it back.'

He put his hands on my waist, staring at me with a devotion that took my breath away. 'I'll be done in late March. We can talk and text in the meantime. When I'm finished, I'll come back and we'll plan what's next.'

'Don't you want to continue to serve on the *Humanity of the Seas*? It's your passion.'

He pressed a gentle kiss to my lips. We'd only been apart a few weeks, but I'd forgotten the tenderness in his touch. How all he had to do was skim a finger across my skin and my entire body went electric. 'Oh, I have a new passion now.'

'Ford...' I grabbed the lapels of his suit. 'What is your plan?'

'Dr Sheridan and I have talked. When I get back, I'm going to work at the clinic during the week. On the weekends, I'll serve as a volunteer physician at one of the community shelters in Nashville.'

'And you'll be happy with that?'

He tucked a finger under my chin. 'Yes, because I know this is where I belong. In Ivy Falls with you, as long as you'll have me, Bird.'

I slung my arms around his neck. 'Yes, that's what I want, because I love you too.' I pressed another kiss to his beautiful lips. 'Just so you know, I had a plan too.'

There was that sweet grin of his I adored. 'Were you also concocting a grand gesture? Maybe flying across the world so you could see this sexy face again?'

'No, I'm a normal person. I was going to make a phone call.'

He threw back his head and laughed. 'My plan was much better.'

I kissed him again and mumbled 'I agree' against his smile.

Epilogue

FORD

Roots

One year later...

After a long day at the clinic, I needed two things: a sweet tea and a kiss from my girlfriend.

I hustled down the brick-paved sidewalks, passing the Dairy Dip and the hardware store. Every few feet someone called out, 'Hey, doc,' and I waved in their direction.

When I'd first come to Ivy Falls that kind of greeting startled me, but over the last year I'd learned to enjoy it, bask in the feeling of being one of the town's own.

Voices rang out around the corner and, when I stepped toward them, I found Tessa and Penny on the sidewalk bickering about the P&P's sign again.

They'd finally won the town's contest at the Fourth of July picnic. Ever since they'd gotten that shiny plaque, they'd been battling over the sign every month. I tried to race inside the bookstore without them seeing me, but they called out my name, stopping me in my tracks.

Tessa propped her hands on her hips, her brownish-red ponytail swinging behind her.

'Don't you like *Come Inside and Espresso Yourself* better than *Coffee and Romance Books. Either Way You Get Something Steamy*?'

Their penetrating stares told me it was a losing question.

'They're both clever,' I offered before dashing inside.

People were too damn serious about the sign contest, and I wasn't getting in the middle of that epic showdown.

My gaze bounced over the P&P's upholstered chairs, couches and small tables. I moved past the children's section and the coffee bar, finally spotting Piper hunched over her laptop with her headphones on. Her head bobbed along to whatever music she was listening to as she took notes.

Like the first time I came into the bookstore, the sight of her stunned me. Her dark hair was styled in a long braid. An old concert T-shirt hung off one shoulder. Every time I looked at her, that same old feeling of a rollercoaster drop washed over me. I still couldn't believe I got to go to sleep kissing her and wake up with her body wrapped in my arms.

She must have felt me staring because she looked up. Her bright smile always made my throat go dry, forced my heart to pick up speed. She crooked a finger in my direction and I obeyed. I pulled out the chair next to her and gave her a peck on the cheek.

'What are you working on?' I asked, taking a long gulp of the tea she had waiting for me.

She slid off her headphones and flipped the book over to show me the title: *The Many Facets of Successful Theater Direction*.

'Stimulating read,' I teased, and she playfully elbowed me.

'It is! I'm learning a lot, and it will definitely help with the kids' show next year.'

She'd had another successful run at the theater this past summer, this time directing a shortened version of *The Little Mermaid*. She'd tried to convince Dex to be Prince Eric, but he took the role of Sebastian instead. The kid had the entire theater in stitches after delivering a few lines. You wouldn't think he'd be able to dance in a crab costume either, but Dex pulled it off.

He'd become a regular for dinner at the little bungalow we rented near the elementary school, and somehow I'd been lassoed into coaching his rec basketball team. A decision his mother had been thanking me about for months. The kids were great, and I found myself having fun with a bunch of stinky, and often foul-mouthed, fourteen-year-olds.

I slid my hand into hers. 'Ready to go? Torran will rip our heads off if we're late for their anniversary celebration.'

'That girl needs to take a chill pill. I thought after Sabrina was born she'd mellow out. It's a good thing I love her and adore being an auntie or she'd be in a constant headlock.'

I took another pull on my drink while she packed up her laptop. When I told her about the battle royale happening near the sign outside, we tiptoed out through the office's back door.

As we hustled down the sidewalk, my phone buzzed. I glanced at the screen and smiled. Another text from Gray showing how proud he was of the 'Head Pro' marker in front of his new parking spot.

I turned the screen to Piper. 'Oh lord, the last thing that man needs is another ego stroke.'

'Tell me about it.' I replied with the middle finger and laughing emoji.

'How did your mom's visit with him go?'

'She said it was good. That she likes the new house he bought. Get this, she actually called it "cozy". Not sure I've ever heard my mother use that word. Gray said he put her to work with decorating, and he'd never seen her so happy.'

'I'm glad she went to visit. The last time we had lunch, she mentioned she missed him.'

With my being gone in Senegal last year, and Gray moving away, my mother quickly learned how lonely her life could become. She'd had several lunch dates with Piper and had eased up on the hints about grandkids. My dad, well, he was still being an asshole.

We turned the corner and I tucked Piper closer into my side. That coffee and vanilla scent of hers slid over me and I wondered if we snuck behind a tree, had a little impromptu make-out session, if it'd be spread around by nine o'clock. Knowing this town, it'd probably be closer to eight. I let out a little groan and had to settle for a kiss on her head.

'Didn't you have an appointment with Mrs V today?' she asked.

'Yes. She's back to form. As soon as I reported that her labs and most recent echocardiogram looked good, she was giving me grief about the scuff on my shoes. How I needed a haircut. That woman never takes a breath.'

'She pesters because she loves.'

'Yeah, well, then she's loving on me a bit too much,' I joked.

'Not possible,' she said, sliding her fingers between mine.

Huckleberry Lane came into view and she leaned her head onto my shoulder. Beck waved to us from the wraparound porch. Torran stood next to him with their little girl tucked in her arms. Their fence was back up around the property and a scattering of new saplings covered both the front and back yards. More than once Torran mentioned how much she missed the old magnolia. How she'd dreamed of hanging an old tire swing from one of its massive branches like the one Piper and Beck had as kids. Beck insisted their daughter was nowhere near ready for a swing, but when she was old enough, one of the trees would be steady enough, have deep enough roots, to handle one.

Roots. The word always struck me. Made me think of Ivy Falls and how the families here continued to grow. Planted the seeds of their life into this tiny community.

When I'd first arrived, I didn't know I was searching for a place to settle. A spot to put down my own roots. It wasn't until I found Piper, and then had to leave her, that I realized all I'd ever wanted was a real place to call home. She'd given that to me.

She squeezed my hand and laid a soft kiss against my cheek. Murmured how glad she was that we were all finally together.

'Me too, Bird,' I whispered against the cuff of her ear. 'Me too.'

A Letter From Amy

Dear Reader,

Every book has its challenges, but this one might be the hardest story I've ever had to tackle. It took many late nights and early mornings to get to the end, but now that it's here I can truly say I am so proud of not only this book, but the Ivy Falls series as a whole.

I knew as I planned this series that the final narrative I would tell would belong to Piper. It was critical to me that I tried to represent her experiences as truthfully as possible. In order to do this, I spent an immense amount of time researching recovery, as well as asking for guidance from therapists, who read early versions of this book and gave me critical feedback. My goal was to always tell Piper's story as authentically as I could. It certainly does not reflect everyone's story, as those are very personal, but I have tried my best to make her voice clear and real on the page.

This book also tackles subjects like grief, divorce, pregnancy, and the death of parents. If for any reason these subjects make you uncomfortable, I hope you will read with care.

There are many wonderful romance books on the shelves vying for readers' attention. I'm honored that you have spent your time with my novel. I have loved creating the world of Ivy Falls and hope that once you experience this sweet little town you will find comfort there and want to return over and over.

Enjoy and happy reading!

Amy

Acknowledgments

First, I want to say thank you to my family. There has never been a time when you've looked at me and wondered why I'm doing this. You see my passion, my love of the written word, and are always firmly behind me. Big hugs especially to David, Olivia and Ryan for being my biggest cheerleaders, and to Jon and Camilla, who proudly display all my books in their home. I really lucked out in the in-law department. For my sisters and brothers and mom, who always ask about what I'm writing and then buy a bunch of copies of my books for their friends and extended family. Thank you for your love and support.

A big thank you to my team at Hera. Jennie Ayres, you are an editing rockstar and your support for this series means so much to me. Ross Dickinson, who catches my inconsistencies and leaves the nicest comments in the margins. And to designer Diane Meacham, who makes me smile every time I see a cover draft.

This book tackles some serious topics. It was important to me to put in the work to make sure everything was as authentic and accurate as possible on the page. Thank you to David for making sure all my medical terms and diagnoses were correct. A big nod of thanks also to Brock and Lissy for reading an early draft of this book and making sure I portrayed Piper's recovery accurately. I'm so grateful for your time and professional feedback.

One of the things that keeps me going as an author is my local writing community. I've experienced some rough publishing days over the last year and you've lifted me up and reminded me why I love this job. You actually had my back when those who were supposed to support me let me down. Kim Tomsic, Dianne White and Karen Chow, thank you for being there for me at a time when I desperately needed guidance and kind words. Beth Revis, for taking my frantic phone call and delivering the best publishing advice. Joanna Meyer, who is the calmest and gentlest soul on this planet, I am so lucky to call you my friend. Kelly deVos, who has read every single word in this series. I am still very grateful for that day you reached out online and asked if I wanted to have coffee. Also to Ginger Scott, who lets me talk her ear off and is always full of words of wisdom. Massive thanks to Sarah Chanis, who spent one very long lunch teaching me everything she knows about working in children's theater. Big shout-out to the Friday Write Ladies (Maddie, Kara, Joanna, Karen and Nicole) – thank you for letting me be a part of your crew.

One other aspect of this work that is incredibly important to me is the readers. Thank you to those who've posted gorgeous photos of my books, left reviews, came to my events, and sent me messages and DMs to tell me how much you loved my characters. Those moments of light and joy mean everything to me.

Welcome Home to Ivy Falls *Playlist*

'Leaning On Myself' – Anna of the North

'Be Someone' – Benson Boone

'butterflies' – Isabel LaRosa

'You Keep Me Up At Night' – THE DRIVER ERA, Ross Lynch, Rocky

'Wild Horses' – The Sundays

'Risk' – Gracie Abrams

'Golden' – Harry Styles

'Make Me Feel' – Elvis Drew

'Delicate'★ – Taylor Swift

'High In Low Places' – Beach Weather

'Off She Goes' – Bad Suns

'Sand' – Dove Cameron

'HOMESICK' – MICO

'OWN WORST ENEMY' – Yarin Glam

'Pieces' – Andrew Belle

★As of this printing, *Reputation* (Taylor's Version) has not been released yet!